Death
Dates the
Oracle

Nocturne Falls
Book 15

USA TODAY BEST SELLING AUTHOR
KRISTEN PAINTER

DEATH DATES THE ORACLE:

Nocturne Falls, Book Fifteen

Copyright © 2023 Kristen Painter

ISBN: 978-1-941695-81-4

Published in the United States of America

Welcome to Nocturne Falls, the town that celebrates Halloween 365 days a year. The tourists think it's all a show: the vampires, the werewolves, the witches, the occasional gargoyle flying through the sky. But the supernaturals populating the town know better.

Living in Nocturne Falls means being yourself. Fangs, fur, and all.

Eamon Underwood isn't what you'd call a social butterfly. In fact, he avoids people altogether, outside of his job at his uncle's funeral home, where Eamon is the mortician. For him, being around the dead is easier than being around the living. Mostly because of his very curious gift that enables him to see just how long a person has left to live. That knowledge makes personal interaction far too difficult.

Until he meets Troula Kouris. And sees...nothing.

Troula comes to Nocturne Falls to join her crazy-cat-lady aunts as an oracle, one of the rare descendants of the original Greek oracles. She's been preparing for it all of her life. Unfortunately, just before she leaves for Nocturne Falls, she gets an ominous prediction that leads her to believe becoming an oracle could be fatal. Or maybe the real danger is the darkly handsome neighbor who lives next door.

When Troula and Eamon make a curious connection that leads to romance, it seems the fates want them together, despite the risks. Can a little orange kitten really solve all of their problems? Or will it all end in a catastrophe?

For Jack, the best ginger boy ever. And to everyone who's ever had their heart stolen by an orange cat.

A whiff of freshly spun cotton candy drifted past. Troula Kouris turned into it and inhaled. Was there anything else that smelled as good as just-made cotton candy? She needed some of that. Not the silly business of having her fortune told.

"Come on, Tru. It's just for laughs. And it's your birthday!" Cindy Prentiss, another of the waitresses at Tru's uncle's restaurant, tugged on Tru's arm, pulling her toward the tent that had a banner outside proclaiming: Madame Fatima, Seer of the Ages, and then in smaller print: $20, Cash Only.

"It's a waste of money. No one can really tell the future," Tru lied and shook her head in answer to her friend's question. The happy chaos of the county fair swirled around them. Noise from the rides and the people on them. Food vendors hawking their wares. Music booming from the stage.

Add to that the sights and smells of the fair, and the place was like a human kaleidoscope of sensory input. She inhaled the scent of cotton candy again. "Plus, my birthday isn't until tomorrow."

Cindy kept her grip on Tru. "I know that, but we're

celebrating tonight. Before you head off to your aunts'. And I know it's not really real, but it's fun."

"I don't know ..." Tru frowned. It wasn't that she didn't believe in such things as fortune telling and soothsaying and all that. She did. She believed in it more than most, because she had aunts who sort of made their living that way. The aunts she was going to visit tomorrow.

In fact, she was about to be able to see the future herself. But having a stranger tell her fortune seemed like it might be a borderline violation of supernatural rules. Would a vampire bite another vampire? Okay, it wasn't exactly the same thing, but there was no telling if this Madame Fatima was real or just out for a quick buck.

Probably the quick buck. There were only a small handful of people gifted with the genuine ability to peek through the veil of time. And an even smaller handful who were directly descended from the Greek Oracles and could accurately make predictions that would come to pass. There were a few other things Legacy oracles could do. But she'd learn more about that in the next few days.

Tru knew all about the oracles, because she was one of them. She was a legacy. "I'd rather get a cotton candy."

"We'll get a cotton candy after." Cindy shot her a look. "Seriously, let's have some fun. Don't be so uptight."

"I am not uptight."

Cindy laughed. "No, you're really not. But don't you think it would be a hoot? Plus, it's my treat. For your birthday. Listen, with the way you look tonight, she's probably going to tell you that you're about to meet a man. Like right here at the fair."

Tru laughed. "Yeah, okay. I do look good tonight, don't I?" She'd taken extra time with her hair and makeup, knowing Cindy's propensity for selfies every five minutes. Tru did not want to look like a wreck on the eve of her thirty-third birthday.

"Yeah, you do."

Tru walked with Cindy toward the tent. Cin was like a dog with a bone when she got her teeth into an idea. And the sooner they got it over with, the sooner Tru could get some cotton candy. And maybe ride the Cyclone again.

Cindy whipped out her phone at the tent's entrance, posed beside Tru, and held the phone in front of them with her outstretched arm. "Say cheese!"

"Cheese," Tru dutifully replied as Cindy snapped away.

After that, they went in. Inside, the tent was pretty much what Tru had expected. Scarves and tapestries and trippy wall hangings transformed the interior into an Aladdin's cave. Loops of beads, shards of crystal, and little mirrors dangled from overhead, casting around the light of the numerous candles like sparks. A few strings of fairy lights added to the atmosphere, while the scents of vanilla, musk, and patchouli perfumed the space.

Overlapping Oriental rugs covered the floor, and piles of fat, square cushions made up the seating area around a low table that was probably an old cable spool cut in half and draped in more scarves and tapestries.

At the center of the table, cradled in an upright claw of patinaed brass, sat a *serious* crystal ball. The largest Tru had ever seen. Not quite the size of a soccer ball but definitely bigger than a softball. Maybe this woman was legit. A crystal ball that size wasn't cheap. She knew, because she'd priced them out recently.

Which was totally something all soon-to-be oracles did right before their thirty-third birthday.

The draperies at the center of the back wall parted, and a woman walked out dressed in a paisley caftan trimmed in black lace. Her eyes were heavily lined in kohl, her purple-streaked hair tied back with a length of patterned silk, and she wore as much jewelry as Tru figured it was possible for one person to wear. Rings, bracelets, necklaces, earrings, even a jangly chain belt—she was covered in silver links, and beads of semi-precious stones like moonstones and rose quartz.

The woman looked at both of them, then spoke to Tru. "You wish to know your future?" she asked in a heavy, slightly Middle European accent.

"Sure," Tru said, playing along but thinking about cotton candy. She was undecided on whether to get the pink or the blue.

The woman held out her hand. "You must cross Fatima's palm with silver."

Cindy dug in her purse. "I don't have that much change."

Tru snorted. "It's just a saying. I'm sure paper money works just fine."

Fatima nodded. "Fatima also takes credit cards, PayPal, and Venmo."

Cindy whipped out a twenty-dollar bill and handed it over. "Here you go."

"Please." Fatima gestured toward the table as she tucked the cash deep into her cleavage. "Sit."

Tru and Cindy settled onto the big floor cushions as Fatima did the same. Tru was surprised at how sturdy the cushions were. She'd half-expected to feel like she was just sitting on the floor.

Fatima put her hands flat on the table on either side of the crystal ball. "What do you want to know?"

Tru shrugged. "I guess what my future holds?" She already knew about her immediate future. Tomorrow, she'd be off to Nocturne Falls, where her aunts, Cleopatra and Delphina, made their home. Once there, Tru would go through the ceremony of the oracles with them to claim her powers.

She'd apprentice with them for at least a few months, until her powers matured. Then she'd be a full-fledged oracle, capable of seeing through the veil of time. What happened after that was up to her, but most likely, she'd move to Nocturne Falls permanently and work with her aunts.

"You must have questions," Fatima insisted. "Something more specific. Come now. What would you like to know?"

Tru shrugged again. "My birthday's tomorrow. How about what will my thirty-third year bring?"

"Focus on that. Fix it in your mind." Fatima nodded at the crystal ball. "Then put your hands on top of the crystal, palms down."

Tru did as Fatima asked. The crystal was cool to the touch. Tru glanced over at Cindy, who was grinning.

"Pay attention," Fatima demanded.

Tru looked straight ahead again. "Sorry."

"Now," Fatima said. "Close your eyes and open yourself to the spirit world so that your future might become as crystal-clear as the ball under your hands."

Tru was a little disappointed in having to close her eyes. Mainly because she was curious about what Fatima was going to do next. With a sigh, she closed them.

Mostly. She left them open a slit. Just enough to see what Fatima was doing, which wasn't that hard with the fake lashes Tru was wearing. She'd bought them for herself for her birthday and decided the fair was as good a place as any to try them out.

They were a little heavy and probably way too Kardashian for her, but they seemed to be doing a great job of hiding the fact from Fatima that her eyes weren't completely closed.

Fatima put her hands on the crystal ball just below Tru's. "Spirits, open the doorway between worlds. Show us what lies ahead."

Tru did her best to focus on the question like Fatima had told her to do while also watching the woman's hands.

Suddenly, the crystal ball filled with inky blackness.

Fatima hissed like she'd been burned, then let out a strangled cry and pulled away.

Tru opened her eyes all the way. The black swirled and pulsed with a life of its own. There was no heat or any feeling of movement, but her hands seemed to be glued to the crystal. "What is that?"

Fatima hissed at her, the slightly European accent gone in favor of one that was slightly more New Jersey. "Get out."

Tru yanked her hands free as Cindy jumped to her feet. "We paid you. Tell us what it means."

Fatima crawled backwards toward the draperies, grimacing. "It means ... your friend is about to meet death."

The quiet of the recording booth felt like an oasis to Eamon. The stillness was nearly a palpable thing. It wrapped around him like a cloak of invisibility, soothing and perfect in its tranquility. If only he could spend all of his time in here, his fortress of solitude.

But people refused to stop dying.

He took a sip of hot tea, then tapped the Record button and leaned into the mic. "Death comes for all of us. But sometimes, it comes sooner than expected. An accident, an unexpected illness, and, occasionally, murder. That was the case for Sarah Lynn Trent of Camden, Illinois. Join me, Eamon Underwood, your host, as I dig deeper into the mysterious and unsolved slaying of Sarah Lynn Trent on this season of *Murder Most Foul.*"

He hit the button to start the intro music.

Just then, the small, low-wattage bulb on the desk lamp flashed twice. On, off. On, off. With a sigh and a gentle roll of his eyes, Eamon pressed Stop on his recording. He knew too well what that signal meant.

He picked up his cup of tea and went to the door, already knowing what he'd find on the other side.

His uncle, Seamus Underwood. The older man

smiled at him. "Morning, lad. I'm sorry to interrupt you, but ..."

Eamon nodded. "Who is it this time?"

"Samuel Young. Resident of the retirement home. I've sent Clark to fetch him."

The retirement home usually meant one thing. "Natural causes?"

"Aye." Seamus shrugged. "The man was ninety-four."

Eamon felt some relief. There was some comfort in those who'd made it that long. "I'll get ready." He hadn't planned on going into the funeral home today, but then, Death had its own plans and followed no one's timetable.

And as the undertaker, he had no choice.

"Good lad. I'll be there in a wee bit to deal with the family. Blue skies all day today."

"Thank you." Eamon went off to his room, which was just across the hall at the back of the house. He showered and dressed in his usual black jeans, black shirt, and black sports coat. He put his sunglasses on his head, grabbed his keys and wallet, and went downstairs, his now-empty mug in his hand.

The big Victorian that he shared with his uncle had more than enough space for the two of them. Eamon had considered getting his own place, even looked at a few online, but living alone would mean dealing much more frequently with people.

Living with his uncle allowed him to bypass a lot of personal interaction. And his uncle was good company. And a good man. After all, he'd opened his home and business to Eamon when he'd left Scotland behind for a fresh start in Nocturne Falls.

Didn't hurt, either, that Eamon had someone to watch football with. Someone who understood *real* football. And someone whose impending death he couldn't see.

Such was his special gift, one landed upon him by a lineage of men who'd been too attracted to the wrong women. Banshees and pixies and selkies. A few witches here and there. Tales of a grim reaper, which Eamon thought had to be true, and vampires, which Eamon wasn't so convinced of. Even rumors one of his great-great-grandfathers had taken up with a *cait sith*, a witch who could transform herself into a cat.

Why were all these powerful supernatural women interested in the Underwood men? Because, according to legend, there had once been an Underwood ancestor capable of transforming himself into the most desired of all magical creatures. The symbol of their homeland: The rare and elusive unicorn.

Load of nonsense, if you asked Eamon. A unicorn? Not bloody likely. He flat-out refused to believe it. He knew there were all kinds of supernatural creatures in the world, but there was no way the Underwoods were descended from a line of unicorn shifters.

That was something someone had conjured up along the way to make them all feel a little better about themselves.

What he did know to be true was that all of the strange bloodlines had left the Underwood men with a curious mix of mostly inconsequential supernatural gifts. They'd become magical mutts, essentially. Whether they'd had any real power of their own to begin with was still in question, but now some had none. Some could do a wee bit of magic. A few more had been gifted with the Sight. And then there was Uncle Seamus, who could predict the weather with an uncanny knack.

Eamon had his own burden to bear. He could see things he had no desire to. Like how long a person had left to live.

He climbed into his black Dodge Charger, the windows heavily tinted, as much as the law would allow, and drove to the funeral home. He pulled around back.

The hearse was already there, a sign that Clark was, too. He might have even had Mr. Young wheeled in and on the prep table by now, too.

Eamon parked and went inside. "Clark? I'm here."

Never hurt to announce yourself, Eamon had discovered. Clark was a good worker, seemed to have no issues with anything, but he could be the jumpy sort. Or maybe that had more to do with where he worked.

"Eamon. Morning." Clark stood next to the gurney, which had come out of the hearse and currently held Mr. Young. In a body bag.

"Morning. Seamus filled me in. I'll just go suit up and meet you in there." Eamon kept his gaze focused on Clark's mouth and nose. Any higher and he'd risk seeing the ghostly hourglass that hovered over the young man's head and the sands trickling through as his allotted time ran out.

He saw them over everyone, save those who shared his Underwood blood. The gift, such as it was, had turned him into a recluse.

Trouble was, Eamon liked Clark. He didn't want to know if he had years or months or hours left, because that was part of Eamon's questionable gift. Besides seeing the hourglasses, he also knew, without understanding why, just how long a person had left.

It was too great a burden to bear. Sure, if it was years, that'd be grand. But if it wasn't … Eamon kept his gaze low as he walked to the prep room where Clark would soon be bringing the body.

There was no one else in the funeral home yet, but keeping his head and eyes down had just become habit.

He opened the wardrobe cabinet and hung up his sport coat, putting his sunglasses, keys, and wallet on the top shelf. Then he took out a Tyvek jumpsuit and put it on over his jeans and T-shirt along with a face mask, clear protective glasses, and latex gloves.

Behind him, Clark brought Mr. Young in and easily moved him to the prep table, removing the body bag as he did so. Clark wasn't a big guy, but he was strong, thanks to whatever kind of supernatural he was. Eamon had never asked and didn't plan to. People deserved their privacy.

"Need anything else, Eamon?"

Eamon shook his head but stayed facing the

wardrobe, occupying himself with the zipper on the jumpsuit. It was as good an excuse as any not to make eye contact. "No, I'm all set. Thanks."

"I'll be up front if you need me."

"Fine." He shut the wardrobe door. "Seamus will be in soon."

"All right." The soft shush of the prep room doors announced Clark's departure.

Alone, Eamon turned to his new client. He gazed at the man, studying him. Mr. Young's eyes were shut, but he had a kind expression on his face, his mouth ever so slightly curved in a gentle smile. Almost as though he'd been ready to go. Maybe he had been. The man had been on the Earth nearly a century.

How many of his friends and family had already gone ahead of him? How many was he leaving behind?

Eamon gave the man a smile in return. "Hello, Mr. Young. Ninety-four isn't bad at all. Good for you. Now, let's get you ready to see your family one last time."

Last night at the fair had seriously upset Tru. She'd walked into Fatima's tent thinking it was all just a joke. But she'd walked out shaken to the core.

She'd almost canceled her trip. How was she supposed to act like nothing had happened? Like she hadn't been told she was about to die? Tru's mother had died from a stroke when Tru was just nineteen. At least, the doctors had said it was a stroke. She'd overheard relatives at the funeral talking about how her mother's gifts had been too much for her to handle.

The same gifts Tru was about to receive. Add to that Fatima's prediction, and Tru had thought about nothing else the entire flight here.

Now, sitting in the back seat of her Aunt Cleo's turquoise blue Jeep, Tru wasn't sure anything made sense anymore. What if becoming an oracle was the thing that caused her to meet death?

She was only thirty-three. She'd barely begun to live.

"You're awfully quiet," Aunt Delly said. Her auburn curls were more burgundy than Tru remembered. She must have changed her color.

"Sorry," Tru answered. She did her best to smile. Probably wasn't that convincing, so it was a good thing neither of her aunts could see her from their seats up front. "I'm just a little tired, I guess."

Behind the wheel, Aunt Cleo nodded. Her salt-and-pepper waves were clipped up in a twist. "Travel wears me out, too."

"Do you think it would be okay if we held off on the ceremony for a couple days?" Tru asked.

"Sure," Aunt Delly said, but she was looking at Cleo. "Right?"

"There are no rules about how soon after your birthday the ceremony has to take place," Aunt Cleo answered. "Just that it must be done in the thirty-third year. The ceremony itself never changes, either." She glanced at Tru through the rearview mirror before putting her eyes back on the road. "We can wait a couple days until you're up to it. Probably not a bad idea. It can be a taxing process, especially when you actually get your powers. Although you might feel invigorated after it. Everyone responds differently."

"Well, I'd like to wait a little bit," Tru said. "Thank you."

Aunt Delly twisted in her seat to look back at Tru. Her eyes were bright and full of happiness. "It's so good to have you here."

Tru's smile was genuine this time. "It's good to be here." If anyone would know what had happened to her last night in the fortune teller's tent, it would be her aunts. She just wasn't sure if she wanted to tell them or not. They were oracles, after all. Although, what if they confirmed what Fatima had told her?

"Are you hungry?" Aunt Delly asked.

"No," Tru said. Then a low growl came from her midsection and made a liar out of her.

Aunt Cleo laughed. "Looks like your stomach thinks otherwise."

"Okay," Tru said. "I guess I am. But I really don't want you guys to go to any trouble." She knew what would happen otherwise. Her aunts would disappear into the kitchen, making a huge Greek feast of salads and dolmas, moussaka, chicken and lamb skewers, maybe even stuffed peppers or pastitsio. They'd set out bowls of olives and hummus along with plates heaped high with pita bread.

For dessert, they'd make baklava. Possibly rice pudding, too. Maybe even some koulourakia, the twisty little orange-scented cookies that went so well with coffee.

It would all be delicious, but the amount of work—and cleanup—a meal like that took ... Tru didn't want to be the cause of that.

"Trouble?" Aunt Cleo snorted through her nose like a horse. "Feeding our niece is trouble? You're about to become an oracle. You need to be fed. Your body needs to be nourished with the foods of our ancestors. It's no trouble."

Aunt Delly twisted to look at her again, making her dangling earrings swing. She had to be nearly sixty, but she acted like a teenager. "Plus, it's already made."

Tru laughed. "All right."

Aunt Cleo slowed the Jeep as they neared the neighborhood, slowing further as she turned down Shadows Drive and approached the house.

Tru leaned forward to get a better look at the place. "I forgot how beautiful your home is."

The gorgeous old Victorian was painted in several shades of green and accented in white. It was like something out of a storybook, especially with the beautiful landscaping and the big, mature trees that provided just the right amount of shade.

The whole street was gorgeous, each house like a designer chocolate in a box of delicious treats. Row after row of Victorian and Georgian houses lined each side of Shadows Drive.

"We love it," Aunt Cleo said, parking in the driveway and turning off the Jeep. "And we love living here. Mostly."

"Mostly?" Tru's hand stopped on the door handle. "What's that mean?"

"Oh, nothing," Aunt Delly said. "It's fine. We just have a questionable neighbor."

Tru furrowed her brow. "Questionable?"

"He's a vampire," Aunt Cleo said. "And very shady."

Tru laughed, then realized her aunt hadn't meant that as a joke. "Oh. How do you know that?"

"Well, he probably is," Aunt Cleo said. "He skulks around."

"He *skulks?*" Tru's brows bent. "Is that an exclusive vampire trait?"

Aunt Delly pursed her lips. "It could be. Plus, he only wears black, and he always wears sunglasses during the day."

"So he goes out during the day?" Tru frowned. "Can vampires do that?"

"Maybe," Aunt Cleo said. "There's all sorts of new technological breakthroughs these days. Who knows what they can do?! Maybe there's some new kind of vampire sunscreen out there. I'm just saying you should steer clear."

Tru nodded. Her aunts were just looking out for her. But she was a little worried about them. "Is he bothering you?"

"No." Aunt Delly glared at her sister. "He's just unsettling, that's all. We wouldn't have stayed if he was a problem. And the man he lives with seems nice. Not sure exactly, but I think it could be his dad. Or maybe older brother. Anyway, let's get you in and settled and you can meet our gang."

Tru got out. The "gang" was the horde of rescue cats that lived with her aunts. She loved cats but hadn't had any since she was a kid. She grabbed her suitcase out of the back, along with her carry-on and her purse, and headed toward the side entrance of the house behind her aunts.

"We've put you up on the third floor," Aunt Cleo said. "I hope that's okay. It's quieter up there, and the cats are less likely to bother you there. Plus, the whole floor will be yours."

"It's fine. I don't mind steps. They're good exercise. And I don't think the cats will bother me." Tru didn't have any pets currently, because the apartment she shared didn't allow them. But that didn't mean she was against them. She thought animals were great.

"The stairs are definitely exercise," Aunt Delly said. She opened the door. "All right, all of you away from the door, now. Shoo. Get back."

Tru walked in behind her aunt and just stared at the feline abundance. There were cats everywhere she looked. At least five. No, wait. Six. Or seven. "So, uh, how many cats do you guys have at the moment?"

"Fifteen," Aunt Cleo answered without hesitation. She pointed to the ones in front of them, naming them as she went. "The calico is Dolly, then those two brown tabbies are Mr. and Mrs. Shrimps. The white longhair is Angel. Pickles is the gray and white one. Captain Carrot is the ginger, naturally, and then there's Big Head Ed, the tuxedo. That gray tabby is Princess. The rest you'll meet eventually. Dr. Booples and Frankie and Little Joe and Butternut and—"

"Fifteen," Tru repeated softly. That was a lot of cats. More than she'd been expecting. She inhaled. Somehow, the house didn't smell. Although it was a big house. Maybe a house of this size could handle that many cats. Well, obviously, it could. Or at least it seemed to be. "How do you keep them all straight?"

Aunt Cleo shrugged. "They're our kids. It's not hard."

"Probably sounds like a lot," Aunt Delly said. "But it's not. Not really. And that includes our newest baby, Nemo. He just showed up on our front porch one day, no mama, no brothers or sisters. Our vet says he's about two months old. We had to take him in. He's the cutest little orange nugget. You'll meet him. He's probably sleeping on the catio."

"Catio?"

Aunt Delly answered. "It's an outside screened porch that the cats have access to through a cat door in the laundry room. That way if we're not home to let them onto the main screened porch, they can still get fresh air. Of course, we can access it, too, but it's really their own space. Anyway, none of them are outside cats, so be sure not to let them slip out, even if they tell you it's all right."

Tru nodded. "Got it."

"Do you want a tour? Or do you remember where everything is?" Aunt Cleo asked.

"I think I remember." Tru hadn't been here since she was a teenager. Back when her mom had still been alive. "I'll just take my stuff upstairs and maybe lay down for a few minutes. If that's all right?"

"Of course it's all right," Aunt Cleo said. "That will give us time to heat everything up for dinner. Half an hour?"

"Half an hour sounds great." Tru gathered her things and started up the steps. A few cats went with her. There were more on the landing of the second floor. An enormous fellow with blue eyes who was mostly white with touches of apricot on his face and paws gazed at her from his seat on an upholstered bench against the wall. The tag on his collar read, "Butternut."

Tru paused. "Hi, Butternut."

He blinked at her.

She smiled. "You are very handsome."

He flopped over and looked at her from his new, upside-down viewpoint.

She laughed and gave his belly a tickle. "You're funny, too. Maybe you can be the new man in my life. Between us, it's been a while." She adjusted her grip on the suitcase handle. "Guess I'll see you later."

She took her suitcase up the next flight of steps to the third floor. It was as nice a space as she remembered from her youth. The stairs opened onto an area that was set up like a little reading nook, then there were two rooms with a spacious shared bathroom in between. The other half of the third floor was storage, which made sense, since it had once been the attic.

Her room was the largest of the two, but it had been made over since her last visit here. The pink teen-girl vibes were gone, replaced by pale blue walls, crisp white furniture, and a big, dark blue and white rag rug over the hardwood floors. Paintings of Greece adorned the walls, pairing beautifully with the dark blue and yellow accents throughout.

Tru smiled. It was a gorgeous room. The bed was

stacked with plump pillows. Then one of the pillows moved, startling her. She laughed at her own silliness.

A little orange cat stretched and yawned.

"Were you under the pillows? I bet you're Nemo." She set her things down and went over to pick him up. "Oh, you're so soft."

He pushed his head against her face, making her smile. His little purrs started immediately.

Her heart melted as she cradled him in her arms. She was so glad she hadn't let Fatima's prediction change her mind about coming. At this moment, her aunts' house seemed like exactly where she needed to be.

With Mr. Young taken care of, Eamon washed up, shed his protective clothing, and gathered his things from the wardrobe. Instead of going to see his uncle, who might very well be busy with Mr. Young's family and the planning of the funeral, Eamon sent him a text. It was just easier.

Headed home unless you need me.

Seamus's response came quickly. *All good here. Just wrapping things up. Shouldn't be more than a half hour behind you. Thoughts about dinner?*

Something easy, Eamon responded. *Pizza?* They ordered in from Salvatore's often. He shrugged on his sports coat. Maybe too often. But they were two single men, and takeaway was easy. Of course, both of them knew how to cook a few things. But whipping up a cottage pie or even eggs and chips just seemed like too much work some nights.

And when there was footy on, pizza went so well with a cold pint. Tonight, Aberdeen was facing Motherwell in what was sure to be an epic battle. Being able to watch all the best games was the main reason they had such an elaborate setup with their streaming services. VPNs made all sorts of things possible.

Seamus's reply was a fast thumbs-up.

Eamon snorted softly at the emoji. Seamus never said no to Salvatore's. *I'll order our usual then.*

He tucked his phone and wallet into his pockets, put his sunglasses on, and went out to his car.

He waited until he got home to order the pizza, trying to estimate when it and his uncle would arrive. He placed the order for their standard, a large meat lover's, along with two salads, something neither of them was that fond of, but they tried to force down a little veg now and then. He added an order of Salvatore's donuts, too.

Those were really just knobs of pizza dough fried, then shaken in cinnamon and sugar, but they were brilliant after a long day. Especially dipped into the chocolate sauce that came along with them. He and his uncle had definitely had a long day and deserved the sweet treat.

Anyone who thought that those working in the funeral arts didn't feel anything for their clients, or their clients' families, was wrong.

It was hard work. Some days harder than others. The job required compassion and empathy and respect. Mr. Young might have lived a long life, but there was no doubt in Eamon's mind that he'd left behind friends and family who'd loved him dearly and would certainly miss him.

With the pizza ordered, Eamon went upstairs to take a proper shower. He turned the water on to let it warm up, then shed his clothes, depositing them into the hamper just under his bedroom window. Which was when he noticed a light on in the third floor of the house next door.

He'd never seen a light on up there. He stared for a moment, but it didn't really concern him. It was just curious. Maybe one of the cats had turned it on. The two women that lived over there were absolutely barmy about cats.

He went off to shower. He probably stood too long under the hot water, but it felt brilliant. He thought about his podcast. He'd need to make more headway tomorrow. Hopefully get the whole first episode recorded. Then his mind shifted back to Mr. Young.

And then back to the light in the window next door.

He dressed in lounge pants and an Aberdeen T-shirt, then went downstairs. The pizza wasn't too far out, according to the app.

His uncle shouldn't be, either.

While he waited, Eamon did a few chores. Loaded the dishwasher with the dishes from last night's dinner, which were still in the sink. Took out the trash and put a new liner in the bin. Wiped down the counters. Picked up a few random bits and bobs in the living room.

Finally, he filled a pitcher with water and went out onto the back porch to give his uncle's beloved plants a drink. He left the lights off, preferring the dark, although the sun hadn't quite set, so there was still more than enough light to see by.

He worked his way around the porch, stopping when

he was about half done to go back in and refill the pitcher. Eamon wasn't much on plants one way or the other, but he had to admit that the pots of flowers, especially the geraniums with their spicy scent, really made the back porch look and smell nice.

He drained the pitcher into the last one, a big spider plant cascading with babies, then just stood there a moment, listening.

There was a fence separating his uncle's yard from the yard next door, meaning he couldn't see into their property. But he could hear them. The two women must be having dinner on their back porch. But there was a new voice. One he didn't recognize. Also female.

He listened closer. The new woman's voice held the fullness of youth and a trill of joy, but there were occasional moments of ... doubt. Was that what it was? Aye, doubt seemed to edge certain answers or comments. Maybe a wee bit of anxiety.

Whoever had joined them wasn't completely happy. Something was bothering her.

Since starting up his podcast, he'd learned a lot about the nuances of inflection and tone in the human voice. He strived to keep his full and rounded, not letting his accent get in the way of being understood. He'd practiced a lot.

He'd developed a real understanding of the emotions a voice could convey, as well.

Then he picked up something new from the conversation. The younger woman called one of the older women "aunt."

The crazy cat women had their niece in to visit. No doubt also a crazy cat woman, if she was staying with them. *You'd have to be*, he thought. Those two nutters had a hundred cats over there. Maybe more.

Devilish things. He'd never had a cat, but he knew all about the old tales of the creatures stealing people's breath and being bad luck. He crossed himself and went back inside just as the doorbell rang. He didn't answer it, though. Just looked at the doorbell camera on his phone. The pizza was being delivered. He still didn't need to answer it. He'd paid and given the driver a tip through the app already.

Living in the age of "contact-free" had made his life so much easier. Only when he saw people face-to-face did he see the hourglass hovering over them. Seeing them through any kind of lens erased that, be it a camera or the television.

He waited until the man's vehicle was pulling out of the driveway to head to the front door and retrieve their food. As he was doing that, his uncle arrived.

Eamon gave him a wave, then took the food into the kitchen. He got out plates, plus forks for the salads, then fired up the telly and found the channel for the game.

His uncle walked in, loosening his tie. "Long day. Mr. Young will have a beautiful service, though. You did a wonderful job with him."

"I appreciate that. Nice family?"

Seamus nodded. "A son and a daughter, lots of grand-children, plus a younger brother and a good deal of his family. It'll be well-attended."

"That's always nice." Eamon left the pizza box closed.

"Just let me shower and change and I'll be down to eat."

"Of course."

Seamus was a man of his word, returning fifteen minutes later, dressed much like Eamon was and smelling of the bay rum soap he favored.

They put a couple of slices of pizza on their plates, salads somehow overlooked, grabbed a beer each, then settled into their spots in the living room. The game was still in preshow, with the actual kickoff a couple of minutes out.

The commentators were just filling airtime with the usual chatter. Eamon glanced over at his uncle. "The cat ladies have a visitor."

"Oh?"

Eamon nodded. "Their niece, best I can tell."

Seamus smiled. "That's nice." He was always cordial to the sisters next door. Mostly, Eamon thought, because he fancied one of them, something Seamus had never confirmed nor denied.

"There's no way we're related to them, right?"

Seamus made a face at him. "Did ya hit yer head, lad? They're Greek. We don't even come from the same continent."

Eamon snorted softly before taking another bite. You

wouldn't find him sniffing after any woman. Not when he could see how long she had left on this Earth. He'd tried it once, and it hadn't gone well, so he was content to be without a partner.

Especially not with one who was doolally over cats.

The food had been as good as Tru could have hoped for. Better, maybe. She'd eaten far too many dolmas, the rolled grape leaves filled with a mix of rice, ground lamb, and spices. She'd had too much of everything, really.

The homemade hummus, fragrant with lemon and garlic, then the moussaka, a delicious casserole of eggplant, more ground lamb, cheese, and bechamel sauce. They'd had that with a salad of cucumbers, tomatoes, red onions, olives, and feta cheese drizzled with olive oil and vinegar, then sprinkled with fresh dill.

All of it accompanied by pita bread and Greek wine.

They'd laughed and talked and told stories. Now, as Aunt Delly came out with a platter of baklava squares and Aunt Cleo followed behind with a bottle of ouzo and three small glasses, Tru just laughed at the idea that she had space for more.

She shook her head. "I don't have room for any of that."

"There's always room for dessert," Aunt Delly said, putting the platter down on the table.

Aunt Cleo set the glasses next to it, pulled the stopper from the bottle, then poured the clear, anise-flavored liqueur into the glasses. "You can watch your diet tomorrow. But tonight, we are celebrating. Not just your birthday but you being here with us again. Hopefully for good this time."

Tru nodded. "It's been too long."

Her aunts nodded in agreement. Aunt Cleo passed out the glasses of ouzo, then lifted hers as she took her seat. "Here's to our little family reunion and to the arrival of a brand-new oracle."

Tru tentatively raised her glass. She wasn't feeling quite as enthusiastic about becoming an oracle. Not since the whole "about to meet death" business. "To our reunion."

"To us," Aunt Delly said.

Tru tossed back the ouzo. It burned a slow fire down her throat, warming her insides like a licorice-scented blaze.

She'd been a little tipsy before the ouzo, which was strong stuff. Now she was glad she was seated. "No more of that for me or I'll end up sleeping out here."

Somehow, the glasses got filled again and another toast made and drunk to.

When that toast was over and the shots of ouzo gone, they helped themselves to pieces of baklava. They sat and ate and chatted some more until Aunt Cleo yawned.

Tru nodded. "I'm right there with you. Ready for bed."

"I'm sure you are," Aunt Delly said. "You've had a long day."

"And a lot to drink," Tru added. "More than usual. A lot more."

Aunt Cleo stood and started gathering things up to take inside. "Dishes can wait until morning. Let's just get them in."

They worked together, clearing the table in short order. Aunt Delly put out food for the cats and topped off their water bowls while Aunt Cleo tidied up the kitchen a little.

"What can I do to help?" Tru asked.

"Nothing," Aunt Cleo answered. "You're a guest. At least for tonight. Tomorrow you can start acting like a working member of the household."

Tru smiled. "Okay. I'll say good night then. Love you both."

"Love you, too, sweetheart," Aunt Delly said. A black cat wound around her feet.

Tru hesitated on her way to the steps. "Will I have cats sleeping with me?"

"You might," Aunt Cleo said.

Aunt Delly nodded. "If you don't want them to, shut your door. If you do, leave it open."

"Okay. See you in the morning." Tru started up the steps. She already knew she was going to leave her door open. The idea of having a little warm body to snuggle with sounded very comforting.

She should have told her aunts about what had happened in Fatima's tent, but they'd had such a happy evening, filled with memories and stories, and Tru hadn't wanted to ruin any of it by sharing Fatima's words.

Thankfully, their powers of precognition only came through touch. And then only with non-oracles. So until Tru was ready to share, they wouldn't know.

Still, she needed to tell them soon. Tomorrow, maybe. Over breakfast. Then they'd have the whole day to talk about it and try to understand what it could mean. She knew better than to ask her aunts to use their gifts to read her future. As a rule, oracles didn't read other oracles. Although maybe that didn't apply to her, since she hadn't gone through the ceremony yet.

She reached the third floor and went into her bedroom. She'd opened the window a couple of inches before going down to dinner, just to get some fresh air in the room, but it was a little too cool now. She closed it, then unzipped her suitcase and got busy unpacking. She wasn't really in the mood, but it needed to be done. If she left everything in there, it would be a wrinkled mess. She was also hoping to sober up and thought the activity might help.

Everything seemed to take longer than necessary, which seemed like it had everything to do with what she'd had to drink. Finally, she got everything hung up or put away in the dresser. She didn't feel like the ouzo had worn off any, though.

With her suitcase emptied, she grabbed a nightgown and made her way into the bathroom to wash her face, brush her teeth, and get ready for bed.

She was going to sleep like the dead tonight. No, wait, not like the dead. Just like a very tired person.

Yes, that was better. A very tired but still alive person.

She brushed her teeth and was about to take her makeup off when she thought she heard a cat meow. In this house, it probably hadn't been a figment of her inebriated mind. Maybe one had come up to sleep on her bed.

She returned to the bedroom and had a look but didn't see one. None on the landing, either. The meow came again, but it was softer this time. Like the cat had gotten farther away. Or was outside.

Her gaze snapped to the window. Oh, no. A sudden panic washed over her. She'd had the window open. What were the odds ...

She ran around the bed to the window, yanked it back up, all the way, and peered out. There was no screen. It was dark outside now, and the trees around the property blocked out a lot of light. "Kitty?" she whispered.

Please don't be outside, please don't be outside, please don't be—

A little meow answered her.

Oh, boy. She understood Fatima's words now. She was going to die because her aunts were going to kill her. Worse, there was only one cat she'd seen so far that could fit through the narrow opening she'd left.

Nemo. The new kitten. *Their baby.*

She was in so much trouble.

She grabbed her phone and shined the flashlight

onto the roof in time to see the little orange fuzzball making his way to the ground via the house's intricate detailing and gingerbread accents.

She had to get Nemo back before her aunts found out. Hopefully, they were already in bed. Asleep.

Tru went downstairs as quickly and as quietly as she could. Which would have been easier if she hadn't had that last shot of ouzo.

It was giving her determination, though. She was going to get the kitten back into the house before anyone was the wiser.

The downstairs was dark and quiet, which boded well for her aunts already being in bed. She slipped out onto the back porch, down into the yard, and kept her voice down. "Nemo. Here, baby. *Psp psp psp.*"

Phone in hand, flashlight on, she panned the backyard to see if she could spot him.

She did. Just as he went through a gap in the fence and into the neighbor's yard. She swallowed and felt a sudden chill go through her. Wasn't that the neighbor her aunts had said was a vampire?

Would he … eat Nemo? There couldn't be that much blood in a kitten. They were so small. But maybe that made them extra tasty? *Please don't let that be true.* It had to be just the ouzo giving her those ideas. *Stupid ouzo.*

She had to go after him.

Panicked, she stuck her phone in her back pocket, then hopped up onto a bench along the fence and heaved herself over into the neighbor's yard.

She hit the ground with a soft thud, landing in a flower bed and crushing what might have been marigolds. She hadn't been aware vampires had any gardening skills. When did they do it? At night?

Focus.

She tried to get her bearings. Thankfully, the vampire's house was dark, so maybe he was in bed. Except weren't vampires nocturnal? Hmm. He could be out then. Looking for his dinner. Even better. Although not for whoever he found.

She shuddered and tried to concentrate on the task at hand. The ouzo really seemed to be kicking in. Never again. That stuff was way too strong. She brushed off the marigold bits and crept along the fence toward the spot where the kitten had slipped through. She found the gap but no cat.

She really wanted to turn her flashlight back on, but that might draw attention to herself. She supposed she had no choice.

Reluctantly, she pulled her phone out and tapped the flashlight app, nearly blinding herself. She squinted to get her night vision back as she turned the phone toward the yard and took a good look around.

A dash of orange between some bushes caught her eye. He was running toward the house.

"No, not that way! Come to me! Do you want to get eaten?" It was hard to yell for a kitten when you were trying not to make any noise. If Nemo became a vampire's midnight snack, her aunts would definitely kill her.

She turned the flashlight off, shoved the phone into her pocket, and went after him, praying she got to him before the bloodsucking neighbor did, fear coursing through her at the very idea.

Then a new thought hit her. Maybe the vampire was how *she* died.

Eamon was just about to head up to bed when a flash of light in the backyard caught his eye. Someone was out there. He glanced toward the stairs. The house was dark, and his uncle had already turned in.

As much as Eamon avoided face-to-face contact, in the case of an intruder, he'd make an exception.

He quietly moved out onto the back porch. There was enough light for him to see by, one of the few benefits of his muddled supernatural blood. A dark shape was nearly at the path that led up to the door of the back porch.

He left the lights off as he soundlessly made his way closer to the door. "Can I help you?"

A little gasp answered him. He reached out and flicked on the outside lights, illuminating the trespasser.

A young, attractive woman stood slightly hunched over in the yard. As intruders went, not at all what he'd expected.

She blinked at him, eyes slightly glassy and transfixed. On him. She seemed to focus suddenly, and a new emotion appeared. Fear.

"Can I help you?" he repeated.

Her gaze darted around, but otherwise she stayed very still. "I'm, um, looking for Nemo."

"Sure you are." Eamon stared at her as he crossed his arms. "And what does this Nemo look like?"

"Um ..." She held her hands about ten inches apart. "He's about this big. And orange. With stripes."

That voice. She was the crazy cat ladies' niece. Had they put her up to this? He was in no mood. "And let me guess—your name is Dory."

She blinked at him again, genuine confusion in her eyes this time. "What?"

He pushed open the screen door and walked down the path, stopping a few feet away from her. The tang of alcohol drifted past him.

So she'd had a few. Maybe that explained—but then another realization struck him like a blast of arctic air, freezing him in place. He was looking right at her. And there was no hourglass over her head.

He felt bolted to the spot. "Are you ... a ghost?"

"A ghost? You think I'm dead?" Her lower lip quivered. She backed up. "Why would you say that?"

"No, I just—"

"Please don't bite me," she whispered. "I probably taste awful. I just want to get my cat and go home."

He couldn't fathom why she thought he was going to bite her, but then drunk people didn't always make sense. He sighed. Despite her inebriation, she was very pretty. And seemed perfectly alive. "You're looking for your cat?"

She nodded. "Nemo. He's a little ginger kitten. He

slipped through the gap in your fence. He's not supposed to be outside, but I left the window open. My aunts are going to kill me. Or ... you are. I'm sorry about trespassing. I really am. I just want the cat and I'll go." Then she whispered, "Please don't let Fatima be right."

He had no clue what she was talking about, but she looked like she might start crying. "It's okay," he said. "We'll look for him together, all right?"

"You promise you're not going to eat him?"

Eamon stared at her. "Why would I eat your cat? And why would you think I'd bite you?"

"Because of what you are."

He went still. How did she know what he was? He wasn't even sure himself. Could she tell he saw death in people? "I don't know what you mean."

"I mean because you're a, you know. A vampire."

He stared at her for another second before he started to laugh. He almost couldn't stop. He hadn't laughed like that in a long time. He used the last of his air to get a few words out. "You think ... I'm a ... vampire?"

"I don't see what's so funny about it." She straightened slightly, looking indignant. "Well, aren't you?"

He managed to catch his breath. "Not even close. I'm a —" He'd been about to say an undertaker, but he wasn't sure how much that would help. "I'm a podcaster. And I work part-time for my uncle. But I promise, I'm not a vampire."

Her eyes held a dubious glare.

Amused as he was, he realized she was even more

attractive than he'd originally thought. There was something about her eyes. Then again, he didn't get to look into a lot of people's eyes like this. "Would you like help finding your kitten?"

She nodded. "Yes. Please."

"Let me go get a flashlight and I'll be right back."

"Okay."

He headed back up the path toward the porch. He opened the door, and a little orange streak zipped past. "What the—cat!"

"Hey," the young woman yelled. "Grab him."

Eamon chased after the cat and scooped him up. The little furball went limp in his grasp, snuggling against him. And purring.

Eamon stared down at the kitten, transfixed by how soft and warm it was. "I've got him," he said softly.

The young woman joined him on the porch. "Wow. You must be like a cat whisperer or something. He likes you a lot. I didn't know vampires were so good with animals."

"I'm *not* a vampire." But Eamon smiled at the wee creature. "He's not so bad, either." The little cat kneaded his paws against Eamon's chest. He looked up at the young woman. "I'm Eamon, by the way."

She met his gaze. "I'm Tru. Thanks for catching Nemo. And for not being bothered by me climbing over your fence to get him." She shook her head. "I think I flattened some of your marigolds. I'm sorry about that. I had too much to drink tonight. But in my defense, it is my birthday."

"Happy birthday." *Tru*. He repeated her name in his head, unable to look away from her. How was there no hourglass over her head? And who was this beautiful, tipsy creature that had just appeared in his life?

"Thanks." She pointed at him. Or maybe she was pointing at the cat he was still holding. "I should probably get him back in the house."

"Hmm? Oh, aye, the cat." Eamon handed the animal to her, surprised by how the warmth from his little body disappeared and left Eamon missing the contact.

Tru cradled Nemo in her arms and smiled down at him. "You little stinker. No more running off, okay?"

"He's, uh, pretty young, right?"

"Yes," Tru said. Nemo was the picture of contentment, almost as if he liked being held that way. "He's just a kitten. And full of energy. Although he'll probably sleep after his adventure now."

Eamon looked at her again. He couldn't understand why he wasn't seeing the hourglass. There was no way they were related. "You knew about vampires, so you must be some kind of supernatural yourself, right?"

The happiness disappeared off her face. "I'm not anything. Thanks again, but I should go."

"Aye, sure. Unless you plan on climbing back over the fence, I can let you out through the gate."

She nodded. "That would be great."

He led her out and down the path, then around the

side of the house, where a gate in the fence opened onto the end of the driveway. He held it for her. "It was nice to meet you, Tru." He reached out and scratched Nemo's belly. "You, too, Nemo."

"Thanks for being so understanding, Eamon. And again for the help with Nemo."

He smiled, gazing at her and enjoying the fact that he could. "Anytime."

She slipped off into the darkness.

He stood there a moment longer, staring after her and wondering what kind of creature was immune to his power.

He latched the gate and walked back to the house. He turned the outside lights off and went in.

His uncle was in the kitchen, his robe pulled on over his nightclothes. "I thought I heard something."

Eamon glanced toward the house next door. "Neighbor had a missing cat. All is well now."

Seamus nodded. "Going up then?"

"Right behind you." Eamon followed his uncle upstairs. Was all well? Not exactly. He felt flummoxed by what he'd seen tonight. Or, rather, hadn't seen.

What was so special about Tru? What kind of supernatural was she? What made him unable to see her hourglass? There was no way they were related, was there? He couldn't imagine how.

He had so many questions and so few answers, which meant this wasn't something he could let rest. He had to find out more.

Tru had to come through the gate in her aunts' fence to get back into the house, because she didn't have a key to the front door yet. She'd have to ask them about that tomorrow.

She took Nemo inside, then quickly went back out to the yard, making sure the door was shut behind her. She looked around for something to block the gap in the fence with, just in case Nemo figured out how to get out again.

She settled on a flat, decorative stone from one of the flower beds. She let out a sigh as she picked it up. She'd flattened some of the vampire's flowers.

He might have claimed to not be a vampire, but she wasn't so sure. She'd never met one before. How was she to know?

Didn't vampires have mesmerizing eyes? Because Eamon had those, for sure. And that Scottish accent ... Parts of her still felt like warm butter from listening to him.

Stupid ouzo.

She'd have to buy him some new marigolds to replace the ones she'd smashed. She did *not* want to be in the debt of a vampire. Not one who had clearly used his charms of seduction to make her think he was handsome and sexy.

Ew. So gross. Except she didn't think he was gross at all. Proof of how powerful he was, she supposed.

She carried the round stone over to the fence and wedged it into place in front of the gap so that nothing could get through. Satisfied with her work, she went back in, locked the house, and headed upstairs.

The drinks she'd had at dinner finally seemed to be wearing off, leaving her exhausted and ready to crash.

Back on the third floor, she finished her interrupted routine, washing her face and changing into the nightgown that was still sitting next to the sink. When she came back out to the bedroom, Nemo was curled up on one of the pillows.

She shook her head. "I didn't see or hear you come up. You are way too quiet."

She climbed into bed, leaning over to give the little cat some pets. She kissed the top of his head. "You gave me such a scare, you stinker."

He smelled of a man's fragrance. Like soap or body wash. She knew exactly where that had come from. Eamon.

She turned the bedside lamp off and looked toward the house next door. Just because Fatima's words hadn't come true tonight didn't mean they wouldn't. Living next to a vampire wasn't something Tru could just brush off.

She'd have to tell her aunts in the morning. She put

her head down on the pillow and tried to work that conversation out in her mind.

The next thing she knew, she was opening her eyes to daylight. She hadn't remembered falling asleep, but she'd been really tired.

She stretched and looked around. Nemo was nowhere to be seen. None of the cats were. She pulled on some leggings and a big T-shirt, knotted her hair into a messy bun, and went downstairs in hopes of coffee, although she didn't smell any.

She found Aunt Delly in the kitchen, using a Keurig to make a cup for herself. That explained why there hadn't been much smell.

"Morning," Tru said. A line of cats were eating at the bowls against the far wall, happily devouring their breakfast.

Aunt Delly turned. "Morning. How did you sleep?"

"Pretty good. I don't actually remember falling asleep. That's how tired I was." She looked around. "Where's Aunt Cleo?"

"Giving Butternut his inhaler."

Tru furrowed her brow. "Butternut uses an inhaler?"

Aunt Delly sipped her coffee before she nodded. "Yep. He's an asthmatic. Takes it like a champ, though."

"He's a beautiful cat. I met him on the second floor last night as I was going upstairs."

"On the padded bench?"

Tru nodded as she walked over to make a cup for herself, getting a mug down from the cupboard.

Aunt Delly smiled. "That's his favorite spot. He likes to keep an eye on things."

Aunt Cleo came down the steps. "Meds done, litter boxes cleaned, water bowls refilled." She grinned at Tru. "Morning."

"Morning. You guys must have quite the routine going to keep up with all the cats, huh?" Tru put a new K-Cup in the machine, Sumatran dark roast, stuck a cup under the spout, and hit Brew.

"We divide the work," Aunt Cleo said. "Doesn't take much time at all now."

Aunt Delly shrugged. "It's just part of our day, you know? And some of these cats wouldn't be around if not for us."

Tru walked over to the windows while she waited on her coffee. There were a few cats out on the screened porch and a couple more in the catio. "Nemo slept on the bed with me last night. Not sure what time he left, but he's such a sweetie."

Aunt Cleo nodded. "He is."

The Keurig sputtered out the last few drops. Tru walked back to get her cup, added some of the creamer Aunt Delly had left out, along with some sugar, then sipped it, careful not to burn her tongue. After a few sips, she found the courage she'd been lacking earlier. "There's something I need to tell you both."

"Oh?" Aunt Cleo looked up from the sink where she was washing her hands. When she made eye contact with Tru, she said, "Is something wrong?"

Tru shook her head. She wanted to tell her aunts, but at the same time, she was afraid of how they'd interpret it. And she didn't know where to start. She almost felt like crying.

"We should sit down at the table," Aunt Delly said. She put her arm around Tru. "Come on, it'll be all right. Whatever it is."

"She's right," Aunt Cleo chimed in.

When they were all settled at the table with coffee in front of them, Tru started the only place she could think of. The beginning of it all. The fair.

"Cindy thought we should go to the fair for my birthday. Ride some rides, play some games, eat the craziest foods they had to offer. And we did. It was fun. But toward the end of the night, she suggested I get my fortune told."

Her aunts' faces already held concern. Now they took on a bit of worry.

Aunt Delly leaned in. "Was she a scammer?"

"I don't know," Tru answered.

Aunt Cleo cut her eyes at her sister. "Let her tell the story."

Aunt Delly rolled her eyes. "So bossy." Then she winked at Tru. "That's how the older ones are."

"Delphina."

Aunt Delly pursed her lips. "Go on, Tru. We're listening."

Tru gathered her thoughts. "Her name was Fatima."

"Not her real name," Aunt Delly muttered.

Aunt Cleo sighed loudly.

Tru decided just to plow on. "My friend paid her, then Fatima told me to think of a question I wanted answered and put my hands on the crystal ball. Which was very nice and definitely real, by the way."

Her aunts nodded but kept quiet. For a few seconds. Then Aunt Cleo spoke. "What was your question?"

"What would my thirty-third year bring?"

"Good one," Aunt Delly said.

"So I thought about it as I put my hands on the crystal ball. She told me to close my eyes, but I left them open just a slit so I could watch Fatima. She put her hands on the ball, too, right below mine. Then she commanded the spirits to open the doorway between worlds and ..."

Tru stared into her coffee, the vision of swirling black filling her head. "It was impossible not to see the crystal, too. And as I watched, the inside of the crystal filled with black. Like the darkest ink you can imagine. Fatima freaked out and told me to leave."

When neither of her aunts said anything, she looked up.

Both of them were staring at her, mouths open and something that seemed very much like fear in their eyes. As soon as she looked at them, they composed themselves.

But it was too late. Tru had seen their reactions. "It's not good, is it?"

"It's, um ... well," Aunt Cleo said. "It doesn't sound

ideal. But maybe it was just a trick of this woman's. Meant to get more money out of you for another reading."

"She told me to leave," Tru repeated. "And when Cindy pressed her for an answer, Fatima said it meant I was going to meet death."

Aunt Delly looked at Aunt Cleo. Neither one of them seemed to have any answers.

Tru thought she should tell them the whole truth. "There's more."

"More?" Aunt Delly blinked a few times.

Tru nodded. "I think I may know how this death is going to come for me."

"Tru," Aunt Cleo began. "If you're going to say like your mother—"

"How can I not think that?" Tru sighed. "Mom couldn't survive her powers. What makes you think I'm any different?"

"No one knows for sure that's what caused your mom's stroke," Aunt Delly said.

"I know, but I also know a lot of people in the family think it was." Tru held her hands up. "But if that's not it, then I have a second theory."

Her aunts just waited.

Tru thought about last night. Parts of it were slightly muddled in her memory. No doubt thanks to the ouzo. "It could also be your neighbor."

"Old Mrs. Flambeau?"

"No, the other one. The Scottish one." What was his name? "Eamon. You know, the *vampire*."

Eamon made himself a cup of tea and carried it up to his studio. His uncle was off to the funeral home, so Eamon had high hopes that he'd be able to knock out a good portion of the first episode of his podcast's new season today. Not the editing; that would come later. But laying down the initial tracks was where it all started. He had to do that before anything else.

When he could, he liked to work ahead, banking episodes. In fact, in a perfect world, he'd have an entire season done before the first episode aired. Hadn't happened yet, but maybe someday.

Trouble was, there was no way of telling when Seamus might need him at the funeral home, so being ahead of schedule was much better than risking falling behind.

His sponsors, who were his bread and butter, wouldn't like it if he missed an episode. Neither would his listeners, of course, and they were really who he wanted to please. More listeners was always one of his goals.

Not the main one, however. That was something very different. He hoped that shining light on one of these unsolved cases might someday lead to a resolution. Justice for the victims. Closure for the families.

For all the death he saw and could do nothing about, that seemed like the greatest possible outcome he could achieve. A way of balancing things.

He settled into his studio chair and, for a moment, drifted off into the memory of last night and the woman he'd met. Tru. What sort of name was that? And why couldn't he see the sand of her life trickling away?

"Enough of that, you daft fool." It didn't matter. He had work to do. He got himself organized. He had his script ready on his tablet, his tea next to him, and the perfect quiet surrounding him.

He took another sip of tea, cleared his throat slightly, then hit Record and leaned into the mic, his voice lower and more stern than usual. "I'm going to find you, and when I do, slice you into pieces so that no one else will ever find you."

He used a moment of silence as punctuation, his voice changing to its usual timbre. "That was only one of the menacing calls Sarah Lynn Trent received from her stalker. Imagine the fear that young woman would have felt. She didn't know her caller, although at one point she said the voice sounded familiar. But then, Sarah Lynn worked two jobs to support herself and her eight-year-old son, Conner."

He sat back. Maybe the opening line had been too menacing. He wanted to recreate, not frighten. But he also wanted to put his listeners in Sarah Lynn's mind, help them feel what she might have been feeling. Which obviously would have been fear. It was a fine line.

Nothing bothered him more than podcasters who relied on cheap tricks or gimmicks to sell their stories. He thought the proper telling of the human experience ought to be enough. Well told, obviously, which was what he strived for.

He was about to do another take when his phone lit up with an incoming call. He kept the phone on silent but face up so he could see the screen. Just in case his uncle needed him.

This call was not from his uncle. It wasn't a number he recognized, either, and he was about to let it go to voicemail when he realized the call was coming from the U.K. It had to be family.

He answered. "Hello?"

"Eamon!"

The voice was vaguely familiar, but he was at a loss to place it right away. "Yes?"

"You don't know who this is, do you?"

"No, I don't. Sorry."

"It's yer cousin Callum, ya muppet."

Eamon snorted. "Cal, how are you? It's been an age."

"Aye, it has been. I'm well. You still at Seamus's?"

"I am. You?"

"Funny you should ask. Because I'm standing on the porch just now."

Eamon blinked. "You're here? In Nocturne Falls?"

"Aye. Now get off yer arse and let me in." The call ended.

Eamon went downstairs with greater speed than usual. He couldn't believe Cal was here. He liked his cousin a lot. The man had dedicated a good portion of his life to the Underwood genealogy, trying to trace their supernatural bloodlines for a variety of reasons.

Eamon had always held out hope that, someday, Callum might find something that could cure Eamon of his particular set of powers.

He flung the front door open, and sure enough, there was Cal. "Well, look what the devil dragged in. I can't believe you're here. Does Seamus know?"

Cal shook his head. "No. I meant to surprise him. Is he not here?"

"He's at the funeral home waiting on a delivery of flowers." Eamon stepped out of the way. "Come in."

"Do you think he'd mind if I stayed for a bit? I've been traveling a lot lately, and I'd love to put my feet up for a couple days, spend some time with you lads."

"I'm sure he'd love it." Eamon had never known Seamus to turn anyone away, much less family. Eamon wouldn't mind it, either. He was eager to see if Cal had uncovered anything new and interesting about the family recently.

Cal picked up the leather hold-all by his feet. "That would be grand. So would a cup of tea."

Eamon smiled. "I'll get the kettle on."

Wasn't long before they each had a cup of tea and were sitting in the living room, catching up.

"Do you want me to call Seamus?" Eamon asked. "I'm sure he'd come home."

"No, I don't want to interrupt his work. And I'd rather surprise him."

"I can guarantee you'll do that. What brings you to the area?"

"I've been in the States about a month now, doing research for a new book." Cal sipped his tea. "I figured I'd never be closer to the two of you than I am right now, so I might as well drop in."

"A new book?"

Cal nodded. "It's about famous Scots and their contributions to American history."

"Sounds interesting."

Cal's eyes lit up. "Did you know Elvis Presley and Johnny Cash both have Scottish roots?"

"Really?"

"I swear it. I'm thinking about using one of them on the cover. Maybe both."

"That would definitely sell books." Eamon hesitated. "Anything new on the Underwoods?"

Cal's smile didn't reach his eyes. "A few bits here and there. I know you're hoping for a cure. Or at least a solution."

Eamon's sigh was soft, but there was nothing he could do to keep his disappointment in. "Either would be nice."

"I know." Cal leaned forward, resting his elbows on

his knees. "The best I can tell you is that I think at some point, I *will* find a cure. At the very least, someone or something that can ease your burden."

"I would be forever in your debt."

"We're family," Cal said. "There won't be anything to repay."

Eamon smiled. "Seamus is going to be thrilled to see you."

Cal sat back. "How do you like living here?"

"It's grand. More room than either of us need."

"I meant the town," Cal explained. "I must confess that part of the reason I came here was I was curious about this place. It's quite a haven for the supernatural."

Eamon gave a noncommittal shrug. "I don't go out much, if I'm being honest. It's too unsettling to be around people, no matter who or what they are."

"I can imagine," Cal said. After a moment of thought, he spoke again. "Vampires might be all right though, eh? Being that they're already dead and all. You know, it could be helpful for me to know who you can see death over and who you can't."

"I try *not* to look at people. And it's not death that I see, exactly ..." But Eamon hated talking about it and didn't elaborate. He knew Cal was just trying to help. And Eamon wanted help. He supposed he'd have to talk about it some. "There's nothing above the bodies I work on at the funeral home, so maybe vampires would be all right. I know there are some in town, it's just that I generally avoid everyone, so I may have already seen one and not realized it."

Cal seemed deep in thought. "How about the witches next door?"

"Witches?" Eamon glanced in the direction of the house. "Is that what they are?"

"Well, just my guess, based on the horde of cats in the windows. Witches can transform into cats, can't they?"

Eamon shook his head, the image of Tru filling his mind. "I don't know." Was she a witch? If so, why hadn't she used magic to find Nemo? Although a spell would certainly explain the way he was feeling. The way he couldn't get her out of his mind. The way he'd gone to bed thinking about her, only to wake up and find her still drifting through his thoughts.

"What is it?" Cal asked. "There's something on your mind, isn't there."

Eamon nodded. Cal had always been perceptive that way. "There's a woman visiting in that house. The niece of the two who own it." He stared past Cal into the backyard. "I met her last night. And when I looked at her, there was nothing hovering over her."

Cal's brows lifted. "So maybe your power doesn't work on witches? This is something we need to investigate further."

Eamon wasn't convinced Tru and her aunts were witches, but investigating further sounded all right to him.

Tru's aunts were both staring at her like she'd suddenly turned blue. "What?"

"How do you know about the vampire?" Aunt Delly asked.

"You told me about him," Tru said.

Aunt Cleo shook her head. "We didn't tell you his name. At least, I didn't." She looked at her sister. "Did you?"

"Not that I recall," Aunt Delly said.

Both aunts looked at Tru again, eyes slightly narrowed this time. Aunt Cleo looked a little more upset than Aunt Delly. "Out with it, Troula."

Tru sighed. "Okay, fine, I wasn't going to tell you this, but Nemo got out last night. It was my fault. I left my window open upstairs. He got out, shimmied down all the doodads on the house and made it to the backyard."

Aunt Delly's eyes went wide. "But I saw him this morning."

"I got him back in." Tru took a breath and tried to brace herself for the next part, which they really weren't going to like. "But not before he slipped through a gap at the bottom of the fence and made it into the neighbor's yard."

Aunt Cleo put a hand to her mouth. "The vampire's yard?"

Tru nodded.

"He could have been eaten!" Aunt Delly looked like she was about to cry. "Or you could have been. Or bitten. Or something." She turned toward her sister. "Cleo!"

Aunt Cleo's face was frozen in a mask of disapproval.

"I'm fine," Tru quickly reassured them. "And so is Nemo. I think maybe ... maybe the vampire wasn't interested because I probably reeked of ouzo." Was that what had kept her safe last night? Did slightly drunk people have unappetizing blood? Interesting, if so. "Anyway, nothing happened, and I promise you, the events of last night will never be repeated. With Nemo or with me going over there. I blocked the gap in the fence, too."

"That's good." But Aunt Delly didn't look convinced.

Tru knew she shouldn't tell them the rest, but there was every chance they'd figure it out on their own. They *were* oracles, after all. "Also, I think he used magic on me."

"What?" Aunt Cleo blinked. "What kind of magic? A glamour? What did he do to you?" She lowered her voice. "Did he touch you?"

"Aunt Cleo! Not like that." Tru felt heat in her face. The very idea that Eamon had put his hands on her ... She shoved that out of her head. "I just think he did something to make me believe he was handsome and sexy and—he wanted me to like him. I think. Or maybe he was trying to make me fall under his spell, I don't know. But I clearly outwitted him, because I made it back here in one piece with Nemo."

"Thank heavens," Aunt Delly said. "I'm pretty sure this town has rules about that sort of thing."

Tru wasn't sure what she meant. "Rules about trespassing? Look, I wouldn't have done it except for Nemo."

"No," Aunt Cleo said. "About vampires. About them not being allowed to bite humans, unless things are consensual, obviously. There are blood banks and such for their *needs.*"

"Oh." This town was certainly interesting.

Aunt Delly crossed her arms. "All the same, you have to stay away from him. He could very well be the predicted death."

Aunt Cleo touched the evil eye amulet around her neck. "Don't say things like that, Delphina. Don't even put them out there in the universe!" She shook her head. "But Delly's right. You need to stay away from him. He hardly ever leaves the house, so you should be fine here, but all the same, if he approaches you or tries to use his magic on you again, you tell us. We'll take care of him."

Aunt Delly nodded. "That's right."

Tru had a feeling she knew what they were talking about—one of the other oracle powers. "You mean you'd curse him?"

Neither aunt spoke for a moment. They exchanged a look. Then Aunt Cleo answered her. "If we had to, yes. To protect you, by all means."

"Wouldn't that be prohibited by the town's laws, too?"

"Maybe." Aunt Delly lifted her chin defiantly. "But so what? If they make us leave, we'll leave. You're the next generation of oracle. We have to protect you. There won't be another legacy of age for five more years."

Aunt Cleo got up. "For starters, you need a *mati*." She pointed at her sister. "Better get one on Nemo's collar, too. Maybe all the cats. There's no telling what that vampire might have planned." Her attention returned to Tru. And Tru's throat. "Where *is* your *mati*? Why aren't you wearing one?"

Tru instinctively put her hand to her neck, even though she knew there was no evil eye charm there. "I just got out of the habit, I guess."

Aunt Cleo sighed with mild disapproval. "I suppose working at Yanni's restaurant kept you protected enough."

Tru nodded. "There were plenty of them around." The little blue eye icon had even graced the menu. It was pretty much a standard Greek thing.

"Do you have one with you?" Aunt Delly asked. "Otherwise, I've got one I can lend you."

"No, I don't, so thanks," Tru said.

"Get it," Aunt Cleo told her sister. "Then we'd better perform the *vaskania* over her anyway. You never know what that vampire did to her."

Tru pursed her lips. "Do you really think he could have—"

"Yes," both aunts said.

"Okay. But I haven't even had breakfast."

"Evil doesn't wait until you've eaten," Aunt Delly said. "Besides, we were going to run out and get doughnuts from Zombie Donuts. But first, we need to get you out from under whatever spell he's put you under."

Tru agreed. But she also felt oddly bothered. As if part of her wanted to stay under his spell. Which was probably just more proof his magic was real, because who would want to be in the thrall of such a tall, handsome, dark-eyed …Shocked by her own thoughts, she shook herself. "Yeah, let's do this."

Clearly, Eamon's magic was far more powerful than anything she'd encountered before.

Delly got the *mati* for Tru to wear, which she clasped around her neck right away, then her aunts went to work assembling a few things. A shallow glass dish with some water in it, a teaspoon, and a dark green glass bottle filled with olive oil from the motherland.

They turned Tru's chair slightly so they could have better access to her.

Aunt Cleo, as the eldest, began.

She filled the teaspoon with oil, then made the sign of the cross with the teaspoon over the bowl of water, all while whispering words in Greek that Tru couldn't hear well enough to make out.

Wouldn't have mattered. She'd already been taught an incantation for removing the evil eye by her uncle, Yanni, just as another male member of the family had undoubtedly taught one to Cleo. Maybe her father.

Tru imagined that someday, she'd teach the one she'd

learned to a male cousin. That's how they worked. The incantations were passed down through time across the genders. That was how they kept their strength. How the words built power.

Next, Cleo moved the teaspoon in the sign of the cross in front of Tru's forehead. It was the strangest thing, but Tru could have sworn she felt lighter suddenly. As if something had been lifted off her.

She'd learned long ago not to question the old ways. The power was real. It reminded her that becoming an oracle was her destiny. Something she was going to have to face sooner or later.

With that done, Cleo dipped her finger into the oil and let a drop fall into the water, all while continuing to whisper the incantation. Again and again she did it, three drops in total. Each one spread across the water so thinly it was no longer visible. Proof that Tru had definitely been under the influence of something.

Tru yawned.

Aunt Delly nodded. "That's it. Let it out."

Aunt Cleo yawned, too. She stepped back and nodded at the dish. "All right, drink."

Tru lifted the bowl and took three measured sips, draining the water.

Aunt Delly put her hand on Tru's shoulder. "How do you feel?"

Tru smiled. "Fine."

"Maybe you should go rest for a bit. We'll be back with the doughnuts before you know it."

"All right." Tru went out to the screened porch and settled onto the chaise, where the sun was just making its presence known. It was hard not to look at the fence she'd climbed over last night.

Had Eamon really been that handsome?

Maybe not.

But also ... maybe he had been.

Tired from his travels, Cal had gone upstairs to one of the guest rooms to lie down. He hadn't even been interested in breakfast, which Eamon was now working on.

He had a couple of rashers of bacon on the griddle, along with two eggs, and in a small pan on the stove, he was warming a tin of beans. There was bread in the toaster, too. If only he had some blood sausage, it'd be a proper fry-up. But then, if he ate blood sausage, that would only add to people thinking he was a vampire.

He chuckled to himself. For some reason, his appetite was strong this morning. As he cooked, he thought about Cal's suggestion that Eamon try to kindle a friendship with the women next door.

He wasn't so sure how he felt about that.

For one thing, he got the sense that they weren't exactly open to the idea. After all, Tru had thought he was a vampire, information her aunts must have given her, which meant they believed it, too. For another, on the rare occasions he saw one of them, they reacted in one of two ways. They seemed to either make a concerted effort not to notice him, or they stared directly at him while clutching their necklaces.

He didn't pretend to understand either response. The

toast popped up, so he snagged it, spread both pieces with butter, then put them on his plate to be topped with beans.

And, just to complicate matters, the aunts' response changed if Seamus was with him. At least the response from the younger, redheaded aunt did. She usually snuck a smile at Seamus. Who usually made no attempt to hide his own smile in return.

But maybe Eamon would get the chance to speak to Tru again. He could ask her about Nemo.

Eamon stared at the baked beans without really seeing them, absently giving them a stir. Nemo might be the key to seeing her again. That was something to think about.

He loaded his plate with the eggs, a couple of rashers of bacon, then a hearty topping of beans on the toast and took his plate, utensils, and his mug of tea out onto the porch to eat. It was a beautiful day. No sense wasting it.

He put everything on the table, then went outside to check on something. Namely, the gap in the fence the little cat had come through. Tru had mentioned it, and Eamon found it just past the midline of the property.

It had been plugged up with something. A decorative stone. Took a wee bit of wiggling, but he got the stone out and the gap open again.

Pleased with his deviousness, he went back to the porch and his breakfast.

As he ate, he contemplated the idea of becoming

friends with Tru. Not more than that. No significant other for him. He'd tried that once.

Losing Sophie Ballentine had broken his heart. And he'd almost broken hers. Permanently. No more. He couldn't do it. He couldn't be the reason the life of someone he was involved with was cut short.

Friends, however, he'd be willing to make an attempt at. But would she? Tru had been afraid of him initially. He couldn't blame her. Not when she'd thought he was a vampire. She'd genuinely thought he'd eat Nemo. Was that a thing? Did vampires actually eat cats? He hoped not. He hated to think Nemo might be in real danger.

He frowned at his toast before cutting a piece and taking a bite. The savory goodness of the beans along with the slight smokiness of the toasted bread reminded him of home in the best possible way. He didn't really miss Scotland, but he got nostalgic, all the same.

He thought while he chewed. Tru didn't still think he was a vampire, did she? He had explained he wasn't one.

But she'd been visibly tipsy. Maybe she didn't even remember coming over here.

He pondered that possibility. If that was true, it could work to his advantage. It would give him a chance at a fresh start.

He used the last corner of his toast to sop up a bit of yolk and beans, then carried his plate and mug back into the kitchen.

There was only one way to find out what Tru thought about him, and that was to make contact again.

But how? He didn't even know how long she was visiting for.

He did know what room she was staying in, however. He thought about what to do with that information and came up blank.

Just then, the side door opened and Seamus came in, a newspaper under his arm. "Smells grand in here. Any of that left?"

Eamon nodded. "Beans and bacon. I can throw on some eggs and pop some bread in the toaster for you. It'll be done in a jiff."

"That would be brilliant. Thank you." Seamus went straight to the kettle to fix himself some tea.

"Flowers arrive all right?" Eamon turned the griddle back on as well as the burner under the beans, then fetched two eggs from the fridge and the bread from the counter.

Seamus nodded. "Aye, and a lot of them. Mr. Young will have no shortage of blooms at his service."

"Good." Then Eamon laughed as he put two slices into the toaster, realizing he'd forgotten the biggest news. "One of your guest rooms is in use."

Seamus frowned. "What now?"

"Callum is upstairs having a rest. He meant to surprise you, but I don't want him coming down the stairs and giving you a heart attack."

Seamus's eyes rounded. "Callum is here? I didn't even know he was in the States."

Eamon cracked two eggs on the griddle. "He's here

researching a book. Plus, he's interested in the town. Figured he'd come for a visit at the same time."

"That's marvelous. Haven't seen him in an age." Seamus ran a hand through his thick head of graying hair. "Any news for you?"

Eamon knew what his uncle meant. "Sort of. He thinks I should get to know the women next door." He glanced at his uncle. "Do you think they're witches, by the way? Cal does. But I'm not so sure."

Seamus seemed to turn that over in his mind for a moment. "I don't know, really. I'm not sure what they are. That redheaded one is a looker, though."

Eamon suppressed a grin. "Aye, I've seen you smiling at her."

"Well, I'm a man, aren't I? I might be pushing sixty-two, but I'm not dead."

Eamon just shook his head. "I don't think they like me."

"Stuff and nonsense. How can they not like you? They've never met you."

"The one that was over here last night, the one who came after the cat, she thought I was a vampire."

Seamus looked Eamon up and down. "Ya do wear a lot of black. And when you go out during the day, you're always in sunglasses."

Eamon shrugged one shoulder. "I like black. I never have to think about what goes together. And the sunglasses just make it harder for people to see I don't make eye contact. And easier for me not to see ... you know."

"I know. And I'm not criticizing. Just pointing out why they might think what they think."

"You have a point. Maybe I should just go over and introduce myself and clear it all up."

"Maybe." Seamus gestured at the griddle. "But not till my breakfast is done."

Eamon grinned and got his uncle's breakfast finished, leaving him to put his own beans on the toast. Then he ran upstairs and took a good look at himself. Put a comb through his hair. Brushed his teeth for a second time.

Changed out of his T-shirt and into a newer shirt, a button-down. Still black. He glanced out the window. The blinds were open in the third-floor window, but there were no lights on. Of course, it was daytime, so that meant nothing.

She might not even be home.

He went downstairs, oddly nervous. Where had those nerves come from? He'd never been nervous in his life. Seamus was sitting at the table, eating his breakfast and reading the paper. All Eamon was doing was going next door to introduce himself and make sure they knew he wasn't a vampire.

They should be nervous.

He stopped before heading out. They probably were. Or would be, if he appeared on their front porch without warning. He'd have to talk fast.

Before he changed his mind, Eamon went out the

front door and across the wide expanse of yard that separated the two homes.

He went up the steps and knocked, then saw there
was a doorbell. He rang it, too. These were big houses. He
knew firsthand that the sound didn't always carry.

A muted voice called out, "Coming."

Tru's voice, he was sure of it.

His nerves increased.

The door opened, and Tru stood there, gaping at him.

He was thrilled to see that the lack of hourglass over
her head hadn't just been a fluke. "Hi."

She didn't say anything. Just stared, wide-eyed and
leery. Then her hand crept toward her neck and a blue-
eyed charm on a silver chain.

11

"I'm Eamon. From next door? I wanted to come over and introduce myself properly. See how Nemo was doing."

"I remember," Tru managed to get out. Her fingers closed around the *mati* now hanging around her neck on a thin, silver chain. Every warning bell in her body was going off. "He's fine. What are you doing here?"

"Uh, like I said, just wanted to make a proper introduction for myself. And check on the wee mite. Make sure he hasn't escaped on you again."

"No, he's fine." So was Eamon. Clearly, her aunts hadn't gotten all of his magic out of her system, because Tru still thought he was incredibly handsome. That accent had to be part of his spell, too. This was not good. How long did it take to buy doughnuts?

Eamon rubbed at his chin. "Listen, I think your aunts believe that I'm a vampire. Maybe you do, too? I just wanted to say, again, that I'm not. I'd be happy to talk to them. I'd like to, actually. I'd hate to think anyone was afraid of me for something that wasn't true."

"Saying you're not a vampire sounds exactly like something a vampire would say."

He laughed, then seemed to realize she was serious.

He gestured toward the sky. "Well, I am out in the daytime. That has to prove I'm not a vampire, right?"

Tru shrugged. "I have no idea."

Her hand stayed on the *mati* at her throat. She was glad Aunt Delly had given it to her, but right now, it might not be enough.

He bared his teeth. "I don't have fangs."

She stayed safely inside the house. Vampires had to be invited in, if what she'd seen in movies was true. "Neither do vampires unless they need them."

He sighed. "What can I do to convince you that I'm not a vampire?"

"I have no idea, but it really doesn't matter, because—"

"Look, I know your aunts are witches. And that doesn't bother me. This town has all sorts of creatures in it. None of them bother me. But you're the first one I've wanted to get to know better."

"Why me?" The very presence of him on her aunts' front porch made her fearful.

He looked away a moment. When he faced her again, there was a darkness in his eyes that hadn't been there before. Not an evil darkness. One that looked very much like ... sorrow. That threw her. "Because you are the first person outside of my family whose death I haven't been able to see."

Her mouth came open, and her fear was forgotten. She let go of the *mati*. "What?"

He held his hand up. "I shouldn't have said anything.

Never mind. I just ... thought ..." He shook his head and started down the steps.

She came across the threshold. "Wait. What do you mean?"

He didn't look at her. Instead, he kept his eyes fixed on his own house. "There's no name for what I am, but that's my ability, thanks to the jumble of bloodlines that run in my family. I can see how long a person has left to live. It's why I rarely leave my house and do my best not to interact with anyone. But then you came over last night, and I couldn't see what I usually see when I looked at you."

He shot a quick glance in her direction, almost like he wasn't sure he should make eye contact. "Like I said, outside of my family members, that's never happened before. It made me think you were worth getting to know."

With the death prophecy she'd gotten from Fatima, Tru really had been thinking that Eamon could be a part of that. What he'd just told her had blown her mind. If he couldn't see death when he looked at her, how did that affect Fatima's prediction? She had to know more. "Why would you share that with me?"

"I didn't know how else to prove I wasn't a vampire and that you're in no danger from me."

Being able to see how much life people had left seemed like it would be a heavy burden to bear. "If you can't see my timeline, does that mean I'm not going to die?"

He shook his head. "I have no idea. I can't tell you what it means." He smiled. He had such a nice smile. "I just can't see a little hourglass over your head the way I can with everyone else. No sands draining away, no sense of how long you have left. There's just ... nothing."

"What if you concentrate really hard?"

His brow furrowed. "No. But I don't want to see it. That's what I'm trying to tell you. It's a relief not to."

"I understand that, but ... someone told me I was going to meet death in my thirty-third year. I was thinking maybe you could give me some insight."

His brow creased deeper. "Someone threatened you?"

"No, it wasn't a threat. It was a prediction. She was a fortune teller."

He scoffed. "You don't actually believe that nonsense, do you?"

She crossed her arms, eyes narrowing. "Depends on the circumstances. And who's giving the prediction."

He pursed his lips. "I sense I've stepped into delicate territory. I've upset you. Can you tell me why before I dig a deeper hole?"

"My aunts aren't witches. They're oracles. Real oracles. Descendants of the original Greek oracles. What they predict really does come true."

"That is truly impressive. Does that mean you're one, too?"

"Yes. Sort of. I haven't gone through the ceremony yet." She dropped her arms to her sides. "And now that you're not the death I thought you were, I might not."

She sighed heavily, feeling like a weight had pressed down on her. If Eamon wasn't the death she was supposed to meet, that could only mean her death would come the same way her mother's had. Because her mind couldn't handle her powers.

"You all right?"

She shook her head. "No. I really don't think I am."

Eamon pointed behind her. "Is that—"

A streak of orange shot past them and out into the front yard.

"Nemo?" he finished.

Tru stared in disbelief. "You have got to be kidding me." She gave Eamon a look. "Grab him!"

She reached back to close the door, then joined the chase, because that was the only way to describe what was happening. As soon as Eamon had gone after Nemo, the little cat had bolted toward the driveway that ran along the side of the house.

Her aunts had taken Cleo's turquoise Jeep and left Delly's little red convertible.

Eamon was on the ground next to it, looking underneath the vehicle. "He's done a runner, but I think he went under here." He glanced back at Tru. "I didn't know kittens could move that fast."

"Neither did I." She went around to the other side of the car and crouched down. She could see half of Eamon. Still handsome. "Do you see him?"

"I did." He pointed toward the front of the car. "But then he went that way."

The gate into the backyard was at the end of the driveway. "Can you keep an eye on him? I want to open the gate to the backyard and see if we can get him to go that way. Should be easier to catch him in an enclosed area. I blocked the gap in the fence last night so he won't be able to get out."

Eamon seemed to hesitate before he said, "Okay, I'll make sure he only heads in that direction."

She got up and opened the gate, then stood a few feet back and called for Nemo. "Here, kitty-kitty-kitty."

"I hear movement," Eamon said.

"Maybe I should run and get a bag of treats. The sound might bring him out."

"Worth a shot. I'll watch for him."

Tru ran inside, found a supply of treats in the laundry room, and came back out, shaking them. "Nemo, where are you? I have treaties."

"Keep it up," Eamon said. "It's working."

She walked back through the gate, jostling the bag to keep the sound going. "Here, baby. I have kitty snacks. *Psp psp psp.*"

A little orange shape darted from underneath the car and into the backyard. Eamon followed, closing the gate behind him. He looked impressed. "Nicely done. That worked like a charm."

"Yeah. Now we just have to get that stinker back in the house."

"There's two of us and one of him. We'll get him."

"We'd better, or my aunts aren't going to be happy with me." Tru shook the bag again.

Nemo was swatting at something in one of the bushes, but the sound got his attention. He looked at Tru and acted like he was about to run toward her.

Then a bird swooped past and landed on the fence.

Nemo ran after it. The bird took off, and Nemo followed, going back through the same gap Tru thought she'd sealed off.

Tru shook her head. "There's no way he should have been able to get through there. I put a stone in the way."

Eamon made a face. "Yeah, about that ..."

Delphina loved Zombie Donuts. You'd have to be crazy not to. They were so delicious. Cleo liked them, too, but she said they were no good for either of their waistlines. Delphina wasn't as concerned about that.

When it was their turn to order, she smiled at the young man behind the counter. "Just give us a dozen assorted. Some chocolate, some cream-filled. Whatever looks good. We like them all."

He nodded and went to work filling a box for them.

Next to her, Cleo shook her head. "I'm worried about Tru."

"I am, too," Delphina said. "We can't let her go through the ceremony if it's going to hurt her."

"I know," Cleo said. "It's enough that the memory of Maria weighs on all of us. We can't lose Troula, too."

Delphina nodded. "So true."

"But I'm more worried about that man next door."

Delphina glanced at her sister. Cleo had never liked vampires, not since she'd been hired by one to predict some investments for him. He'd tried to lure her into becoming his pet. "Your past is coloring your views."

"With good reason. Look what happened to me!"

"What *almost* happened to you. And nothing's going

to happen to Tru, either. And come on, all vampires aren't bad. We live in a town founded by them."

"The Ellinghams are lovely, but there are some bad eggs out there, Del. We don't know what the one next door intends. Tru's already had an encounter with him and come away tainted."

Delphina knew her sister was referring to the proof the oil had shown them. "That could have been from her visit to the fortune teller. We don't know."

"I do."

Delphina looked toward the heavens and pressed her lips together. Her sister was so stubborn sometimes. "If you like, I could go next door and talk to them."

She wouldn't mind getting to know the older gentleman who lived in the house with the potential vampire. He had kind eyes and the sweetest smile, but every time Cleo caught her looking at him, she said Del was inviting trouble.

Hardly. A little flirting had never hurt anyone.

All Delphina would have to do was touch him, ask a few questions, and she'd know what his intentions were. Good or bad. It was that simple. At least for her. Not all oracles could read people that easily, but it was one of her special gifts.

The young man behind the counter presented them with their box of doughnuts. "Here you go."

Delphina picked them up and shot Cleo a look. "Pay the man."

With a slight sigh, Cleo took her wallet out as

Delphina backed through the door and went out to the car.

Cleo didn't have any special gifts, but her predictions were sharper and truer and looked more deeply into the future than Delphina's. But Delphina could see backwards much better than Cleo. Delphina wasn't bothered by that, but the past wasn't nearly as interesting as the future.

Cleo came out and opened the rear door of the Jeep for Delphina. She slid the box of doughnuts onto the seat, then went around to the passenger side and got in.

Cleo slipped behind the wheel and buckled up, then started the car.

"I'm not saying speed, but those doughnuts are still warm." Delphina checked herself in the mirror before pushing the visor up.

"We're not that far from home."

The sweet, doughy scent filling the car was making Delphina's mouth water. She glanced back at the box. "Do you think we got enough?"

"A dozen doughnuts for three women? I think we got plenty." Cleo pulled out of the parking lot and got them on the road to home. "Why aren't you as concerned about Tru? You don't seem to think it's as much of an issue as I do."

"I do think it's an issue. I just don't know what to do about it." Delphina sat back. "I know we need her. Not only because we're more powerful in threes, but there are precious few of us. But we can't and shouldn't push her to go through the ceremony if it could be dangerous to her."

"But what if the ceremony isn't where the danger lies?"

"It's not. It's in her gaining her powers and then her mind and body not being able to handle them."

"That's not what I meant."

"I know," Delphina said. "You meant that the neighbor is the danger. Well, I don't agree. You just think every vampire is out to get you. Or someone."

"No, I don't. The Ellinghams aren't. They were clearly cut from a different kind of cloth. They wouldn't have started this town otherwise. But we know nothing about that vampire next door."

"No, we don't, because you can't be bothered getting to know him or the other man who lives there." Delphina frowned. "Most of the vampires in this world are good people. You know that. You just had one bad experience. One bad apple does not spoil the whole bushel."

"It literally does," Cleo said.

Delphina huffed out a big breath. "Well, just because you had your heart broken—"

"I was *not* in love with Vincenzo."

Delphina just nodded. She knew better. Cleo still had his letters in a box on the top shelf of her closet, tied with a red ribbon. Not that Delphina had been snooping. Just looking for something. "I still say your one bad experience doesn't mean every vampire is bad. Especially not in a town like this. There are rules and regulations in place to make sure of that."

"Maybe." Cleo shook her head. "I'd rather be safe than sorry."

"What if I call one of the Ellinghams personally and ask about him?"

Cleo seemed to consider that. "You don't think they'd protect one of their own?"

Delphina glanced out the window. Her sister was so difficult. Delphina inhaled the smell of doughnuts again to try to calm herself. "What if we try to track down this Fatima and find out what really happened in that tent?"

"Not sure how you're going to do that."

Probably was an impossible task. "Then the only other thing I can think of is we call on the local coven. Maybe one of the witches in town can work some of their magic and see if they get the same kind of reading for Tru since we can't do it ourselves. I mean looking for the death part that she saw in the fortune teller's tent."

Cleo began to nod slowly. "That's not a bad idea. At the least, they might be able to put some kind of protection spell around her."

Or, Delphina thought, she could just go next door and talk to those men and see what they were really all about. Touching them shouldn't be too hard to do. "I'll make a call when I get home. One of them lives just down the street. I met her out walking the other day. She's got a cat, too."

"Just one?" Cleo smiled.

Delphina laughed. "Yes. Just one. But I'm sure she'd help us. She was a lovely young woman. Pandora."

Cleo glanced over. "She's Greek?"

"No. Not sure what she is. She just has a good Greek name."

"Well, go ahead and talk to her," Cleo said. "But I hope she really can help us. Pandora's legacy to the world was unleashing a host of troubles upon it. We already have more than enough on our hands."

13

Eamon grimaced when Tru looked at him. "I moved the stone."

"Why? It wasn't on your property."

"You're right. It wasn't. I'm sorry. I thought if one of the cats came back through to my side, I'd get to see you again."

The tiniest hint of a smile played on her mouth. "Is that what you thought?"

He nodded. She was so beautiful. He was touched in the head to think there could be anything between them, but wouldn't that be something. "I'm an eejit, I know."

She lifted one shoulder in a cute little half-shrug. "It wasn't the worst plan. But now we do need to go over to your house."

"Aye, we do."

They went back out the gate, making sure it was secured behind them, then cut across the yard to Eamon's and through his gate.

Nemo was in his yard, chasing a butterfly.

"Look at the wee mite. Not a clue about the trouble he's caused."

Tru laughed. "Nope. I don't think he'd care anyway."

"Probably not, the blighter."

Slowly, they walked toward Nemo, both of them obviously hoping to get close enough to grab him.

The little cat looked at Eamon, meowed, then trotted up to him. Eamon picked him up and gave him a scratch under his chin. "Hello there, ya troublemaker."

Nemo pushed into Eamon's hand and purred. Eamon could only smile. "He's really sweet when he's not trying to set a land-speed record."

Tru laughed and shook her head. "Once again, you seem to have the touch." She tickled Nemo's belly. The little cat closed his eyes. "He really likes you. More than he likes me, I think."

"I find that hard to believe."

At the sound of a car arriving next door, they both turned their heads.

Tru's smile disappeared. "That has to be my aunts. I need to get us both back in the house."

"Here." Eamon put Nemo in her arms. He wasn't sure if Tru was worried about her aunts seeing that Nemo had gotten out again or seeing Tru with him. Either way, Eamon didn't want to be the cause of any friction.

Tru took the cat and headed for the gate. Eamon followed.

Her aunts were getting out of the blue Jeep. The older one, who was on the driver's side, opened the rear passenger door. The younger one waved at them, then seemed to realize Tru had Nemo in her arms. "What are you doing outside with him?"

The older aunt turned, a large pastry box in her

hands. She immediately frowned. "Good question. And I'm not talking about the cat."

"It's not what you think," Tru said. "Nemo got out again, and Eamon helped me catch him."

The redheaded aunt touched her necklace. She wore the same pendant as Tru. Both aunts did. "That was nice, but we should all go inside now. We got doughnuts."

The older aunt handed the box off to her sister before charging toward Tru. Eamon had stopped walking a few feet from his uncle's property line. He stayed where he was, wishing he'd just gone back inside. He didn't need to make eye contact with them to know they weren't happy.

The older aunt positioned herself between him and Tru. "What do you think you're up to, vampire?"

"Aunt Cleo, don't," Tru started.

Eamon did his best to smile and not look at the hourglass over the woman's head. It was tricky with women. You had to be careful not to end up staring at their chests. Staring below the belt was no better. He kept his gaze toward the ground. "I'm not a vampire. And I'm not up to anything. I mean no one any harm. Especially not Tru."

Just as he'd done with her, he lifted his hands toward the sky. "If I was a vampire, I couldn't be out in the daylight, now, could I? Look at me. There's no smoke coming off my skin. I'm not about to burst into flames."

He lifted his gaze enough to see if that had done the trick.

The angry brackets around her mouth softened slightly, but then she shook her head, obviously unconvinced. "Why won't you make eye contact? That alone makes you seem suspect."

Tru, who hadn't gone inside, came over and put herself in front of Eamon, Nemo still in her arms. "Aunt Cleo, leave him be. He's got a lot more going on than you understand. But he's not a vampire."

"Really?" Cleo said. "Because you sound like you're back under his spell."

Eamon rolled his eyes. "I have no spells. I have no magic. None that can do harm, anyway."

The redheaded aunt put the box on the porch, then marched over to them. "Enough of this now."

Eamon nodded, gaze back on the ground. He really just wanted to go inside. "I'll leave you all alone."

"Not so fast." The redheaded aunt grabbed his wrist. "Are you a vampire?"

"Aunt Delphina." Anger edged Tru's voice.

"Let her be," Cleo said. "Go on, Del. Make him answer."

"Are you a vampire?" Delphina repeated.

"No," he spit out. Heat and something that could only be described as power radiated from the woman's touch. He didn't think he could have freed himself from her grip even if he'd wanted to. "I swear I'm not."

"Do you mean any ill will toward Tru or toward any of us?"

"None whatsoever. I swear it on my ma's life."

"Who's the older man that shares the house with you?"

"My uncle, Seamus. It's his house."

"Why don't you make eye contact with anyone?"

"For the reasons Tru said." He hated talking about this. He kept his eyes low. "I can see when people are going to die."

The woman took a breath, and her voice softened. "You can tell that with me?"

"Yes," he whispered. He knew the question that would come next. Cold dread filled his belly.

"How long do I have?"

He shook his head. "Please don't make me look."

She released his wrist as she turned away from him. "He's telling the truth."

He'd had enough. He glanced at Tru but said nothing. Just gave her a long, hard look. Then he turned and walked back to the house.

14

"There aren't enough doughnuts in the world to make up for what you two just did." Tru couldn't remember a time she'd been this angry. Maybe not since her mother had died. She stood glaring at her aunts, who were sitting on the couch. "That was completely uncalled for."

"It *was* called for, Troula." Aunt Cleo refused to back down. "You might not think so, but we have to protect you."

"Not at the expense of someone else. Who is completely innocent, by the way. Someone we might be able to help. Someone we *should* help, because if there was ever someone in need, it's that man next door."

Nemo had passed out in one of the cat condos in the living room, where they were having the conversation, but he was awake now. He was one of five cats in the room. Apparently, arguments were interesting.

Aunt Delly shook her head. "But we didn't know his situation. We do now."

"Because you basically subjected him to a lie-detector test against his will."

Aunt Cleo threw her hands up. "What would you have done in our position? If you'd come home and seen the legacy oracle you'd sworn to your dying sister to protect in the company of a man who could have potentially been the end of her?"

Tru sat down. "You spoke to my mother before she died?"

Aunt Cleo stared at her hands and nodded. "She was coherent for a few minutes before you arrived. She made us promise to protect you."

"And to help you find a good man," Aunt Delly said.

That sounded like her mother. Tru wished she'd been able to talk to her. "Why didn't you tell me this before?"

Aunt Cleo looked at Delly. "We thought you'd be upset that you didn't get to speak to her yourself."

Tru nodded. "I would have been. I am now." She sighed and sat back. "I'm still mad at both of you. Eamon didn't deserve that. He's twice helped me get Nemo back in. And he's done nothing to make me feel unsafe in any way."

"How did Nemo get out again?"

Tru realized Aunt Delly was changing the subject. "He slipped out the door when Eamon came over to talk."

"To talk about what?" Aunt Cleo asked.

"He wanted to talk to you two. He wanted to explain that he wasn't a vampire. To all of us."

Aunt Delly cleared her throat. "Well, he's done that now."

Tru cut her eyes at her aunt. "Because you made him. That was quite a parlor trick you pulled out there."

"We all have our gifts."

"Not all of us," Tru said.

"Listen, about that," Aunt Cleo began. "In light of what we learned from Eamon—about him not being a vampire, I mean—I think we should postpone the ceremony. At least until we can figure out if this Fatima was on the right track. Because if he's not the death she foresaw ..."

"Yeah, I know." Tru wasn't going to argue that. "And I swear, the crystal ball filled with black. I saw it with my own eyes. I don't think she could have done that."

"Neither do we." Aunt Delly offered a quick little smile. It was almost enough to make Tru feel bad for yelling at her. "There's a witch who lives down the road. Pandora. I was telling Cleo I might reach out to her, see if there's any help the local coven might be able to give us. I'm sure they could do something."

"Witches?"

Aunt Cleo nodded. "We're not too far removed from them, you know. There are some who would consider us kin."

"But we don't do magic or spells or ..." A long-haired black cat walked through the living room. Tru pointed. "Which one is that?"

"Cher," her aunts answered simultaneously.

"You do have more than enough cats to qualify." Tru didn't like the idea of calling in outside help. It would mean opening herself up to them. Telling them what had happened. Talking about her mother's death. It all felt so intrusive. It *was* intrusive. But she supposed if she ever wanted to become an oracle, they'd have to do something.

She slouched a little. Did she still want to become an oracle? She'd spent her life preparing for it. She'd gone to school and studied communications with a minor in mythology to learn how to talk to people when she worked for them, but also so that she could understand the nuances of omens and signs. That was about all the world of non-oracles could help her with. Everything else she'd have to learn once she became a full-fledged oracle.

But after graduating, instead of teaching or working in a field more suited to her degree, she'd gone to work at her uncle's Greek restaurant so that she could be near her family until she came into her powers. Her father, heart-broken by her mother's death, had returned to Greece and the rest of his family there.

She hoped to be able to visit him someday, but there was no telling where life as an oracle might take her. It might very well be her end.

She'd never considered that her gifts might be the death of her. Not until Fatima. Until then, she'd just assumed that her mother's stroke had been an abnormality. Even if it had been caused by an overabundance of power.

She'd never imagined that could happen to her. Now she had to consider that it might.

She looked over at her aunts. They were watching her, waiting for her to do something, clearly worried that they were going to upset her again. "So you want to contact this witch?"

They both nodded.

"Pandora," Aunt Delly said again.

Tru arched her brows. "You see the irony in that, right?"

"I mentioned it," Aunt Cleo said.

Tru got up. "Go ahead and talk to her. See what she thinks. In the meantime, I'm going to go out for a walk. I need to clear my head."

They just nodded, as placid as little mice.

Tru hesitated. "You both owe Eamon an apology. You get that, right? I also want you to think about how we might help him. That seems pretty important, too. Why else would the Fates have put us next door to him?"

Their nods were a little less convincing. She scowled as she walked out of the living room and went into the kitchen. "I need some fresh air."

What she really wanted to do was talk to Eamon, but she thought she ought to give him a little time to cool down. She'd certainly needed some, and he'd seemed pretty mad when he'd walked away. Something he had every right to feel.

If she offered to help him now, he'd probably slam the door in her face. Well, she didn't really think he'd do that. He seemed better-mannered than that. But he'd undoubtedly turn her down.

Maybe she'd stop by later this evening. Her aunts should be the ones apologizing, but she would do it, too.

Eamon and his uncle didn't need all the drama. Not with what Eamon was already dealing with.

She stood by the kitchen table, looking down at the box of doughnuts. She opened it and had a look at the selections. She wasn't all that hungry now. The scene outside had caused her to lose her appetite, but her stomach was growling, and the doughnuts smelled good.

She grabbed a paper napkin from the holder on the table, then picked a chocolate with rainbow sprinkles and another that looked like apple crumb.

Balancing them on the napkin in one hand, she went out the front door, down the driveway, and out to the sidewalk. She took a bite of the crumb. Not apple crumb, spiced pear. And surprisingly delicious. She stared at Eamon's house. It was impossible to tell what was going on inside.

She hoped he wasn't mad at her, but if he was, she wouldn't blame him. Cleo and Delly *were* her aunts. She could have done more to stop them. She could have at least tried harder to rein them in.

Probably without success, but she could have tried. She was as mad at them as she was at herself.

With a sigh, she started down the street.

Eamon had been sitting in his studio for what felt like an hour, staring at the script on his tablet, but he had yet to speak a word. He was lost in his own head, reliving the feel of Delphina's hand on his wrist and the barrage of questions she'd shot at him.

To say he was angry would be an injustice to the full truth of what he was feeling. Angry, aye. But also hurt. Shocked. Violated. Betrayed.

He probably didn't have a right to the last one. Tru owed him nothing. They weren't friends. They were barely acquaintances. But he'd been so starved for human companionship that he'd allowed himself to think otherwise. He'd read more into her sweet smile and lighthearted laugh than he should have.

More fool he.

He'd thought retreating to his fortress of solitude would be the balm he needed. All his recording studio had done so far was remind him of how very alone he was. How alone he would always be.

Silence surrounded him as much as the blanket of misery he'd draped himself in. He was a pathetic creature with a questionable skill that did no one any good.

He should never leave the house again. Maybe ...

maybe he'd get a cat. Now there was a thought he'd never imagined having. He didn't think Seamus would mind.

If Nemo had been around, Eamon would have picked the wee beastie up and held him close, letting that insistent purr rumble through him as he did his best to forget that a world existed beyond the front door.

What was wrong with that?

Other than it meant he'd become a lonely old woman.

The words on the tablet blurred. He'd never hated his existence more than he had in this moment. He wondered, if he could see his own hourglass, where the sands would be. How much longer could he live this life?

This house was his prison. This room that had once been his escape felt less like a fortress of solitude and more like solitary confinement.

In that moment, he would have done anything or given anything to rid himself of his heritage. Being a vampire would have been better.

He closed his eyes, trying to purge the darkness edging in around him, only to open them and find the desk lamp blinking.

On, off. On, off.

Eamon took a deep breath, letting it out as a long sigh. Then he scrubbed his hands across his face and went to the door.

Seamus was on the other side. He smiled. "We were thinking about takeaway for lunch. Cal and I are too busy talking to cook, and it's already gone half twelve. What say you?"

Eamon shook his head. He hadn't told Seamus a word of what had happened. "I'm not hungry."

"Not hungry?" Seamus's eyes narrowed, and he gave his nephew a longer look. "What's wrong, lad? You look bothered."

Eamon glanced back at his worktable, searching for a lie that would make everything all right. "The, uh, recording's not going like I'd hoped."

"Dinna fash," Seamus said. "It'll all come together."

Eamon nodded, but not worrying was easier said than done. He didn't want to upset his uncle. He also didn't want to retell the story of what had happened outside, either. He'd gone through it enough in his head already. "I guess I could eat. I'll just pack up and come down then."

"Good." Seamus headed for the stairs.

Eamon turned everything off, plugged his tablet in to charge, and closed the door. Regardless of how he felt, he didn't want to spoil Cal's visit. He went down to the living room, where the other two men were looking at Seamus's collection of takeaway menus.

Eamon tried for a light tone. If he faked it long enough, it might eventually be true. "So, what's for lunch?"

"We were thinking about getting some curries from Curry Kitchen and then watching the match."

There had been a game they hadn't been able to

watch live because of the time difference. Whenever that happened, they recorded it.

"Sounds good." Curry Kitchen was a newish Indian restaurant in town. Eamon and Seamus had ordered from there many times since the place had opened a few months ago.

"You want your usual?" Seamus asked.

Eamon nodded. "That would be great. I just remembered I need to go do something. Be back in a minute."

"No worries," Seamus said.

Eamon slipped out the back porch door and down the path to the yard. He stood for a moment. The sky was pure blue, with only a few puffy white clouds here and there. He took a few breaths, hoping the fresh air would erase some of the heaviness on his spirit.

Then he walked toward the rear of the yard, found the gap in the fence, and crouched down. He reached through, grabbed the stone, and wedged it into place again.

He brushed his hands off and went back to the house. Seamus was on the phone, ordering. Cal was in the kitchen, fixing a cup of tea.

Eamon went to make himself one.

Cal glanced over. "What were you doing out there?"

Eamon hadn't been aware Cal was watching him through the window. "Fixing part of the fence."

Cal nodded. "Did you talk to the witches next door yet?"

Eamon almost told Cal they weren't witches, then

decided it wasn't important. "No. I don't think I'm going to."

Cal frowned. "Why not? They could help you."

"I don't think so. The youngest one isn't even a witch yet."

"No? Fascinating. How does she get to be one?"

"I don't know."

Cal grinned. "Maybe you could be her first spell once she comes into her power."

Eamon understood his cousin just wanted to help, so he forced his mouth into a tight smile. "I've been this way all my life, Cal. If there was a cure for me, it would have shown up already. No one can change what I see."

"I don't think that's true. My research has shown that—"

"I appreciate you want to help. But don't waste your time on me." He hesitated, thinking he'd sounded a bit harsh. "I don't want to get my hopes up for something that's not going to happen, you know?"

"I ken that, but what if there is a chance?"

"I'm ... all right the way I am." Which might have been the biggest lie he'd ever told.

"You're sure?"

Eamon nodded as he poured water over a teabag. "I am."

Cal looked like he wanted to say more but didn't.

From the living room, Seamus called out. "Food's ordered. I'm gonna queue up the game."

Cal picked up his tea. "If you change your mind ..."

"You'll be the first to know." Eamon put the kettle back. Maybe the game would be a good distraction from having to talk about anything else. He hoped. He was inches away from going back upstairs and locking himself away for the rest of the day and night.

He took a seat in the living room, but not long after, there was a knock on the door.

"Curry Kitchen's gotten faster," Seamus said, getting up. "But I suppose we're VIPs by now, eh, Eamon?"

Eamon forced a smile. "I suppose so."

Seamus went out to get the food. He came back a moment later. "Eamon? There's a young woman here to see you."

"Me?"

Seamus nodded. "Pretty lass. Don't keep her waiting."

Eamon frowned but got up and went to the door.

Tru was standing on the front porch. She started talking as soon as he was in earshot. "Look, I know you're mad but—"

He stepped outside and closed the door behind him so his uncle couldn't hear. "We don't have anything to say to each other. Don't worry about it."

"You might not have anything to say to me, but I need to apologize to you. So do my aunts, although I haven't quite shamed them into that yet. I am really sorry for what happened today. My aunts are very protective of me. Oracles are rare. Still doesn't excuse their behavior, but I hope it explains it a little."

He just stared at her, the pleasure of being able to

look at her face lightening his mood. "Do they still believe I'm a vampire?"

"I don't think so."

He stood there a moment longer. "Well, you've apologized."

"Right." She twisted her hands together. "Would you like to come over for dinner sometime?"

He almost laughed. "No." He opened the door to go back in and nearly knocked Cal down.

"Sorry," Cal said. "I, uh, thought I saw the delivery car." He smiled at Tru. "Hello, there. I'm Callum, Eamon's cousin. Nice to meet you."

Eamon didn't buy for one second that Cal had seen the food arriving. Cal had seen Tru and that was all the reason he'd needed to come to the front door.

Eamon was well aware of what Tru looked like. He didn't blame Cal one bit.

"Nice to meet you, Callum," Tru said. But then she looked at Eamon again. "No? Really?" She blinked at him. She knew she'd heard him right. She just didn't believe he'd turned her dinner invitation down. "Because of my aunts? I swear, I'll get them to apologize."

Eamon sighed. "Cal, if you could just give us a second."

"Sure, sure," Cal said, smiling at Tru for all he was worth. "Pleasure to meet you." He went back inside, adding a little wave for good measure before Eamon closed the door again.

"Your cousin seems nice." Tru arched her brows, wondering if he'd picked up her implication that since Cal was nice, Eamon ought to be, too.

Of course, Cal might not have Eamon's gift of seeing how long people had left to live. She supposed that could sour anyone's mood.

Eamon shook his head. "It *is* because of your aunts, but not because they haven't apologized. I can see hourglasses over them. I can't spend a whole meal trying not to see what's right in front of my face."

Tru paled slightly. "I know you said that out in the yard, but I just ... So you can see them?"

He nodded. "Aye."

"Why them but not me?"

"I don't have the slightest. Now, if you'll excuse me—"

"Do you think it's because I'm not really an oracle yet? Like, maybe I'm in some kind of limbo?"

Again, he shook his head. "I don't know."

"How long do they have left?" She chewed her bottom lip. "It's okay. You can tell me."

"No, I can't. For one thing, I did my best not to look. For another, that doesn't feel like information I should be sharing with anyone, but if I was going to, shouldn't I tell the person whose life I'm talking about?"

She frowned. "I didn't expect you to have rules about it. But I guess I understand. I just worry about them, you know?"

"Sure, I understand. And I don't really have rules. That just seems like information only one person should know. The person involved."

She still wanted to know. But then again, maybe it was better not knowing.

"I should go back in. Thank you for apologizing."

She wasn't ready for him to leave yet. She reached out and grabbed his arm. "Eamon. I know you're mad about what happened. You have every right to be. But don't you think there's more to you not being able to see my time-line? Don't you think it's something worth investigating?"

He hesitated, his gaze briefly resting on her hand on his arm, then he made eye contact again. "It's probably just what you said. You're in limbo right now. Once you become an oracle, I'm sure things will change."

She let go of him reluctantly. "I might not become an oracle."

"Do you have that choice?"

She hadn't really asked, but why wouldn't she? "I do. I mean, it's my decision, isn't it? Although my aunts would be really disappointed. The next oracle doesn't come of age for five more years. And oracles generally work best in threes. But ..." She shrugged even as she realized she really did have a decision to make.

"How long do you have to decide?"

"Until my next birthday." It seemed like he was softening up. She decided to ask her question again. "Are you sure you won't come to dinner? I'd hate for things to be bad between us. We are neighbors, after all."

"Aye, we are."

She was winning him over. She could feel it. "Maybe you could bring your uncle, too." She grinned suddenly. "Don't say anything, but I think my Aunt Delly likes him."

Eamon snorted. "I've seen him looking at her, too." He ran a hand through his hair. "Look, I'll think about it, all right?"

"Okay." She pulled her phone out. "Then you'd better take my number so you can let me know what you decide."

Once she had his number, she'd be able to get ahold

of him, and she wasn't giving up on the idea that she could help him.

They exchanged numbers, and as he was hitting Save, his gaze narrowed. "Was this all a ploy to get my number?"

She smiled. "No. But would that have been so bad?"

He studied her for a few seconds, then shook his head. "No."

The tension had definitely eased. She was glad about that. "I don't know much about the supernatural world outside the realm of the oracles, but there is something else my kind believe in. The Fates."

He didn't say anything.

She figured she might as well go on. "There's a reason your uncle's house is next door to my aunts. A reason we met. A reason you can't see an hourglass hovering over me."

"And you think that is what?"

She took a breath, hoping she didn't ruin the new peace she'd established. "I believe it's because there might be a way that I can help you. Or maybe it'll take my aunts and me. Oracles have different specialties when it comes to their individual gifts."

"Mm-hmm." He didn't seem convinced.

"You don't believe that."

"I've had this gift all of my life. Other men in my family have odd powers too. None quite as dark as mine, although there are stories of a great-uncle who caused those around him to cry if they stayed near him long enough."

She grimaced. "That doesn't sound like fun."

"He actually had several people request in their wills that he attend their funerals. He made a good living for a while as a professional mourner."

"Is that how your uncle got into the business?"

Eamon nodded. "Aye, it was. It became a family thing. But my point was that if there'd been a cure, why hasn't anyone found it yet? Callum's been looking for ages, and he's not the first one. What taints the blood of the Underwood men canna be undone. It's ... sweet of you to want to try, but don't waste your time on me."

Her heart broke a little at his words. Did he really think he wasn't worth the effort? "Trying to help someone could never be a waste of time."

He stayed quiet a moment. "You really believe that, don't you?"

"Of course I do." She gestured toward her aunts' house. "It runs in the family. How else do you think my aunts ended up with fifteen cats?"

His eyes rounded. "Is that really how many they have?"

She nodded.

His eyes narrowed. "Wait. Did you just equate me with a stray cat?"

She laughed. "Yes. And no." Although he did give her similar vibes. He seemed so desperate to find his place in the world. Something his gift seemed to be keeping him from. "I'm sure I've kept you from your family long enough, but please let me know what you decide about dinner. Or maybe you and I could just do lunch sometime."

He shook his head but seemed a little sad about it. "I can't go out. Too many people. Hourglasses everywhere."

"Then maybe you could come over and we could eat at the house. Just the three of us."

He made a face like he didn't understand. "The three of us?"

"Yeah." She smiled. "You, me, and Nemo."

Eamon went back inside and shut the door, but instead of going back to the living room, he leaned against the door and paused to compose himself. Tru had that effect on him. She disconcerted him.

Why did she have to smell so good? And be so beautiful? Why did her smile light up her whole face that way? Why, of all the people in the world, was she the only one immune to his ability?

He sighed. And now her number was in his phone.

She wanted to help him. So did Callum, but for some reason, Tru's offer seemed easier to accept. With her, he actually thought she might be on to something. Cal was just working on a hunch, as best as Eamon could tell.

He should have said yes to lunch. Lunch with her, even if it was just them sitting on the back porch, sounded grand. Especially with Nemo keeping them company. Or he could have invited her over here. Seamus wouldn't have minded. Nemo could have come, too.

Eamon smiled, thinking about an afternoon with Tru and that wee orange beastie. There were far worse ways to spend an hour or so. Like the way he usually spent his day.

The doorbell rang, making him jump. Thinking she'd

come back, he yanked the door open and stared straight into the face of the Curry Kitchen delivery boy.

He couldn't have been more than eighteen. But that's not what Eamon noticed first. The lad's hourglass was nearly empty.

Eamon felt like he'd been punched in the gut. He averted his eyes, but there was no erasing what he'd seen. The sick feeling in his belly spread to his heart. "What's your name?"

"Scotty Hawkes. I'm from Curry Kitchen. I've got your food."

"Right. Just a—" Eamon took a step back, still reeling from what he'd seen. "Seamus," he called out. *"Seamus."*

His uncle appeared a few seconds later. "I heard the bell." He dug in his pocket for his wallet as he smiled broadly at the young man. "Hello, there."

Eamon tried to think. There had to be something he could do. Today had already been wretched. He couldn't bear the thought of knowing this boy was close to death and ignoring it. He reached for the door so that Seamus couldn't close it. "Scotty. Don't go yet."

"Was the order wrong?"

"No, it's just ..." Eamon didn't know what to say.

Scotty gave him a polite smile as he hitched a thumb toward his Toyota Corolla. "I got three more deliveries to make."

"This is important."

Seamus, bag of food in hand, gave Eamon a look. "Something you want to share?"

Eamon nodded. "His time's running out." He looked at Scotty. "Do you believe in the paranormal?"

Scotty grinned. "Is this a trick? Yeah, sure, I believe. My dad and I are—never mind. Why?"

Eamon did the best he could. "Because I can ... sense things about people. And there is serious trouble coming your way. But I have some friends who can help."

"Tru?" Seamus asked, looking at Eamon.

"Aye," Eamon said. "Get her aunts, too. Get them all."

Seamus put the food down and slipped out the door. Eamon got Scotty to stay with the promise of an extra tip. A few minutes later, Seamus returned with Tru and her aunts.

They all came up the steps and stood around Scotty.

Tru looked the most concerned. Delphina was second, but Cleo just looked mildly put out. Tru glanced at Scotty before shifting her attention to Eamon. "What's going on?"

"If at all possible, one of you needs to find out what's going to happen in this young man's future."

Scotty looked at the group around him. "You guys are freaking me out."

Tru gave him a big, bright smile. "Sorry about that, but I promise you, it's all going to be just fine."

Cleo's eyes narrowed in Eamon's direction. "Did you see something?"

Eamon just nodded, hoping she'd understand. He didn't want to put into words that the young man's life was nearing its end. Not in front of Scotty.

Cleo came around to face Scotty and took his hand. She closed her eyes, and it seemed for a moment that she became more radiant, glowing with an pearlescent shimmer. She opened her eyes again and let go of him. "Do you give me your permission to speak freely about what I saw?"

"Yeah, sure," Scotty said.

Cleo nodded. "You're supposed to go camping over the weekend. With your father."

Surprise lifted Scotty's brows. "Yeah, that's right."

"And you've planned to go whitewater rafting while you're there."

"Yeah, me and my dad, like you said. We go every year." Scotty laughed. "Did he put you up to this? My dad is such a joker."

Cleo's face was solemn and serious. "No, he didn't."

"Come on," Scotty said. "How would you know?"

"I'm an oracle. I know things others cannot." Cleo's expression grew stern. "Del."

Del came forward and took hold of Scotty's arm. She began to glow with the same radiance Cleo'd just had. After a moment, Del released him. "I'm an oracle, too. Capable of seeing the past and the future and truths about people, just as my sister is. Do you also give me permission to speak freely about what I saw?"

"Sure," Scotty said.

"Good. Because what I saw is your past, which is how I know you and your dad are werewolves. You go camping a few times a year, mostly so you can run wild and give your wolves some freedom." She smiled. "You always have the best time."

All traces of disbelief left Scotty's face, and for a split-second, a flash of blue lit his eyes, but it was gone as soon as it appeared.

Wolf, Eamon thought. He'd never seen that before.

Cleo gave Scotty a smile. Maybe to soften what she said next. "Don't go rafting. The river's swollen with the recent rains, and the rapids are more treacherous than usual. If you go, there will be an accident. Neither you nor your father will survive."

"What?" Scotty's knees buckled.

Seamus grabbed him and eased him down onto the bench on the front porch. "It's all right, son. It's all right. Do you want something to drink?"

He shook his head. "I want to call my dad."

Cleo sat on the bench next to him. "If you want me to talk to him, I'd be happy to."

"Okay," Scotty said. "Yeah."

Eamon leaned against the foyer wall, feeling relieved but spent. He'd never done anything like that before. It was exhausting and terrifying. But the sense of relief outweighed both of those things.

Tru stepped into the house and came up to him. "That was amazing. And it proves to me that what you have isn't a curse. It's a gift. You saved *two* lives just now."

Eamon glanced through the doorway at Scotty, who was on the phone. The hourglass over his head was full.

Full. Scotty had a long life ahead of him now. Eamon smiled. "His hourglass changed."

Tru's smile was huge. "You absolutely saved him."

Eamon shook his head. "Your aunts did that. I never could have convinced him."

"Just proves my point," Tru said. "We were meant to know each other. This"—she wiggled her finger back and forth between them—"was meant to be."

"I still don't want this gift. It's too much."

"I know. But you still did a very good thing." She stared at him like she had something else to say. Then she leaned up and kissed him. On the mouth. "Thank you."

The kiss shocked him so much, he had no voice for a moment. "Um, aye, you're, uh, welcome. Thank you."

Delphina stuck her head inside. "I'm so sorry I doubted you. Please forgive me."

Eamon nodded. With the taste of Tru's lips lingering on his, he would have forgiven all kinds of things in that moment.

Cleo spoke to Scotty's dad, then handed the phone back. After a moment longer, Scotty hung up.

He adjusted the Curry Kitchen trucker hat he was wearing. "Me and my dad owe you guys." He glanced at Eamon and stuck his hand out. "Thank you. My dad says if you ever need your car worked on, it's on the house. He owns Hawke's Body Shop."

Eamon shook his hand. "I'll keep that in mind."

It was odd being acknowledged for something he'd always considered a burden.

Scotty thanked them all, then said goodbye and went off to deliver the rest of his food.

Eamon was about to say goodbye to Tru and her aunts himself when Seamus cleared his throat softly.

"Why don't you ladies join us for lunch? We have more than enough." Seamus smiled at Tru's aunts. Well, mostly at Delphina. "We bought extra to have leftovers, but we'd be happy to share them with you. So long as you like curry."

Delphina answered before anyone else could get a word out. "We'd love to." She looked at Cleo. "Maybe we should get a bottle of ouzo?"

Tru put her hand up to stop them. "How about we just have water?"

18

Tru sat next to Eamon, feeling like she might overflow with joy. Things had worked out far better than she'd hoped. She'd never imagined they'd all be sitting around a table together, sharing a meal so soon.

She glanced at him. He was still working hard not to look over her aunts' heads, which she understood. But he looked happier. She leaned closer. "Maybe later, we could take a walk together."

He nodded. "I'd like that. Especially if we don't run into too many people. But it's a little better at night. I can't see the hourglasses quite as clearly."

"That's good. Text me when you're ready to go, and I'll meet you on the sidewalk." She just smiled at him.

He smiled back. "You look happy."

"I am."

"Me, too."

Callum lifted his glass. "Here's to Eamon, Cleo, and Delphina for their combined efforts. Saving two lives is a remarkable feat."

"Here, here," Seamus said.

Tru raised her glass. "What you three did today was nothing short of astonishing."

As they all drank, she hoped, more than anything,

that today would be a turning point for Eamon. That he'd see how useful his gift could be. Even if it made him uncomfortable. But maybe that would lessen over time, too.

Callum set his glass down. "So, the three of you are oracles, descendants of the original Greek Oracles. Doesn't that make you minor goddesses? Forgive me, but my grasp of Greek mythology isn't what it should be."

"No," Aunt Cleo said, but she looked amused. "The Oracles weren't goddesses. They were considered the mouthpieces of the gods. Messengers, of a sort. But not goddesses."

Seamus looked at Delphina. "You could have fooled me."

Aunt Delly blushed, which Tru didn't find surprising. Delly leaned closer to Seamus. "I love your accent."

Tru glanced at Eamon again and smiled while cutting her eyes at his uncle.

Eamon gave her a little nod to say he'd seen the exchange.

"The curry is brilliant," Callum said. "Well done."

"Thank you," Seamus said. "I am very good at takeaway."

They all laughed.

Aunt Cleo nodded. "It is very tasty. We hadn't tried Curry Kitchen yet, but I would definitely order from them now."

Callum's fork paused midair. "So what exactly does an oracle do? Predict the future?"

"We can," Aunt Cleo answered. "We can also see into the past. Some of us, like my sister, more clearly than others."

"Which," Eamon said, "was how you were able to see that Scotty and his father are werewolves?"

"Right," Aunt Delly said.

"Although you can do more than that. Can't you?" There was no animosity in Eamon's expression, even though Tru knew that he was referring to Aunt Delly had done to him earlier.

"Some of us can," Aunt Delly said.

"Like what?" Callum asked.

Aunt Delly looked at her sister, obviously unsure how much she should say. There was nothing super-secret about being an oracle, but they didn't exactly put a neon sign in the front window proclaiming, "Fortunes Told!"

Aunt Cleo sipped her water. "Besides our ability to predict future events, we often have a secondary power that is more uniquely our own. Being able to see more clearly into the past. Using one person's future to see into another person's life. Generally a family member or a close friend, in that case. Sometimes being able to understand when a person is telling the truth. Every once in a while, an oracle will be granted the ability to read the future of objects or places instead of people."

Callum made a face. "How would that work with the objects or places?"

"What if you wanted to buy a piece of land to build a business on but you weren't sure it was the right spot? Or what if you found a large diamond but you weren't sure the best way to cut it to give it the greatest value? Or maybe it's something simpler, like you inherited your great-grandmother's quilt and wanted to know its history."

"Aye, of course," Callum said. "This is terribly interesting. Forgive me for all my questions. I'm a researcher, genealogist, and writer. I think it's in my nature to question everything."

Aunt Cleo laughed. "That's quite a combination. No wonder you're so curious. There are many people who go their whole lives without meeting a single oracle. Now you're having lunch with two."

Callum glanced at Tru. "So you aren't one? Will you be?"

Tru nodded. "I'm not one yet. As to whether or not I will be ..." She glanced at her aunts. "I'm still figuring that out."

"Why wouldn't you?" Callum asked. "It seems like such an amazing thing. To be able to predict the future! Who wouldn't want that?"

"Well, it's more complicated," Tru tried to explain. "My mother, who was also an oracle, most likely died because she wasn't able to handle the intensity of her powers."

Callum sat back. "I am so very sorry. I dinna mean to stir up any hard memories. Forgive me."

"No, it's all right," Tru said. "I just have reason to believe I could be in the same boat."

Eamon turned toward her. "I wish there was a way I could help you with that."

Callum nodded. "Why don't you just have one of your aunts see what your future's going to be?"

"Doesn't work that way," Tru said, scooping up some rice and curry on her fork. It was one of the best things she'd ever eaten. She looked at her aunts. "Right?"

Aunt Cleo nodded. "No oracle can read another oracle's timeline. But we are going to talk to a local witch and see if she knows anything that might help."

"Wait," Callum said. "Aren't oracles already witches?" He looked at Eamon. "Didn't you tell me they were witches?"

"No," Eamon said. "You assumed that, and I didn't correct you."

Aunt Delly shook her head. "We're not witches, although I suppose you might put us in the same category, if you really needed to label us. But we don't do any kind of magic or spells or hex people. We simply read what we're shown."

Tru wondered about the oracle ability to curse people, but apparently her aunts didn't think that was the same as casting spells.

"So interesting," Callum said. "The power that's within you two ..." His eyebrows rose. "Amazing."

As Callum continued to ask questions of Aunt Cleo, and Seamus continued to make eyes at Aunt Delly, Tru started up a side conversation with Eamon. "What are you doing after lunch?"

"Recording an episode of my podcast."

"That's right. You mentioned you did that. What's it about?"

"Unsolved murders. My hope, and it's a lofty one, is that someone listening might know something they don't realize is important and that just maybe one of those victims might get justice."

She fell in love with him just a little bit right then. How could she not? "That's a very admirable goal."

"It's always felt like a way to balance all the death I see in the world. Hasn't happened yet, one of the cases being solved, I mean. But maybe someday."

"What's your podcast called?"

He laughed. "Why? Are you going to listen to it?"

"Maybe I already have." She shrugged. "I do like podcasts. Especially the murdery ones."

He laughed a little harder. "It's called *Murder Most Foul.*"

Her mouth came open. "I think I have listened to it! I should have recognized the accent, but I listen to so many. That is really cool."

But then, everything about Eamon was cool. Even if he didn't realize it. Yet.

19

As reluctant as Eamon had been to say goodbye to Tru, he'd also been eager to get back into his studio. Amazing what saving a life could do for a person's attitude.

He had the first episode and part of the second recorded in just under four hours. He was thrilled with the progress and looked forward to editing what he had.

Not as much as he was looking forward to his walk with Tru, however. Before saying goodbye, he'd confirmed that was something he wanted to do as soon as he was finished in the studio.

He changed into track pants, a long-sleeved T-shirt, trainers, then added a ballcap. The brim was very convenient for avoiding seeing anything hovering over a person. All he had to do was tilt his head down and instant shield.

He was halfway down the steps when he realized he'd left his phone on the dresser. He went back up, grabbed it, and sent Tru a text.

Being able to do that was such a novelty. He very rarely sent texts except to his uncle and sometimes Clark. *Ready to walk?*

She answered shortly. *Ten minutes?*

Perfect.

He went into the kitchen and found Cal at the table on his laptop. "Uncle Seamus around?"

Cal looked up and shook his head. "He went to the funeral home to do some paperwork. Said he'd be back in plenty of time for supper and that he plans to make a cottage pie."

"Nice," Eamon said. Seamus made a gorgeous cottage pie.

"Where are you off to?"

Eamon smiled. "I'm going out for a walk with Tru."

Cal nodded. "She might be the answer you've been searching for."

Eamon shook his head. "I haven't been searching for an answer."

"Well, no, I guess you haven't. But that much power? There must be a way she could use it to keep you from seeing what you see."

"She's not even sure she's going to become an oracle. You heard her. It might be dangerous for her. I wouldn't want that."

"No, of course not, but if she finds out from this witch that it's safe, it's something to think about."

Eamon shrugged. "Maybe."

"Even if she couldn't help you, think about what those women could do with their abilities. The stock market predictions alone could make someone a billionaire. The possibilities are endless."

"They might have some sort of ... rule in place about that."

"Maybe. But I bet they'd bend that rule for the right fella."

Eamon wasn't sure what to say. He wasn't interested in using Tru or her aunts as a way to make easy money. He and his uncle lived a good life. Maybe they weren't rich, but they weren't skint, either. "I need to go meet Tru. See you later."

"Later." Cal went back to whatever he was doing online.

Eamon went out the front door. The sky was going that soft purply heather of twilight that reminded him of home.

Tru was just walking out from her house. She waved at him. "Hiya. You look very sporty."

She was in body-hugging electric-blue leggings, white trainers, and a white sweatshirt with a wide neck that exposed one shoulder. Her hair was up in a ponytail, showing off the most perfect neck he'd ever seen. Hard not to stare at it. Maybe he did have a wee bit of vampire in him.

"You do, too." But he wasn't thinking about walking so much as he was of kissing her. *That* was new. But he couldn't kiss her. He shouldn't touch her at all.

She stood on the sidewalk, looking in both directions. "Which way do you want to go? It's been ages since I've been here, so it doesn't matter to me."

"I've never gone for a walk in this neighborhood, so it doesn't matter to me, either."

She glanced at him. "You've never gone for a walk?"

He shook his head.

"What do you do for exercise?"

"You mean besides walking up and down the house steps all day?" He smiled. "I do some calisthenics. Plus, we have a treadmill and some weights. I run a couple times a week, throw some iron around." He shrugged. "What do you do?"

"I was working as a waitress at my uncle's restaurant. That's about all the exercise anyone needs."

"I'll take your word for it." He pointed down the street past her aunts' house. "Let's go that way."

They started walking, falling into pace beside each other.

"The houses here are all so beautiful, aren't they? I mean, look at that one. Look at all the colors."

He nodded. The house was mostly white but had accents of light blue, dark blue, and a medium purple. "Nothing like this at home, I'll tell you that."

"Do you mean Scotland?"

"Aye. It hasn't been home in a long time, but it's hard to think of it as anything but."

"I can understand that." She adjusted her sweatshirt, pulling it up off her shoulder, but that only made it fall off the other one. "Do you think you'll go back someday?"

"You mean for a visit? Or go back to live there?"

"I guess both."

"Maybe to visit. But that's a long trip surrounded by a lot of people. Coming over was hard enough. Not sure I really want to do that again. Going back to live?" He shook his head. "Not unless Seamus kicks me out."

She laughed.

"That's a lie," he said. "Not even then. I like it here. The people are pretty accepting, even if I haven't really made an effort to fit in."

"You have a pretty solid excuse."

He wanted to hold her hand. He stuck his hands in his pockets instead. Kissing her had been great, but at some point, he'd have to explain why that couldn't happen again. He didn't look forward to that, but she'd understand. He hoped. "What about you?"

She tipped her head. "What about me what?"

"You said something about staying here, right? Or will you eventually go home to wherever you're from?"

"The plan was for me to move here, ultimately. To become part of my aunts' business. But that was before the prediction that I was going to meet death. If I don't become an oracle, there's no reason for me to stay."

Even if he couldn't be romantically involved with her, he didn't like the idea of her leaving. They could still be friends. "What will you do if you don't become one? Go back to your uncle's restaurant?"

"Maybe. I don't know. I don't want to be a waitress the rest of my life. It's a hard job. And the pay isn't always great. Not to mention, I went to school for communications. Maybe I could do something with that. But I really did it to learn how to talk to the people who'd be hiring me."

He didn't quite understand. "You mean as an oracle?"

She nodded. "A lot of big corporations hire oracles to help them with their business decisions. And like my aunt was saying about the diamond scenario, there are all sorts of people who use our services. Bigshots. With money. I was sort of hoping to bring a more modern approach to the oracle business."

"As opposed to?"

"My aunts, basically. Which isn't to say that there's anything wrong with how they do things. They're old-school, which a lot of people love. I just thought we could reach a more diverse clientele if one of us was able to put a more current face on things. You know, show up in a business suit as opposed to a flowered skirt and peasant blouse."

"You are younger. Makes sense. What do they think of that?"

"Nothing, because I haven't brought it up. Didn't seem like much point in it." She shrugged. "Not until I know what I'm doing. Which hopefully will be soon, depending on when we can meet with Pandora."

"I hope that all works out. I hope she can help you." He thought a moment. "I know you said you didn't want to, but you *could* always waitress here. Until you found something you liked better."

She stopped walking. "Did you just ask me to stay?"

Eamon stopped walking, too, and now looked like he wasn't sure how to respond. "I guess I did."

Tru hadn't been prepared for that, but it was sweet of him to say, and it made her feel good. Who didn't want to be wanted? "I could certainly think about it. At some point, my aunts will bring in another oracle, though. Namely, my cousin. She'll be of age in five years." Tru stared off into the distance as she thought about that. "I guess in five years, I could have my own place easily enough."

"Listen," Eamon said. "We should talk later about ... that."

"About me staying?"

He nodded, looking very much like his old miserable self.

"What's wrong? You were happy just a second ago. Now you look like something terrible's happened."

He sighed. "Could we go somewhere else? I don't really want to have this conversation standing on the sidewalk."

She pointed to the end of the street, trying to imagine what he might be about to tell her. She really hoped it wasn't that he really could see an hourglass over her head. "There's a dog park over there. With no dogs in it. We could go sit on one of the benches."

"Okay."

They made their way to the park, through the gate, then to the first bench. Thankfully, whoever had had their dogs here recently had picked up after them.

Eamon took a deep breath. "I would love for you to stay, but I need to tell you now that it's not because I want you as a girlfriend."

The wind left her sails. Definitely not what she'd been expecting. "Okay. That's ... fair. But I thought you liked it when I kissed you."

"I did. But I can't be involved with anyone." The muscles in his jaw tensed, making it easy for her to see that this wasn't enjoyable for him to talk about, let alone share with someone. "I had a girlfriend once. Sophie. I liked her enough that I decided I would deal with being able to see her hourglass."

"Did she know? About your ability?" Tru was slightly jealous of the woman, and there was no logical reason for that.

"No. She had no supernatural in her, so there was no reason for me to think she'd understand. I figured it was better not to tell her. Just in case she thought I was off my nut completely and broke up with me because of that."

"So what happened?"

"Things were good. For a while. Then I realized the sand had begun slipping through her hourglass faster."

"Was she sick?"

"No." Eamon's gaze was directed at something far away. "She seemed to be in perfect health. I thought for a while that it was just my imagination. But a couple more months proved it wasn't. Then it occurred to me that maybe I was the reason. Maybe because I was watching it all the time, even if I wasn't meaning to, I was making the sand run faster. I was causing her life to be cut short."

"Oh, no. That can't be right." She frowned. He had to be blaming himself for something he had no control over.

A man entered the dog park with two Labs, one chocolate, one yellow. He waved at Tru and Eamon, then took the dogs off the leash. The pair immediately began to tear around the open space like someone had just turned their motors on.

Eamon lowered his voice, even though the man was on the other side of the park, and kept his eyes aimed toward the ground. "It *was* right. I broke up with her immediately. I made my decision to leave for the States not long after that, but before I left, I went to check on her. She worked at a daycare." He smiled a little. "She was always so great with kids."

"What about her health?" Tru asked.

"Her hourglass was full again, so it had to be me. Somehow, I had been the drain on her life force. There was no other explanation."

The dogs raced by, panting, tails wagging, making her and Eamon both chuckle, despite the discussion.

Eamon glanced over. "And before you think it's just

the effect I have on people regardless of how I feel about them, it's not. Clark, the assistant at the funeral home, is fine, and he's worked for my uncle for four years. Been around me all that time. I think it has far more to do with physical contact."

Tru was silent for so long, she wondered if Eamon thought she wasn't talking to him anymore. The man collected his dogs and left. "I don't know what to say except I'm so sorry that happened to you."

Eamon just sighed.

Tru had never wanted to touch him more. "Maybe we can talk to the witches about that, too. Or maybe my aunts could do something. Look at your past and your future and see if they can figure out what's going on. But I'm not ready to give up on you that fast."

He leaned away. "Tru, don't you see? If you get involved with me, I will be the death you meet. And I don't want that. I like you a lot. I think you're beautiful and sexy, and I would love to be with you. But you're far too valuable to this world for me to be that selfish. I would never want to hurt you. If something happened to you because I was selfish, I couldn't live with myself."

Her eyes burned with unshed tears. She laughed at how absurd she was being. "I don't know why I feel like crying, but I do. This is really unfair. For both of us. I like you, Eamon. But it seems like neither of us is going to get the chance to see if whatever spark we feel means anything. And that sucks."

He nodded. "Aye, it does. I've never wanted to not

have a conversation more than this one. If there was anything I could do to change it ..."

"Maybe there is." She turned, squaring off to face him. "But are you willing to do what it takes if there is a way?"

She expected him to hesitate, but he answered right away. "Absolutely."

"What if it means some kind of sacrifice?"

"So long as it doesn't require anyone else losing their life, or the life of an animal, I'm good."

"Then let's go talk to my aunts and see what we can come up with."

"All right."

"But regardless of what they find, I see no reason not to keep seeing you."

He gave her a strange look. "Are you daft? After what I just told you? I wish I could see your hourglass right now just so I knew if I was affecting you."

"I'm not daft. You said you thought you affected Sophie through physical contact, right?"

"Aye."

She shrugged. "So we just won't touch." She grabbed hold of his shirt, leaned in and kissed him. After a few long seconds, she broke away. "Starting now."

Eamon didn't know what to expect from Tru's aunts, but if it meant there was a possibility he and Tru could be together, he was willing to put up with a lot. The thought of kissing her again was a big motivator.

"Aunt Cleo, Aunt Delly," Tru called out as they walked into the house. "I'm back with Eamon, and he needs your help."

"In the kitchen," one of them answered.

He and Tru went in that direction. The aunts were fixing dinner, but it looked like they'd just fed the cats, because a whole crew of them was lined up eating—except for a three-legged black cat with a white patch on his chest. That one was sitting on the windowsill, eyeing them curiously.

Eamon pointed at him. Or her. "Who's that?"

Delphina looked over from where she was putting pieces of chicken on skewers. "That's Yardstick. He and Nemo get on quite well. You might see them running around together sometimes."

He snorted. "Yardstick? How did you come up with that name?"

Delphina grinned. "Because he only has three feet.

Might not make sense to someone used to the metric system."

Eamon groaned, tipping his head a wee bit so the visor of his hat covered the aunts' hourglasses. "No, I get it."

"It's a terrible name," Cleo said. She was slicing vegetables for a big salad. "But Yardy doesn't mind it, do you, boy?"

Yardy meowed like he actually knew he was being spoken to.

Cleo smiled and looked up at them. "Would you like to stay for dinner, Eamon? It's nothing fancy. Greek salad with chicken."

Delphina leaned to see him better. "Which is the only kind of salad we know how to make."

Tru rolled her eyes but looked amused. "It's really good. Especially the grilled seasoned chicken. But the salad has onions, tomatoes, cucumbers, kalamata olives, feta cheese, and lettuce. Of course."

"Plus, we still have some dolmas," Cleo said.

"What are those?" Eamon asked.

"Grape leaves stuffed with rice, seasonings, and in these, a little ground lamb."

"I've never had those." He nodded. "I'd love to stay. Thank you."

"So," Cleo went on. "What do you need help with?"

He looked at Tru. He wasn't sure where to start. "Maybe you could have a look at my future? See what might happen if…

Tru held his gaze and smiled. "See what might happen if Eamon and I were together."

Both aunts stopped what they were doing. Cleo shook her head. "I'm not sure what sort of reading we would get. Not when it involves a family member."

Tru nodded. "I understand, but couldn't you just read him? Maybe see if I'm even in his future or not? Eamon thinks that he might cause a person's life to shorten if he has too much physical contact with them."

Delphina looked concerned. "Like your uncle?"

Eamon wasn't surprised that's who she'd thought about. "I don't think my ability affects those in my own family. I can't see their hourglasses, though, so I don't know that for sure." A slight panic came over him. "I really hope I'm not affecting him that way."

"I hope so, too," Delphina said.

Cleo put the cucumbers she'd been slicing into the bowl. "We called Pandora and set up a time to meet with her tomorrow, but I'm wondering if there's not someone else who might be better-suited to helping Eamon."

"Like who?" Eamon asked.

Delphina looked at her sister. "Are you thinking what I'm thinking?"

Cleo nodded. "Probably." She looked at Eamon. "There's a retired reaper in Nocturne Falls. A man named Lucien Dupree. He owns Insomnia. It's a nightspot for supernaturals. But seeing hourglasses sounds very much like something he'd know about, considering what he used to do."

Eamon nodded. "There is some reaper blood in my family. There are all kinds of bloodlines, though. Like I mentioned, we're supernatural mutts. Still, I don't know how I feel about talking to man whose job involved gathering souls."

"Like Cleo said, he's retired from the reaping business," Delphina said. "He's no kind of threat, not anymore. He and his wife, Imari, only live a couple blocks away."

"For real?" Tru said. "There's an actual Grim Reaper in this neighborhood?"

Cleo nodded. "This town is filled with all sorts. His wife is a retired genie."

Tru just shook her head. "This place is crazy."

Eamon had to agree. "Do you think he'd see me?"

Cleo went back to chopping vegetables. "Walk down and knock on his door."

"I don't think so," Eamon said. "Just because I can see the timelines of others doesn't mean I have a death wish of my own. Can't we call him or something?"

Delphina gave him a sympathetic glance. "I don't have his number."

"Neither do I," Cleo said. "I see his wife around sometimes, but he's not exactly a social butterfly."

Tru tugged on Eamon's sleeve. "Come on. We can go down there and talk to him. I'll do it. He wouldn't hurt an almost-oracle."

Cleo pursed her lips. "He wouldn't hurt anyone. He's *retired*. And Imari seems very nice."

He looked at Tru. "You really want to do this?"

"Yes. Then, when we get back, maybe my aunts can have a look at your future and figure out what to do next."

He was impressed with her courage. "All right. Let's go." He asked Cleo, "Which house is it?"

"Black house trimmed in peacock colors. You can't miss it," she answered. "Also, the name Dupree is on the mailbox."

"That will help." He and Tru went back out and down the sidewalk. Almost all the homes had lights on now that it had gotten dark. "Aren't you nervous?"

"Sure, but not enough to keep me from doing this."

"Apparently." He smiled at her. "Thanks."

They found the house pretty effortlessly, mostly because the name was on the mailbox and the description made it easy to spot. The black Victorian mansion was brightened considerably by the vibrant shades of green, blue, and teal.

They stood at the end of the path leading to the front porch steps. The double doors were inset with panels of stained glass. Looked friendly enough.

Tru gave him a quick smile, then headed for the doors. He took a few fast steps to catch up. "What are you going to say?"

She shrugged. "I'll figure it out."

She knocked before he could say another word.

The door opened, and a colorfully dressed woman greeted them. "Hello."

Eamon tried not to stare. There was no hourglass over her head.

"Hi," Tru said. "I'm Troula Kouris, and this is Eamon Underwood. We both live down the street, so we're actually all neighbors. Are you Imari?"

The woman nodded, smiling. "I am. Nice to meet you."

"You, too," Tru said. "We were wondering if we could speak to your husband, Lucien? We need to talk to a reaper."

Imari's perfect brows lifted slightly. "Please come in. He's in his study, but I'll get him."

"Thank you."

Eamon and Tru stepped into the foyer. It was a beautiful space with dark teal walls. There was color everywhere inside, something he hadn't been expecting.

"I'll be right back." Imari left them, disappearing deeper into the house.

Tru leaned over and whispered. "She's so pretty! And I love all the colors in the house."

He nodded. "It's not what I'd usually go for, but I like it a lot."

About a minute later, Imari returned. A man followed her. Everything about him, his hair, his eyes, his countenance, was dark. Lucien.

"My wife said that you're neighbors and you wanted to speak to me?"

Tru nodded. "I'm Troula Kouris and this is Eamon Underwood. We both live just a few houses down. And we do want to speak to you, very much. See, my friend Eamon can see hourglasses over people's heads. The remainder of the days they have left to live. And it sounded like something you might be able to help with."

Lucian's eyes narrowed as he looked at Eamon. "Is that right?"

Eamon nodded, again trying not to stare. "Aye, it is."

"How long do I have left then?"

Eamon shook his head. "I couldn't tell you. Neither you nor your wife have one."

Lucien was silent a moment. Finally, he lifted his chin slightly. "So you only see the timelines of mortals?"

"I guess. I do my best to keep to myself. It's not the most comforting thing to walk around surrounded by people with ticking clocks over their heads."

Lucien grunted something unintelligible, then said, "You understand I'm retired."

"I do," Eamon said.

Lucien gestured toward the back of the house. "Come into the living room, and let's talk some more."

After the foyer, Tru wasn't surprised that the enormous L-shaped couch was sapphire blue or that the rug had flecks of fuchsia or that the throw pillows were every color of the rainbow or that the walls were a burnished golden yellow. What surprised her was how well it all worked.

Imari excused herself for a moment.

Tru was happy to study the room while Eamon and Lucien talked.

"There are only two reasons why you'd see hour-glasses like that," Lucien began. He was seated in a large leather chair adjacent to the couch. "You either have reaper blood in you or you're related to a sandman."

Eamon shook his head. "These aren't people about to sleep. It's definitely their life that's sifting through that hourglass."

Lucien took that in stride. "Then there's reaper blood in your veins."

"Along with a host of other creatures," Eamon said. "My family is a melting pot of the supernatural. It's why most of the men have some sort of odd little gift. My uncle, for example, can accurately predict the weather at any given moment."

"Useful," Lucien remarked.

"Indeed," Eamon agreed. "Sadly, mine is neither little nor odd. Or useful. It's big and disturbing."

"I can understand how it would feel that way. Death is … not a comfortable thing for most people."

"In my day job, I'm the undertaker at my uncle's funeral home, so I'm very aware of how difficult death is for most people."

Tru had to interject. "Your gift isn't entirely worthless. You saved Scotty and his father."

Lucien's eyes narrowed. "Explain."

Just then, Imari returned with a tray bearing a teapot and glass cups in metal holders. "Mint tea?"

"I'd love some," Tru said. She was game to try anything new, and it smelled wonderful. Besides that, it would be rude to turn down someone's hospitality in their home.

"Sounds lovely," Eamon said. "Thank you."

Imari poured cups for all of them, passed the cups out along with a bowl of sugar cubes, then sat at the other end of the big couch, crossing her legs under her and holding her cup with such grace that Tru felt like a big clumsy lump.

Imari, with her dark, flowing curls and burnished skin was honestly the most beautiful woman Tru had ever seen. She didn't understand why Eamon wasn't staring at her.

"Go on," Lucien said. "Tell me how you saved these people."

Together, Eamon and Tru explained what had happened, Tru filling in the parts about her aunts being oracles and what they could do.

At the end, Lucien nodded. "That's remarkable. That young man and his father owe you a debt."

"No," Eamon said. "They owe me nothing. I was just glad to help."

"Of course you were. Because you're a decent human being. But there are those in this world who would have done nothing." Lucien sipped his tea. "I don't think I can help you in the sense of removing this gift from you."

Eamon's face fell. He sighed. "I see."

"But"—Lucien lifted his finger—"I might be able to teach you to control it. It all depends on your willingness to learn and how deep this ability lies within you. I'll need to know more about what you can do."

Eamon held his hands up. "I'd love to learn to control it, but I've told you everything I can do. There's very little of me involved in it. I just see the hourglasses over people, whether I want to or not."

"Have you ever tried *not* to see them?"

"All the time. It's why I'm wearing this hat. The brim makes it easier to block them out."

"No," Lucien said. "Not physically. I mean have you ever tried with your mind?"

Eamon glanced at Tru like he thought the man across from him was a little crazy. "No. I wouldn't know how to begin doing that."

"That is what I would like to try to teach you. No

promises, you understand?" Lucien put his tea down. "Without knowing the real strength of the reaper blood in your veins or the powers of the reaper who contributed that blood, there's no way for me to guess how successful this attempt might be."

"Would it help to know the reaper's name?" Eamon asked.

"Immensely. I could look him up and see just what his skills were," Lucien answered. "How would you find that out?"

"My cousin, Callum, has been working on our family's genealogy for years. He's been trying to trace all the different types of magic and creatures and whatnot that are behind all of our curious powers. He might be able to tell me. Or he might be able to find out."

"Then ask him. If he can tell you the reaper's name, all the better." Lucien hesitated. "May I ask why there's been so many different bloodlines in your family? While it doesn't create issues for most creatures, some do tend to stick to their own kind because, as you are witness to, mixing the bloodlines can create issues with the magic. Occasionally, the original magic disappears entirely, lost to the generations."

Eamon glanced at the floor, then shook his head. "We're just mutts. That's all I can say."

Tru had an inkling that there was a reason but he didn't want to say. Maybe because she was there. Maybe it was something embarrassing. Either way, it was his right to share what he wanted and keep the rest to himself.

She just hoped it wasn't information that could prove useful later. She drank the last of her tea, which had been very tasty.

Lucien cleared his throat softly. "See what you can find out from your cousin. In the meantime, I'll do a little research on my end. We should exchange numbers as well. Then we can contact each other with what we've found."

While Eamon and Lucien did that, Tru smiled at Imari. "That tea was really good. Thank you."

"You're very welcome," she said. "It's nice to meet new people in the neighborhood, so I'm glad you stopped by. Although I wish it was under different circumstances. Such a gift as Eamon's sounds like a heavy burden to bear."

Tru nodded. "It sounds that way to me, too."

They said their goodbyes and headed back to Tru's aunts' house. "Did that make you more or less interested to see what my aunts have to say?"

"After talking to Lucien, more. Definitely."

"He's an interesting guy, don't you think?"

"Intimidating, to say the least. An actual reaper." Eamon shook his head. "I never thought I'd meet the likes of him."

"How are you feeling about what he told you?"

Eamon took a breath before answering. "A wee bit hopeful, I suppose. It feels … disloyal to want to remove my ability altogether. That probably sounds like a load of bollocks, but it's the only family legacy I have of the magic that was once in us."

"It sounds perfectly reasonable. Getting rid of it entirely might make you feel disconnected from your family, and your family is really all you've had for a long time."

He nodded, smiling. "Aye, that's exactly it. My family has been there for me. I wouldn't want to do anything that would seem disrespectful. But at the same time, if I never saw another hourglass, I'd be just fine with that, too."

"I get the family thing, because I'm in the same boat. I've been raised with the expectation that I would be an oracle someday. It's not just something my family hoped I would do. It's always been understood that it was my duty. Just like it would be for any daughters I have." Although those chances were getting smaller and smaller every day.

He gave her a long look. "I wish I could hold your hand right now."

She nodded. "I wish you could, too." She'd never thought being unable to hold hands with someone could make her ache inside, but that was exactly what was happening. The comfort of that physical connection would have done wonders for her.

But it was more than that. Eamon had become forbidden fruit. And she'd never wanted a taste of anything so badly in her life.

"The meal was stunning, and that chicken was incredible," Eamon said. He meant it, too. The salad her aunts had served really had been delicious and full of flavors he wasn't used to.

He'd texted his uncle before the meal to say he was at Tru's and wouldn't be back until after dinner. He was glad he'd stayed. He could talk to his cousin when he got home later.

"I'm glad you enjoyed it," Delphina said. She made a happy face at Tru. "I love the words he uses. Stunning! So cute." Then she headed into the kitchen with the big salad bowl, which was mostly empty.

"I probably ate too much." He put his hand on his stomach. Under the table, Nemo rubbed against his legs. The cat had been hanging around him since they'd arrived. "But it was all so good. The dolmas might be my new favorite thing."

Cleo grinned. "We'll make a Greek out of you yet."

Delphina came back with a platter of flaky little squares speckled with nuts and glistening with some kind of syrup.

Recognition hit Eamon. "Is that baklava?"

"It is," Delphina said proudly. "Homemade. Have you had it before?"

"I have. There was a chippie near where I grew up that was owned by a Greek family. They always had it." He smiled at Tru, then at Delphina. "There's no way it'll be as good as this, though."

"Smart boy." Cleo gave him a wink. "What's a chippie?"

"A fish and chip shop," Eamon explained. "Which is how I already know your baklava will demolish theirs."

Tru laughed. "You're awfully charming."

He smiled. He was happy. Truly happy. If nothing in his life changed, he could live like this. There was no question he would prefer a life where being close to Tru and having the ability to touch her were possible, but if that didn't happen, this was still very good.

Delphina cleared away a few more things. "Why don't we make a pot of decaf? And while that's brewing, Cleo and I can take a look at you, Eamon."

Tru frowned. "But you have a Keurig. That doesn't make pots of coffee."

"We have a Mr. Coffee, too," Cleo said. "It's in the pantry. Still comes in handy now and then."

Eamon nodded. "I'm fine with that."

Delphina patted him on the shoulder. "Don't be nervous. It's not going to hurt."

He laughed. "Thank you for the reassurance."

He carried his plate and utensils into the kitchen, where he was promptly shooed into the living room.

Nemo followed him in. Eamon took a seat on the couch and waited for the women. He picked up a small, crinkly ball and tossed it for the cat.

Nemo took off after it. Then he brought it back, carrying it in his mouth.

Eamon pointed at him as he looked at the women. "Do you see this? This cat plays fetch!"

Cleo laughed. "It's not that uncommon in cats. People think it's just a dog thing, but it really isn't."

Eamon shook his head at Nemo. "You're a smart little lad, aren't you, now?"

Nemo dropped the ball. Eamon picked it up and tossed it again. Just like before, Nemo chased it down and returned it.

"This cat is something else."

Tru and her aunts came in. Cleo and Delphina sat on either side of him. Tru took one of the chairs. Nemo sat on the coffee table, watching. Yardy was in the cat condo by the windows, along with another cat Eamon didn't know the name of.

Cleo spoke first. "We're going to have a look at your future. And if you'd like, Del could also look at your past. It may not seem that important to you, but sometimes the past can answer a lot of questions."

He nodded. "I'm open to anything you think might help. Especially if reveals something that will help Lucien better understand what's going on." Over dinner, Eamon and Tru had told her aunts all about their visit to the reaper and his wife.

"That's the goal," Delphina said. "To find bits of information that will help solve this whole puzzle of how to make things better for you."

"What do you need me to do?"

"Just sit back and relax," Cleo said. "The more open you are to the experience, the easier it will be for us."

"All right." He settled in.

Delphina rubbed her palms together. "I'll start."

She took Eamon's hand in both of hers, then closed her eyes and emitted the soft radiance he'd seen before.

After a few moments, she opened her eyes again and shook her head, looking at her sister. "Nothing stood out to me."

"Is that bad?" Eamon asked.

"No, not bad," Delphina said. "In a way, it's good. I didn't see any traumas or incidents that might have contributed to your current ability."

"My turn," Cleo said.

Tru leaned forward in her chair. "How far into his future are you going? Are you going to look for me?"

Cleo cut her eyes at her niece. "I'm going to let his future show me whatever it wants to. I cannot direct what is already there."

"Okay." Tru sat back and gave him a little shrug as if to say she'd tried.

He didn't mind. Whatever they found was just more information. Hard to say what might be helpful.

Cleo took his right hand, the same way Delphina had

taken his left, holding it between both of hers. She closed her eyes, and the glow emanated from her.

Her brow bent, furrowing into lines that he could only interpret as bad news. Whatever was in his future couldn't be good.

With the kind of stealth only a cat could achieve, Nemo stretched his way onto Eamon's lap. Eamon smiled and scratched his head.

"Whoa," Cleo said suddenly. "*Whoa*. What the—" She opened her eyes, instantly pinpointing Nemo. "When did he show up?"

"Just a second ago," Eamon said.

Tru was on the edge of her seat. "What did you see?"

Cleo frowned. "You know I can't discuss Eamon's future with anyone but him without his permission."

"Go ahead," Eamon said. "You can say whatever you need to in front of Tru. I don't mind."

Cleo took a moment, long enough to make Eamon think she didn't want to share what she'd seen. She wiped her hand over her mouth, then spoke. "What I saw was a lot of darkness. Almost like an illness that was diminishing you more and more every day."

"Like Alzheimer's?"

"Sort of. But it wasn't just your mind. It was your body, too." There was pain in Cleo's eyes. She clearly didn't want to have to tell him this. "But then it changed. And in all of my years as an oracle, I've never seen a future change while it was being shown to me. Not once. And that change occurred when Nemo got into your lap."

Eamon glanced down at the beastie. "Och, this cat changes my future?"

Cleo nodded slowly. "That's how I interpret it."

Tru's mouth was hanging open. "What does that mean? How does Nemo change it?"

"It really felt like Nemo saved Eamon's life," Cleo said. "But like I said, this is brand-new for me. I really can't be sure. But there are other oracles I can ask. And I will."

"Thank you," Eamon said. He scratched Nemo's cheeks, which made the wee cat purr like mad.

Cleo nodded. "But until I do, and until I know more, I think you need to keep Nemo close to you."

"You mean take him home with me?" Eamon blinked as he tried to take it all in.

"Yes," Cleo said. "That's exactly what I mean. He does seem to like you, so I think it'll work out."

"But he's your cat," Eamon countered.

"We're never opposed to finding a good home for one of our clowder, outside of a few we consider our personal cats," Delphina said. "It means we have room for another one who might need a home."

Eamon picked Nemo up and cradled him in his arms, staring at the stripey orange creature in disbelief. "Did you hear that, lad? Looks like we're going to be house-mates. I hope that's all right with you."

Nemo stretched out one paw, putting it squarely on Eamon's cheek.

He shook his head as he looked at the women around

him. "You really think a cat is going to save my life? That he's some kind of talisman?"

Tru rubbed her temple. "Do you want to take the chance he's not?"

Eamon smiled and gazed down at Nemo's sleepy face and quivering whiskers. "No."

Tru helped her aunts gather a cat owner starter kit for Eamon: a disposable litter box, a jug of litter, a couple of cans of cat food, a Ziploc baggie of dry food, some toys, and a blanket that Nemo was particularly fond of, along with the folder that held Nemo's health records from his one trip to the vet.

Eamon had gone back to his house to explain things to his uncle and smooth the way for Nemo's impending arrival.

Tru couldn't imagine Seamus would have a problem with taking Nemo in. Not considering the circumstances. Actually, she didn't think he would have minded even without the circumstances. Seamus seemed like the sort of man who'd welcome a pet. Especially one who might be able to benefit his nephew.

A few minutes later, there was a knock at the door.

"I'll get it," Tru shouted. Her aunts were taking care of the rest of the cats—giving medications, cleaning litter boxes, and whatever else the evening routine entailed.

She opened the door. Eamon and Seamus stood there. Seamus was sporting a grin like she'd never seen. He looked ecstatic. She smiled back. "Hello, Underwoods."

"Hello, my dear Tru." Seamus put his hands together in front of him. "Where's the wee moggy? I can't wait to have him running about the place." He went straight past her into the house and called out, "Delphina? It's Seamus. Where are you hiding our new kitten?"

Eamon looked like he was trying not to smile. "I dinna think he'd have this kind of reaction."

Tru laughed. "I love it. And if Aunt Delly wasn't already crushing on him, she will be now. The way to her heart is definitely cats."

Eamon came in and closed the door. "I've never had a pet. What if I do something wrong? I don't know how to look after a cat."

"Cats aren't hard to take care of. Just remember, they have minds of their own. You can't make them do anything they don't want to do. And they're most likely to do the thing you want them to do when you no longer want them to do it."

"So they're like women, then?"

By the twinkle in his eyes, she knew he was teasing her. She smirked at him. "In some ways, they're a lot like men, in that they rarely listen and don't always have the best bathroom habits."

Eamon's eyes rounded. "Is he going to poop all over the house?"

"No, he's going to poop in his litter box. But I was referring to the fact that some cats are diggers and like to do an abundant amount of covering, which can result in litter getting on the floor. And then there are some cats who don't cover at all, and that gets a little smelly. No clue which one Nemo is."

"I guess I'm soon to find out. You know a lot about cats."

"My aunts have been giving me a crash course." She laughed softly. "Also, me and my aunts are a text away if you need anything or have questions."

Eamon nodded. "Aye, that's the most important bit." He narrowed his eyes. "Do you really think Nemo's going to save my life?"

"I've never known any oracle to be wrong. Whatever's going to happen, Nemo's important to you. I don't think keeping him close is a bad idea."

"No, I suppose not."

"Come on," she said. "Let's go get him."

"Seamus or Nemo?"

"Both of them."

They found them in the living room. Seamus was holding Nemo, who was hanging over the older man's shoulder and rubbing his face on Seamus's head. Seamus was smiling and might have been purring a little bit himself. "Look at the wee mite. He already loves his Uncle Seamus, don't you, lad?"

Tru thought she might die from the cuteness.

Aunt Delly seemed positively in love.

Eamon shook his head, chuckling softly. "He's supposed to be my cat, Uncle Seamus."

"I know, but I live in the house, too. There's no harm in him spending time with both of us now."

"You'll still need to get him a scratching post," Aunt Delly said. "A bed or a cat condo wouldn't hurt, either. But you'll need a sturdy litter box and a scooper. That litter box is a throwaway and only made to last about a week. After that, you'll want to toss it. Trust me. More food, too. Cats his age eat a lot. He's a growing boy, after all."

Seamus was stroking Nemo's back. "Maybe you and I can take a trip to the pet store tomorrow. So I get the right things. Would you mind helping me out with that?"

"Not at all." Aunt Delly nodded. "I'd love to go with you."

And so it begins, Tru thought.

Aunt Cleo came in, a cat carrier in hand. "You can return this after you get one of your own, but you should put him in the carrier. I know you're only going next door but just to be safe. You never know when a noise might startle him or something. The last thing we want is him bolting."

Eamon nodded. "Good idea. Especially since we already know he's a runner. What's the best way to get him in there?"

Aunt Cleo smiled as she pinched the door open. "It's not hard. Are we ready? I'll pop him in there if we are."

"Sure," Eamon said.

She held her hands out toward Seamus.

He reluctantly nodded. "Off you go now, lad. Just for a wee bit, then you'll have the run of the whole place."

Aunt Cleo took hold of the scruff of Nemo's neck, her

other hand under his bottom, and put him right in. She closed the door. He didn't fuss or try to escape, which made Tru happy. She didn't want Eamon to be worried that having a cat was going to be difficult.

Not when Nemo was suddenly so important to Eamon's future. How *that* was going to work she had no idea, but if Cleo had seen it, it had to be true.

"That was easy enough." Eamon crouched down to have a better look at him.

Aunt Cleo nodded. "Make sure you add a carrier to your shopping list. You'll want one for any trips to the vet."

Eamon stood. "How often does he have to go?"

"Once a year for a checkup is fine," Aunt Cleo answered. "After he's finished all of his kitten shots and been neutered. As cute as he is, there are more than enough cats who need homes. We don't need him making more."

"Right." Aunt Delly nodded. "Unless you think he needs to go in for something else. Cats do get sick now and then."

"Right." Concern etched lines around Eamon's mouth.

Tru so badly wanted to put a hand on his arm and console him. "He'll be fine. Cats don't get sick that often."

Eamon picked up the carrier by the handle, holding it as gingerly as if it contained eggs.

Aunt Cleo snorted. "You're not going to break him if he gets jostled."

Tru picked up the plastic shopping bag of food and supplied and put Nemo's info folder in it. "I'll help you carry his stuff over."

"Good," Eamon said. "Then you can make sure we set it all up right."

She suppressed a smile. "Happy to help." She looked at her aunts. "Back in a bit."

"Take your time," Aunt Cleo said. "We're going to watch our shows."

Tru walked with Seamus, who had the litter box and jug of litter. Eamon went ahead of them, still carrying Nemo as if he were precious cargo, which indeed he was.

As they went into the house, Cal greeted them from the kitchen table, where he was on his computer. Eamon had texted him about finding out the name of the reaper in their bloodlines. Probably what he was working on.

Eamon went into the living room, where he looked expectantly at Tru. "What do I do now? Just let him out?"

Cal joined them, just watching.

"Sure," she said. "And while he's exploring, we can set up his litter box."

"Shouldn't we do that first? In case he has to, you *know.*"

She shot him a look that seemed to be saying he needed to calm down. "He's in a new place. He's going to want to explore first. In fact, in a house this big, you might not see him for a few hours. There's a lot to look at and sniff and discover."

Eamon set the carrier down. Nemo meowed softly. "What if he can't find his litter box?"

"We'll show it to him, but trust me, he'll find it. Cats are very smart creatures. Sometimes too smart. You'll see."

Cal nodded. "The Egyptians worshipped them as gods, after all."

Eamon sighed.

Tru laughed. "Having a cat really isn't hard. You're overthinking this."

"Aye," Seamus said. "Let the wee lad out already. He's dying in there."

"He's not dying," Eamon said. But he bent down and opened the carrier.

Nemo came right out, looked around, meowed once, then trotted toward the kitchen.

Cal smiled. "He's a ginger. Handsome thing, too."

Tru nodded. "And he's got a lot of exploring to do. Like I said."

Eamon nodded. "I hope he likes it here. But let's get his food and water set up. And his litter box."

Seamus took the food bag from Tru and went after Nemo. "I'll feed the mite. You two take care of the rest."

Eamon shot Tru a look and shook his head.

She grinned and whispered, "Who knew Seamus was going to turn out to be a crazy cat guy?"

After saying good night to Tru, Eamon spent the rest of the evening watching Nemo. And watching Seamus watch Nemo.

After a good bit of exploring, just as Tru had predicted without even using oracle powers, Nemo had settled down on the back of the sofa, one cushion away from Eamon.

Cal joined them in the living room, and they finally put on the game they'd yet to watch.

Eamon looked over at his cousin. "Any joy on that name?"

Cal shook his head. "Nothing definitive yet. I might not be able to narrow it down to one. Might be two or three names."

"That should be all right. Better than nothing, right?"

"Aye," Cal said.

When the game ended and they all decided to turn in, Eamon was once again unsure what to do about Nemo. They'd put his litter box in the laundry room, which was on the first floor. But Eamon felt like he should take the cat upstairs.

Although maybe he shouldn't.

"Take him," Seamus said.

"What?"

"You look like you don't know what to do with him," Seamus said. "If you want to take him up with you, do it. If he wants to come back down, he will. A cat's going to do what a cat wants."

"When did you get so smart about cats?"

Seamus smiled. "Since I met Delphina. Now take him up with you and let's go to bed. I've got a funeral this afternoon."

"Right." Eamon scooped Nemo into his arms and carried him up the steps. They went straight to Eamon's room, where Eamon deposited the little cat onto the foot of his bed. "Now, you don't have to sleep in here. I just dinna want you to get lonely downstairs. I thought you might wake up and think you'd been abandoned or something."

Nemo stretched, then lay down, turned halfway upside down, and curled into a tight little ball. It looked like he was going right back to sleep.

Eamon watched the rise and fall of the animal's body as he breathed. How was such a small thing going to make a difference to Eamon's life? He couldn't fathom it.

Shaking his head, he went into the adjoining bathroom to get ready for bed. He washed his face, brushed his teeth, and changed into the pair of sleeping shorts he'd left hanging on the towel bar.

When he came back out, Nemo had repositioned himself onto Eamon's pillow.

"I guess I'm sleeping on the other side tonight." He

turned off all but the bedside lamp and got under the covers. He took his tablet from the nightstand and turned it on. He was reading a thriller at the moment, a real page-turner.

Eamon was only a few pages in when Nemo got up, came over to his pillow, and plopped down so that his body nestled into the crook of Eamon's neck and shoulder.

Eamon smiled. He patted Nemo's side. His purring vibrated into Eamon. "That's fine, little one."

Sometime later, Eamon woke. The bedside lamp was still on, his tablet was flat on his chest, and Nemo was gone. Not on the other pillow, not at the foot of the bed. Nowhere Eamon could see.

He squinted at the time. Nearly three in the morning. Should he check on the cat? Make sure he was all right? What if he was stuck somewhere? Or had gotten into something he shouldn't have?

Eamon supposed Tru would tell him he was over-thinking it again. With a sigh, he flipped back the covers and went out to do a little exploring of his own.

Seamus's door was slightly ajar, but Cal's was shut. It was possible Nemo had gone in with Seamus.

As softly as he could, Eamon called out, "Nemo. Are you in there, lad?"

He waited a moment but got no response. If anything, he'd half-expected the cat to come out. But no.

Eamon looked in the two other rooms on the second

floor. There was no point in checking his studio; the door was shut. It was always shut.

He started down the stairs, staying to the side closest to the wall where the wood was less likely to creak. On the ground floor, he looked around. It was easier to see down here, because there was more ambient lighting. Buttons on electronics and appliances, that sort of thing. "Nemo?"

He looked through the living room, then checked in the laundry room. The litter box had been used. A point for Tru, again.

He went toward the front of the house, looking in the dining room, the small den, and the fancy parlor his uncle never used.

No sign of the cat.

Eamon returned to the kitchen. He couldn't tell if Nemo's food had been eaten or not. Same with the water.

Cal's laptop was still on the table. Eamon stared at it. He wondered if it was password-protected. He really wanted to see what progress Cal had made with finding the reaper's name. He'd said so little about it that Eamon couldn't help but be curious.

He went over and swiped a finger across the touch-pad. A box popped up, demanding a four-digit code.

On a whim, Eamon tried twenty-three-zero-four. Cal's birthday. But that wasn't the code. He tried again, this time reversing the numbers in case Cal had used the Americanized way of listing a date. Not that either.

He tried a few more times, switching the day for the

year Cal was born. Still no access. He thought a moment. Cal loved history. Especially Scottish history. Was there a date from the past that would appeal to him?

There was only one Eamon could think of. A date even he knew. He typed the numbers in, one-six-zero-five. The year Guy Fawkes tried to blow up Parliament.

Access granted.

Eamon almost laughed. Of course that was what he used. Icons at the bottom indicated Cal had a browser open and a couple of other documents.

Eamon looked at the documents first. One was the manuscript of the book he was working on. The other was the Underwood family tree.

He opened up the browser next. It was a search page listing results to the query, *What are the powers of an oracle?*

Cal had been pretty interested during lunch. No surprise he'd continued researching the subject. That was up Cal's street. He never could let something go until he felt like he knew everything about it.

Being at the same table with two real live oracles must have stirred an interest that he'd had no choice but to give in to.

Eamon closed the documents and browser so they looked just as they had when he'd opened the computer. He went back upstairs, still clueless as to where Nemo had gotten to, but he'd heard no crying, so he had to assume the cat was all right.

When he got back to his room, Nemo was asleep on

the bed, whiskers twitching ever so slightly. Maybe he was dreaming.

Eamon snorted as he got under the covers, doing his best not to disturb his furry new roommate. Clearly, he had a lot to learn about cats.

Which obviously was another point for Tru.

26

Delphina couldn't help but smile from the front passenger seat in Seamus's car. He was a handsome man with a lovely smile and an accent that made her knees weak. And now they were off on a little adventure together. One might even say it was like a first date. "Thank you for driving."

"Of course," he said. "We're only going to the pet shop because of me. Wouldn't be fair for you to drive, would it? Although I must say, that little red convertible of yours looks like a sweet ride."

"Maybe we could go for a drive in it sometime." She glanced at him. "If you'd like to do something like that."

"I'd love it. And thank you for coming with me this morning."

"Happy to. How did Nemo do last night? Is he settling in?"

"According to what Eamon told me at breakfast, Nemo slept on his bed most of the night." Seamus shook his head. "I don't mind telling you this, but don't share it. I'm a little miffed the lad didn't sneak in to see me. Would have been nice, I think."

Delphina smiled. "You could always adopt another

cat, you know. They do very well in pairs or trios. Often better than they do alone."

"Is that right?" He looked over at her.

"Yes. In fact, sometimes a cat will bond with another cat and will go into mourning if separated."

"Och, we dinna take Nemo from his mate, did we?"

"No, no. We wouldn't have let that happen. He certainly had a few friends in the house, one good one in particular, but no one he was inseparable from."

"So he had a pal then?"

"He did. Cats are pretty adaptable, though."

"Hmm." Seamus's mouth bunched to one side. "Do you think he misses his mate?"

"He might. Two cats aren't much different than having one."

Seamus nodded as he parked by the pet shop. "I'll give it a think."

They got out and went inside. Seamus looked around. "Where do we start?"

Delphina pulled out a list. "I wrote down the things we talked about last night. I hope that was okay?"

"Brilliant. Should I get a trolley?"

She grinned. "If you mean a shopping cart, then probably."

He laughed. "Aye, I do."

Together, they got two litter boxes, since Seamus decided they should have one upstairs and one down; two stainless-steel scoopers, which were the most expensive, but Seamus wanted the best; and a large assortment of dry and canned food.

Then they went to look at cat furniture, something the shop had a large selection of: beds, trees, condos, and scratching posts.

Seamus shook his head. "There's too much to pick from. How do I know what he'll like?"

"As far as scratching posts go, he'll use whatever you get." Delphina shrugged. "Cats just like to scratch. They aren't picky. Keeps their nails in good order, too, although they still might need to be trimmed."

Seamus looked at her with a tiny bit of panic in his eyes. "Trimmed? Who does that? Do we have to take him somewhere?"

She laughed. "No, you can do it yourself. I can show you. We'll buy a trimmer before we leave, all right?"

"If you show me."

"I promise I will." Was that his way of getting her to come over? If so, she was all for it. "Now, which of these kitty trees do you like?"

Seamus pointed. "That one."

"The big one?"

He nodded. "Looks class, don't you think? It's got a couple of platforms, a place to scratch, a little dangly bit, and a hidey house. It's got everything."

"It's not going to be cheap."

"What good is money if you can't spend it?" He laughed. "I know, they say the Scottish are tight with their coins, but I don't mind splashing out for something like this. Besides, you get what you pay for."

"That's very true."

By the time they were done, there wasn't anything cat-related left to buy. Seamus had added a fuzzy cat bed, a handful of toys from the pick-and-mix baskets, two flavors of cat treats, a brush, and a crinkly tunnel.

"My nephew's going to think I've gone mad." He grinned. "But I don't care. And this way we'll be ready if we decide to get Nemo a mate."

Delphina nodded. Seemed to her that decision had already been made, even if Seamus wasn't quite aware of it yet.

He paid and got everything loaded into the car. "Would you like to get some coffee or something? I've got some time before I need to get ready for the funeral this afternoon, and I'm a fan of elevenses myself, but if you have to get home ..."

"No, I'd love that. Pandora isn't coming over until twelve-thirty. We have plenty of time for a little stop."

"Grand." Seamus drove them to the Hallowed Bean, a place Delphina didn't come to often enough in her book.

"I love this coffee shop."

"So do I," he said. He parked. "Let's see what treats they've got in store today, shall we?"

They went inside and stood a few feet away from the counter, looking at the various kinds of drinks on the menu, then checking out the sweets and pastries in the display case. There was quite a selection.

"I know what I want," Seamus said, pointing. "I'm going to have a cup of tea with one of those apple fritters."

"Those do look good." She nodded. "I'll have the same."

"Tea, too?" He looked surprised.

"I like tea. Some Americans do, you know."

He laughed. "Right, right."

They went up to the counter and ordered, stepped off to the side and waited for their tea and pastries, then took them to a little table near one of the windows.

The apple fritters were light and flaky, loaded with chunks of tart apple cooked with cinnamon and sugar and glazed with a milky-white icing that tasted of vanilla. In a word, the fritters were perfect.

"Oh, my," Delphina said. "This is decadent. I'm not sure I could eat lunch after this." Totally a lie. She would absolutely eat lunch. But it seemed like the ladylike thing to say when devouring a pastry nearly the size of your head.

Seamus nodded as he wiped a smudge of glaze from the corner of his mouth. "It's gorgeous." He took a sip of his tea, then got a funny smile on his face. "I went a little overboard at the pet shop, didn't I?"

She shook her head. "You did fine. And so what if you did? What's wrong with spoiling an animal that's going to bring you years of companionship? Why shouldn't they be treated nice?"

He nodded. "I agree. But part of me also wants to do

everything in my power to keep Nemo happy. To make sure that whatever he's supposed to do for Eamon, he's around to do. If he's not happy at our house, he won't want to stay."

"I can understand that, but it sounds to me like he's settling in just fine."

His expression grew more serious. "Is there anything more you can tell me about what that thing is? Or what it is that might be going to happen to Eamon?"

She shook her head. "No, I'm sorry. My sister was the one who saw that part of Eamon's future. If she'd seen something specific, she would have said. Unfortunately, we don't always get the clearest visions of what's to come."

Seamus nodded, but his mouth bent in a frown.

Without thinking, Delphina reached across the table and covered Seamus's hand with her own. "You're worried about him, aren't you?"

"I am. I canna help it. I've worried about that lad all my life. Imagine seeing nothing but death all around you. It's a blessing he can't see his family's hourglasses. I think he would have gone mad by now if that was the case."

"Pandora is coming over to meet with him today. I'm sure she'll be able to do something to help."

"I hope so," Seamus said. "He deserves a chance at a normal life. As much as that's possible for him."

Delphina could only nod and hope Pandora's powers had that much capability.

27

Tru was nervous. Not just about Pandora coming over and meeting such a powerful witch, who also happened to be a neighbor, but also about what Pandora might tell her.

Because the truth was, Tru had come to understand that she desperately wanted to be an oracle. She'd realized it watching her aunts working with Eamon. She'd grown up believing it was her destiny, and the thought of not becoming one left her feeling like there was an emptiness inside her.

She didn't want to go the rest of her life wondering what could have happened if she'd become one. She didn't want her powers to be the death of her, either. But if Pandora could give her some kind of protection against that, Tru would be eternally grateful. Also, if Pandora was able to figure out whether or not Fatima's prediction still stood, that would be nice, too.

Anything she could do to help Eamon would be equally appreciated.

Tru finished running the push-sweeper, which did a surprisingly good job of cleaning the floors and rugs. Apparently, her aunts preferred it to the vacuum, since the cats thought the vacuum was the devil.

Aunt Delly was dusting and wiping down surfaces while Aunt Cleo was straightening things and returning the multitude of cat toys to their various storage bins.

Tru looked around. "I think we're in good shape."

"I hope so," Aunt Delly said. "Pandora's due to arrive in ten minutes. There's no time to repaint." She laughed at her own words, making Tru smile.

Tru took comfort in the fact that Aunt Delly wasn't nervous. Or if she was, she wasn't letting it affect her. Tru tried to be that way, too. "No time to adopt out any of these cats, either. I hope she's not allergic."

"She's not," Aunt Cleo said. "She has a cat of her own."

"Oh, that's right. I remember one of you mentioning that."

Someone knocked on the front door.

Aunt Delly headed for it. "I'll get it."

Which immediately told Tru it was probably Seamus and Eamon, arriving early for the meeting. A moment later, when a smiling Aunt Delly returned with the two men, Tru was proven right.

Seamus was in a dark suit and tie. "I have to leave from here and go straight to the funeral home," he explained.

"You look very nice," Tru said.

Eamon greeted her with a nod but no smile. Maybe he felt like she did. Like something was coming and it might not be good.

While Seamus walked toward the living room with

Aunt Delly, Tru stood with Eamon in the hall outside the dining room and just beyond the foyer. "You seem nervous."

He sighed. "It's the not knowing. Are you not nervous?"

"No, I am. For sure. I just hope that whatever she tells us, there's a solution. It's one thing to get bad news; it's another thing not to be able to do anything about it."

"Aye." He managed a quick smile. "More than anything, I hope you're able to become an oracle."

"You do?"

"Don't you?"

She nodded. "Yes. But I guess I didn't think you'd thought about it."

"If it matters to you, it matters to me."

She smiled, his kind words making her feel good. "Thank you. How's Nemo?"

Eamon snorted. "He scarpered through the house this morning like he had an atomic rocket strapped to his backside. I didn't know a cat could move that fast."

"Zoomies," Tru said with a grin. "You can expect them on a regular basis. And it's a good sign. He wouldn't do them if he didn't feel at home. He's happy."

"That's good to hear."

She tipped her head, knowing he'd been concerned about being able to take care of the animal properly. "How are *you* feeling about him being there?"

One side of Eamon's mouth lifted in a smile. "He slept on the bed with me last night. Part of the time he was actually on me, curled up on my shoulder against my neck. It was ... nice. He's a good lad."

Tru laughed softly. "I'm so glad. Cats really can be great companions."

"I'm starting to understand that. Uncle Seamus actually mentioned getting another one at breakfast. Something about Nemo needing a mate."

That sounded like Aunt Delly's influence if ever Tru had heard it. "Cats are social creatures. A companion can keep them from getting lonely." She shrugged. "Lonely cats can be troublemakers. Not intentionally, mind you. But their need to entertain themselves can lead to behavior that humans don't necessarily appreciate."

"Well, it's Seamus's house. If he wants to adopt another one, I'm not going to stand in his way."

Aunt Cleo came to find them. "Come in and sit down. Pandora should be here any moment."

"Right," Eamon said.

Tru led the way. They settled onto the couch in the living room. Aunt Delly was in her chair, and Seamus was next to her in a kitchen chair that had been brought in. Two other kitchen chairs had been added to the room as well. Aunt Cleo was in the kitchen, arranging a few squares of baklava and some cookies on a plate.

There was already a pitcher of lemonade, glasses, a stack of napkins, and some small plates on the coffee table.

Tru looked over. "Do you need help, Aunt Cleo?"

"No, I'm on my way in. Thank you."

The doorbell rang, sending a few cats running. Aunt Delly got up. "I'll get it."

After a moment, she returned with a pretty redhead and a younger woman with purple streaks in her hair. Aunt Delly introduced them. "Everyone, this is Pandora Van Zant and her stepdaughter, Kaley."

Kaley shrugged. "You can just say daughter. It's okay."

Pandora smiled. "I hope you don't mind that I brought Kaley, but she's becoming very adept in her craft and has the rare skill of being able to read auras. I thought it might be useful, but I was also thinking this might be a real learning experience for her."

Kaley nodded. "I'm still pretty much a fledgling, so if you don't want me to be here, like, I totally get that, too."

Tru glanced at Eamon. "I'm okay with it."

He took a breath. "Help is help. Doesn't bother me who it comes from." Then he got to his feet as he looked at Pandora and Kaley. "I'm Eamon. It's nice to meet you, and you're definitely both welcome."

Seamus was already standing, but Aunt Delly and Tru got up as well. They all shook hands. Aunt Cleo offered lemonade and the snacks she'd put out, then everyone got seated again.

"So," Pandora began, talking to Tru. "I understand you and Eamon both need some help. Why don't we start with you? What's your concern?"

Tru had already organized her thoughts about what she was going to say. "I don't know how much my aunts told you, but any day now, I should be undergoing the ritual to become an oracle, like they are. However, right before coming here, I went to see a fortune teller at the county fair back home."

"Was she an oracle, too?" Pandora asked.

Tru shook her head. "I don't think she was anything more than a fair employee. It's not something I'd normally do, either, but my friend convinced me to do it as a fun thing for my birthday."

"And what happened?"

Tru paused, thinking back to that night. "Long story short, she predicted I was going to meet death in my thirty-third year."

"Which is the age you just turned," Pandora said. "Is that right?"

"Yes." Tru stared at the cookie she'd put on her plate. "And before you think it's silly to put any weight behind the prognostication of a side-show psychic, my mother had a stroke when she was forty-three. Most likely because the enormity of her powers was more than her brain and body could handle. After ten years, they just gave out."

Pandora nodded. "The longer I live in Nocturne Falls, the less likely I've become to think anything related to the supernatural is silly."

Aunt Delly sucked her teeth. "I hear that."

Tru appreciated the reassurance. "Thank you. As you can imagine, my concern lies in whether or not I should go through the ritual to become an oracle. I want to. It's something I've prepared for all of my life. But I also don't want to die."

"Of course you don't. Your concerns are natural and very reasonable," Pandora said.

"Yeah," Kaley nodded. "For real, though."

Pandora smiled. "Why don't we start with Kaley reading your aura? It can be a great diagnostic tool."

"All right," Tru said. "What do you need me to do?"

"Just stand up," Pandora said. She looked at Kaley. "When you're ready."

Kaley gave a little nod. She stared at Tru and seemed to sort of space out. Like she wasn't looking at Tru, so much as looking through her. But with great concentration.

Kaley slowly turned her head one way, then the other. Finally, she blinked and took a deep breath. "I have good news and I have bad news. Which do you want first?"

Tru sat down. Next to her, Eamon had stiffened. She made her decision quickly. "The bad news. I'd rather get it out of the way."

"Cool," Kaley said. Then she swallowed. "Then I have to tell you, your aura definitely holds the signs of death."

28

"What?" Eamon stared at the young woman. Well, in her direction anyway. He had no desire to see the hourglass over her head. But looking directly at her or not didn't change what he was feeling. She had to be wrong. He couldn't accept that Tru was going to die.

Delphina gasped and covered her mouth with one hand while the other clutched Seamus's. "Please tell me that's not true."

"Hold up," Kaley said. "She asked for the bad news first. There's more. There's still the good news."

Pandora nodded at the girl. "Go on, just tell them."

"Okay," Kaley started. "What I saw doesn't look like *impending* death. It's more like death is going to be a part of your life. Which sounds weird even as I'm saying it, but I can only interpret what I see."

Cleo straightened. "Death is a part of every oracle's life. We see it when we read people, regardless of whether we're reading their past or their future."

Delphina stood up. "Read my aura. Tell me if you see the same thing in mine that you saw in Tru's. Then we'll know for sure."

Eamon nodded in her direction. "Brilliant idea."

"Yeah, good one," Kaley said. She went quiet, and Eamon snuck a glimpse of her face. She was looking at Delphina the same way she'd looked at Tru. A few moments later, she returned to full consciousness and nodded. "Yep, your aura totally has the same signs of death in the same places. Must be an oracle thing. Which is cool because I learned something today, so thanks."

Eamon let out a sigh of relief and went back to staring at the table.

Kaley spoke to Delphina with a smile in her voice. "You're also pretty lovestruck."

"W-what?" Delphina stammered as she sat down. "I don't think we should discuss my aura any further."

Eamon lifted his gaze in time to see Pandora nudge Kaley as if to tell her that was enough. Kaley nodded, but a hint of a smile still bent her mouth.

Meanwhile, Uncle Seamus was grinning like he'd just won the lottery. Delphina's cheeks were flushed.

Tru exhaled. "I'm glad to hear what you saw was just a normal oracle thing. Does that mean you didn't see anything else in my aura that I should be concerned about?"

"That's what it means," Kaley said. "You've got a really good aura. You're worried, obviously, but all sorts of positives in there, too. You're full of empathy especially."

"Thank you." Tru leaned back against the couch, visibly relieved. "Pandora, is there anything further you'd suggest I do before going through the oracle ceremony?"

"I can certainly try to scry your future, but Kaley's yet to be wrong about an aura. If you want a definitive answer on the possibility of your death, you'd really need to talk to Lucien Dupree."

"The reaper," Eamon said. "We did talk to him. He was going to look into something for me, but I haven't been able to get the information he wanted yet. But we can discuss that later." He didn't want to take time away from Tru. He nodded at her. "We can certainly bring it up to him."

"Maybe," Tru said. She glanced at Pandora again. "If you were me, would you do the oracle ceremony?"

Pandora nodded. "I would. But again, if you want to be sure, talk to Lucien. I can certainly do a spell of protection for you, but I'm not familiar with the process of becoming an oracle. I'd want to do a little research to be sure I wasn't creating magic that could interfere with the ceremony."

Tru looked at her aunts. "What do you think? Have you ever heard of a witch's magic affecting the oracle ritual?"

They both shook their heads, but Cleo spoke. "It's something we can research as well, if you want to do it."

Tru shrugged. "As long as it wouldn't hurt, then I think I would like whatever extra protection Pandora can provide."

Cleo nodded. "Then we'll research it on our side, if Pandora will do the same on hers."

"Consider it done," Pandora said. Then she turned to Eamon. "Now, what can we help you with?"

He'd known he was going to have to share. He just hadn't really reconciled himself to that fact. It was hard to talk about his ability. It still felt very much like he was revealing a dark secret that was better left hidden. He kept his eyes on the pitcher of lemonade, watching a bead of condensation make its way down the side. "I can see how long people have left to live, and I'd rather not."

"In what way can you see that?" Pandora asked.

"I see an hourglass hovering over people's heads. I can tell how much life they have left based on the level of the sand and how fast it's falling. I also believe that having physical contact with someone might cause their life to run out faster."

"What makes you think that?"

"Past experience with an ex-girlfriend."

Uncle Seamus leaned forward. "Sophie?"

Eamon nodded and looked at him. "I realized a few months into dating her that the sand had begun to sift through the hourglass at a much higher rate than before. So I broke things off with her. Right before I moved here, I checked in on her again. Everything had returned to normal."

"Oh, lad, I'm so sorry." Seamus shook his head. "You've not had an easy go of it, that's for sure."

Eamon wouldn't argue that. He rested his arms on his knees and laced his fingers together before speaking to

Pandora again. "I'd like to be sure I'm not affecting my uncle that way. I can't see the hourglasses of anyone related to me. I can't see Tru's, either. Nor could I see Lucien's when we went to visit him. Or his wife's. My take on that is that they're both essentially immortals."

Pandora gestured to Tru. "And in Tru's case?"

He shook his head. "No idea why I can't see hers."

"Very interesting," Pandora said. "Can you see the hourglasses over Tru's aunts?"

He nodded.

"And over me and Kaley?"

"Aye." He hoped she didn't ask how much life those hourglasses had in them. He'd been trying his best not to see them.

"Hmm," Pandora said. Without looking at her more closely, he couldn't tell if his revelation had made her uncomfortable. "Just curious, but is this gift why you work in your chosen profession?"

"In part," he answered. "My family has long been in the funeral services business, so it just made sense. But being a mortician is definitely one of the few jobs I can do without having to stare down someone's mortality all day."

Then he realized how wrong that was and snorted. "Actually, that's not true at all. I work with the dead. I am absolutely faced with mortality. But there's a big difference in someone who's already passed and someone who's still very much alive."

"I understand." Pandora folded her hands in her lap. "Can you tell me a little more about what Lucien's helping you with?"

Eamon nodded. "My cousin, Callum, is researching the name of the reaper in our family history. If he can find that, I'm going to pass it on to Lucien, who will then see if that reaper had powers specific to my ability."

"In order to find a way to release you from that ability, I imagine."

"Aye," Eamon said. "I should also tell you that our family history is a real mashup of supernatural creatures and abilities. Always has been. Because of that, the men in the family tend to have a whole host of random gifts. Although some have none at all."

"And the women?"

He shook his head. "They don't seem to inherit anything. Not sure why, but that's how it goes."

"All right," Pandora said. "That's all useful information. Would you mind if Kaley reads your aura?"

"I'd be grateful for any help. It's why I'm here." He stood as Tru and Delphina had done but kept his gaze down. He didn't need to see Kaley for her to do her job.

Then he heard a soft, "Wow." It was enough to make him look at Kaley's face.

Her brow was puckered, and she was shaking her head, eyes narrowed as if she couldn't believe what she was seeing.

"What?" he asked, unable to contain himself.

"I-I don't know what to make of it."

"What?" Pandora asked.

"Just tell us what you see," Tru said.

"That's just it," Kaley answered. She looked at Pandora, the strangest expression on her face. "I don't see anything."

29

Tru needed more information than what Kaley had given them as Eamon sat down beside her. "Nothing?"

"No," Kaley said. "It's like he's—" She looked at Eamon and went silent.

"He's what?" Tru pushed.

"Like he's fighting himself. That's not a good explanation." Kaley frowned as she stared at Eamon, who was concentrating on the table. "It's like there's an aura there, but for some reason, it's being hidden. Or being suppressed. It's super weird. And even though I couldn't see anything, it also felt ... angry. Or maybe anxious is more accurate."

She shook her head again and glanced at Pandora. "That's no help at all, is it?" She sighed. "I'm sorry. This has never happened before. I told you I was still a fledgling."

Eamon's frustrated sigh punctuated his next words. "You tried. It's not your fault that I am so deeply troubled."

"You're not troubled," Tru said. "You're gifted. Do I need to remind you again that you saved two lives? We'll figure this out." She looked at Pandora. "Won't we?"

Pandora nodded. "We will. Kaley being unable to see

your aura still gives us some information. Maybe not as much as if she did, but it's still valuable."

Eamon snorted. "Oh, really? What does it mean, then?"

Pandora frowned. "I don't know yet. But I'll find out. There are witches far wiser than me in this town, and I'll make this my top priority."

Eamon shook his head again. "I am destined to this life. To this curse." His face was a mask of pain and despair. "Forgive me," he choked out. "But I need to go."

He got up and stalked off, clearly hurting.

For a moment, no one said a thing. But as they heard the sound of the front door closing, Tru jumped to her feet. "I'll talk to him. Please, Pandora, anything you can do to help."

She nodded. "I'm going to call my mom right now and see about convening a special meeting of the coven."

"Thank you."

Pandora put her finger up. "I was about to ask him for a few drops of his blood. I already know we're going to need it to do a deeper diagnosis."

"I'll talk to him." Tru ran out after Eamon. He was just walking through the door of his house. She followed. "Eamon. *Eamon.*"

He'd left the door open, so she went in after him and closed it. She found him sitting on the stairs, head in his hands.

She sat beside him and put her arm around his shoulders.

"You shouldna be touching me."

She smiled. His accent definitely got thicker when he was upset. "I'm a grown woman. Who's about to become an oracle. I do what I want."

He sighed but still didn't look at her. "I dinna realize you had such a stubborn streak in you."

"Well, now you do. Does it change how you feel about me?"

"I have no right to feel anything about you. You should stay far away from me."

She lifted one shoulder. "Yeah, I'm not going to do that. I like you too much."

"Then you're mad."

"I think I like daft better. Sounds more lighthearted."

He snorted in amusement, even though it didn't seem like he wanted to, finally turning his head to see her. "Why are you helping me?"

"Because it's the right thing to do. Because we're friends. And as I mentioned earlier, I like you." Enough that her heart beat faster when she was around him.

"I like you, too, but continuing to be friends seems like a form of torture. I'm not a good person to be around."

"You're a fantastic person to be around."

He narrowed his eyes. "How can you think that? I could actually be the death the fortune teller predicted for you."

"You're not. I already know that." She didn't, really, but she refused to believe that Eamon could do her harm, knowingly or unknowingly. She had no basis for that belief, other than it was what she chose to put her faith in. This man was not her end. In fact, he felt much more like her beginning.

A singsong of little meows came bounding toward them as Nemo came down the steps, his bouncing causing his cries to vibrate with his movement. He stopped right behind Eamon and climbed up onto his shoulders, rubbing his face against Eamon's head.

"See?" Tru said. "Nemo agrees with me."

"You're both daft." His mood was definitely lighter as he reached up and grabbed the little cat, bringing him onto his lap. "What am I going to do? I dinna think I can live the rest of my life this way."

"You're not going to, because we're not giving up. Are we?" Tru scratched Nemo's head.

"Are you asking me or the moggy?"

She laughed. "You. Are you giving up? Doesn't seem very Scottish. I thought you people were fighters. You know, *Braveheart* and all that." A sudden image of Eamon in a kilt took her mind in a whole new direction.

His eyes narrowed. "I am not giving up."

"Good. Pandora needs a sample of your blood to do some more investigating."

"Blood, eh?"

She nodded. "You up for that?"

"Aye." He looked into her eyes. "If I thought it was safe to kiss you, I would. Right now. I am a lucky man to have a friend like you."

She breathed through the impulse to kiss him anyway. She didn't want to upset him just to satisfy her own personal desires. But kissing him would have been very nice. "I like being your friend. I'm really glad we met."

Nemo swatted at a loose strand of her hair, making them both laugh.

"Is Pandora still at your aunts'?" Eamon asked.

"Yes."

"Then let's go back over there and get this done. I feel like a right eejit."

"Don't. No one else thinks that. What you live with every day is unimaginable to the rest of us."

They both stood. Eamon gave Nemo a quick cuddle, then put him on the steps. "I'll be back, lad."

Then he nodded at Tru. "All right. Let's go see about this sample."

Together, they walked back over. Again, she found herself itching to touch him. To hold his hand, mostly.

Not being able to do that made her want to more than ever.

They went in and found everyone in the kitchen. Conversation stopped.

Eamon cleared his throat softly. "I'm sorry for running out."

Seamus nodded. "It's all right, lad. You came back is what matters."

Eamon turned himself in Pandora's direction. "I understand you need some of my blood."

"I do," she said. "Having your blood will enable me to cast some very specific spells in the hopes of gaining more detailed information about what's going on with you."

"Then let's do it."

"Great." She procured a rolled leather kit from her purse and set it on the counter, where she unwrapped it to lay flat. The kit contained several small, corked vials, some alcohol wipes, and lancets.

Tru wanted to support Eamon in any way she could, even though the sight of blood made her a little queasy. "Maybe you should test mine, too. Just to be sure about the death thing. If you can do that."

"Absolutely," Pandora said. She took out a wrapped lancet and stripped off the cellophane. "Who wants to go first?"

"I will," Tru said, already wincing. "Just do it fast, okay?"

30

Tru's reaction to having her finger jabbed and blood taken amused Eamon to no end. It touched him, too, because it was plain she didn't want to do it by the way she squinched up her face and refused to watch.

When it was all over, she pressed her finger and thumb together and looked absolutely wounded.

He would have given anything to kiss her finger and make it better. She was the genuine article, that one. Her name suited her well, because she *was* true. Pure of spirit, inside and out. He wasn't sure he'd ever known anyone quite like her before.

Of course, he didn't know that many people on purpose. But she still seemed like a rare bird.

He decided right then and there that if Pandora could suss out a way to keep him from hurting Tru's lifeline in any way, he'd not only take it, but he'd stop caring about seeing hourglasses over everyone's heads. At least he'd try.

Because being able to be with Tru, to touch her, and hold her hand, and kiss her, that would be enough. Having her in his life could probably make any burden bearable. Even seeing how long those around him had left to live.

He held out his hand to Pandora. She pricked his finger, then squeezed it over one of the vials until she'd collected a fair amount.

"All done." She offered him a bandage.

He shook his head, refusing it. "I'm good. Now what do we do?"

"Now you wait while I go home and cast some spells. I have to show a house at three—I'm a Realtor by trade—but I'll have answers for you as soon as I'm physically able. In the meantime, if you can pursue the reaper information with Lucien, then go for it. Any additional information we can gather can only help us."

He nodded. "I'll mention it to Callum when I get back. I can't do much without a name." He hesitated, then glanced at her hourglass before making eye contact with her. "Thank you for this. You have a very long life ahead of you."

She smiled. "That's good to hear. I'll be in touch as soon as I know something. Your uncle gave me your number while you were gone."

"Good." He'd spend the rest of his afternoon and evening working on his podcast. Might as well get as much done as possible.

They said their goodbyes, then he headed for the door himself. "I'll see you back at the house, then, Uncle?"

Seamus, who was deep in conversation with Delphina, nodded absently. Abruptly, he straightened. "Wait, no. I have to leave for the funeral."

"See you after that, then," Eamon said.

Tru fell into step beside Eamon. "Are you interested in taking another walk tonight?"

He wanted to. But the thought of being that close to her without being able to touch her seemed like a self-imposed form of torture. "I don't think we should."

Her smile disappeared as they stopped by the door.

He scrambled to explain himself. "It's not that I don't want to, but things feel so up in the air right now. Once we know something, then ..." He lowered his voice. "I canna be responsible for anything happening to you, Tru. It would end me."

She sighed but nodded all the same. "Okay. I get it. And you're right. Until we know what's going on with both of us, maybe we should just keep our distance."

She seemed hurt, and he didn't know how to fix it. "I'm sorry. I know you don't like it. I don't, either. But again, I won't be the reason you come to harm."

She stared at him a second, looking very much like she wanted to say something else, but then just shook her head as if she wanted to disagree with him but couldn't. "I know."

He clenched his hands to keep from taking her face in them and kissing her senseless. "We'll have our answers soon. Pandora said so. Then we'll know if you're truly safe around me."

She looked back toward the kitchen. "You're right. But waiting is hard."

"Still a load of bollocks, though, eh?"

She smiled but her eyes narrowed, making her seem miffed that he'd amused her when she was trying to be mad. "Yes. That."

"Eamon, what do you think of Yardstick?" Seamus walked toward them with the black and white cat in his arms, apparently unconcerned about any hair getting on his suit. "Delphina told me he and Nemo were good mates. And the poor wee thing only has three legs. He ought to have a home of his own, don't you think? Somewhere he doesn't have to fight for his food."

Eamon cut his eyes at Tru. "Is there any chance your aunts would let a cat go hungry?"

"None." Her smile improved. "But being one of two cats would probably be easier for him than being one of fourteen."

"That's exactly right," Seamus said.

Eamon held Tru's gaze. "You're not helping."

"Good," Tru said, crossing her arms and looking remarkably unrepentant.

"I think we should give him a try," Seamus said. "Yardy might blossom in a quieter house."

Eamon sighed good-naturedly. "I've never heard you use the word 'blossom' in all your life, Uncle Seamus. Might that have been Delphina's suggestion?"

"And what if it was?" Seamus stroked the cat's head, making the beastie close his eyes and lean into the caresses. "It's my house, init?"

Eamon smiled. "It is. And if you want to bring Yardy over, then you should."

Seamus looked surprise. "You mean that, don't you?"

"I do," Eamon said. "Who am I to stand in the way of anyone's personal happiness?"

Seamus grinned. "Be a good lad and run home and fetch the new carrier, would you? It's in the laundry room on the shelf. Then I best get going."

Eamon nodded. "I will." He looked at Tru. "Be right back."

"I'll see you later. I have a few things I need to do."

"All right." He watched her go. She patted Seamus on the arm, gave Yardy a scratch on the head, and wished him a good life in his new home. Then she disappeared back into the house.

Was she upset with him? Or upset at their circumstances? Or both?

Either way, he couldn't do much about it. He went straight out and to his uncle's house, got the carrier and came back, feeling worse about what had happened the more he thought about it. What was he supposed to do? Just accept that he might be shortening her life?

That was ludicrous. He brought the carrier into the oracles' house and set it on the floor in the living room, where Seamus was sitting on the couch with Yardy on his lap. Delphina was next to him.

She glanced at Eamon, but he kept his gaze down. "She went upstairs. Do you want me to call her?"

"No, it's all right. She's not too happy with me right now, I don't think."

"She'll get over it," Delphina said.

"I hope so." Eamon opened the carrier door so his uncle could put Yardy in when he was ready. "Uncle Seamus, if you don't need me, I going to be in my studio the rest of the day."

"You go on then, lad. I'll be over with our new moggy, *then* I'll be getting to work."

Eamon just nodded and went back home. He wasn't exactly in the mood to record, but it needed to be done. And it was the only thing he could think of that might actually keep his mind off of Tru.

He found Cal, who was packing up his laptop, at the kitchen table. "Going somewhere?"

Cal nodded. "Off to the town's library for a bit. Need to do a little research that the internet just can't help me with. How did it go with the witch today?"

Eamon stuck his hands in his pockets. "She needs to dig deeper to find out what's going on with me. No real answers yet." He didn't feel like having a whole conversation about not having an aura. He had no idea what it meant himself.

"Hopefully soon," Cal said. "Don't lose faith."

"Listen, how soon do you think you might have the name of our reaper ancestor?"

"I'm close," Cal answered. "Maybe by the time I get home."

"That would be good." He frowned. "How are you going to get there?"

"Already called a Ryde. It should be here in three minutes."

"I hope you find what you need."

Cal nodded. "So do I."

Cal left, and Eamon went upstairs. He glanced into his bedroom. Nemo was asleep on the bed. Eamon left him be. He couldn't take the cat into the studio with him because of the noise, and he didn't want to have to shut him out. Better to let him sleep.

Once in the studio, he got to work. It kept his mind off of Tru. A little. Halfway through the episode-in-progress, he just didn't want to keep recording. He forced himself, calling upon every ounce of professionalism in his body, and finished the episode.

He'd been recording for two hours. That was plenty of time. He deserved a break. Maybe a cup of tea and some biscuits. He shut everything off and went downstairs. The television was on in the living room, but Uncle Seamus had to be at the funeral home, making Eamon think his uncle had put the telly on for the cats. Yardy was curled up in Seamus's chair, asleep. Nemo was in the new cat tree, positioned by the windows so it would get some sun, also asleep.

Eamon skipped the tea and biscuits. The noise of him puttering in the kitchen would only wake them up.

Instead, he went through to the screened porch, then left it behind to sit on the steps, where the late afternoon sun was still making contact.

He sat in the warm rays, the screened door behind him, and just let it bake him. He could see why cats liked this so much. The heat was sort of mesmerizing. It put him in a state of motionless pleasure. If only the sun could bake his troubles away.

A nearly soundless meow turned his head.

Nemo was at the door, squinting into the sun. He opened his mouth again, releasing another tiny, needy chirp.

"You want to come out here, lad?" Eamon got up and opened the door enough for Nemo to slip through.

The gap in the fence was plugged. If the cat wanted to run around in the yard, Eamon didn't see any harm in it. Not while he was keeping an eye out.

Nemo rubbed against Eamon's leg, then trotted down to the grass, where he flopped over and rolled like a dog.

Eamon grinned. It was so easy to forget his cares around this goofy bit of orange floof. Kind of like being around Tru. He sighed and leaned his elbows back on the step behind him. If Pandora and Lucien couldn't help him, what was he going to do?

He used to think he'd be fine living the rest of his life in semi-solitude, keeping himself to himself. But that was no longer possible.

Not after meeting Tru.

31

Tru had finished the book she'd brought within minutes of going upstairs. That was all the excuse she needed to borrow Aunt Cleo's Jeep and head into town. To the library, to be exact. She had fond memories of the place from when she'd visited years ago, but she still used the navigation app on her phone to find her way there.

And if she couldn't hang out with Eamon while they waited on Pandora's findings, books were the best way to escape and kill time.

She parked and went in, already knowing she was going to have to renew her library card. She went to the front desk first and took care of that, then began to wander, which was easy to do at the library. She really didn't know what kind of book she wanted, other than one that would distract her.

Because that was exactly what she needed. To be distracted from the fact that she wanted to be with Eamon and couldn't be. She understood why, of course. And he was right. Until they knew whether he could be prematurely shortening her life, it was best they keep some distance.

But knowing that and being okay with it were two different things.

It was her own fault for liking him more than she should. If he turned out to be as bad for her as he seemed to think he was, she was going to be the most miserable person on the face of the planet.

She shouldn't have let herself get so crazy about him. She knew that. But blaming herself didn't make her like him any less.

She did a slow walk through the history section, reading titles as she went. She thought something historical might really transport her, but nothing jumped out at her, so she kept going, working her way through half the library without pulling a single book.

Not the most productive trip to the library, that was for sure. For a break, she went over to the reading area, found a magazine, and sat in one of the big comfy chairs. Her hope was that she might be able to lose herself in an article. She found one about what a visit to a fitness camp was really like.

Might be interesting. Although not if it was written by a woman with no pounds to lose. But Tru read on, eager to focus on something other than thoughts about the man she couldn't be with.

As she neared the end of the article, which was far more interesting than she'd imagined it would be, a familiar voice pulled her concentration away. It seemed to be coming from one aisle over, meaning she couldn't see the person, only hear them.

There was no mistaking that accent, but she wanted to see for herself.

She shifted one seat closer, since it was empty, and found a gap between some books on a higher shelf. She stood up like she was adjusting her position and got a better glimpse. Eamon's cousin, Callum, was talking quietly to a librarian in the midst of the craft and DIY section.

She sat back down, a little frisson of panic running through her. Like she didn't want him to see her. It was a public library that she had every right to be in, so why she felt that way, she had no idea.

She held the magazine in place to hide behind and listened closely.

"I know you have them," he said. "You must in a town like this."

"I'm sorry, sir," the librarian said. "We have some books on learning magic tricks, but that's all."

Callum sighed in obvious frustration. "What do you need me to do? Swear an oath that I'm a supernatural, too?"

"I really don't know what you're talking about."

Neither did Tru. What was Callum after?

"Do I need to get someone to vouch for me? Is that it?"

"Anyone can get a library card."

Another frustrated sigh from Callum. "Vampires built this town, but you want to pretend like there's not a private room filled with grimoires, spell books, and old magical texts? Secret histories? Inherited diaries of curious creatures? Are you telling me that in this town, you don't have a reserved section for all things ancient and arcane? Really?"

Tru's eyes widened. Was that what Callum wanted? She knew he was trying to find the name of Eamon's reaper ancestor. Did that have something to do with him wanting access to the books he'd mentioned? She had no idea, but she wanted Eamon to get that name, too. Anything that might help.

The librarian let out a little snort that might have been a stifled laugh. "Maybe I should get the head librarian."

"If that's what it takes to get access, then by all means. I'm a published author. A well-known researcher. I'm not sure what else I can tell you to make you understand I'm qualified to see those books."

Tru glanced over. Through the gap between the bottom of one shelf and the books on the shelf below it, she could see a slice of their torsos.

The librarian shifted, moving from one foot to the other like she wanted to leave, but Callum didn't budge. She finally said, "We do have a rare books room."

Callum laughed like he'd been right all along. "Whatever you want to call it is fine with me. How do I get in there?"

"Access to the rare books room is by appointment only."

"Then let's go make me an appointment. The soonest

available. In fact, if you can let me in right away, I promise not to bother you again."

"I can't guarantee anything until I look at the appointments."

Tru lifted the magazine a little higher. Now she was curious about what was in that rare books room herself. Using her peripheral vision, she watched Callum go up to the front desk with the librarian.

After a brief exchange, Callum was issued a pair of white cotton gloves and led toward the back of the library. He was quickly out of sight.

Tru put the magazine back on the rack where she'd gotten it, then slipped into the stacks to see where the rare books room might be.

She found it at the back of the library. A glass door and a large window separated the small room from the rest of the library. She stood between the shelves of Arts and Recreation, pretending to be interested in a book on hiking the Appalachian Trail. It gave her the perfect vantage point to see what Callum was doing.

He was browsing the shelves in the rare books room, his back to her. For no real reason that she could think of, she took her phone out and snapped a picture of him. He stopped in front of a particular book, tilting his head to read the spine better.

He sort of nodded, then pulled the book out and took it to a table in the center of the room. It was a large volume with a dark leather binding and gold lettering too worn to read from Tru's vantage point. He opened it to the very beginning, running his gloved finger down a table of contents.

He flipped through to about the middle and leaned in to read.

She was too far away to make out anything on the pages.

He glanced toward the door, making her snap back behind the shelf. She waited a second before looking again. He was taking pictures of the pages with his phone. Then he closed the book and put it back on the shelf.

She studied the spot where it went, memorizing it.

He left the rare books room, closing the door securely behind him. She scooted around the shelf to see what he did next, but he just returned the gloves to the woman at the front desk and left.

She went to the front desk and put on her friendliest smile as the librarian on duty came over. "Hi, there. Would it be possible for me to have five minutes in the rare books room? I don't have an appointment, but I swear I won't be in there long."

"You do normally need an appointment."

Tru dug out her library card. "I know, and I should have made one. I just didn't realize I'd need to have a look at something in there. Just five minutes. Maybe not even that long. I'll be quick, promise."

The librarian sighed. "Just a moment." She pulled out a clipboard with a pen attached and passed it over to Tru. "Sign in."

Tru scrawled her signature on the first free line, but her attention was on the name above hers. C. Underwood, but the C was written with such a loopy, flowing style it could have been an E. Had Callum done that on purpose? Or was his handwriting really that flowery?

The librarian took the clipboard back and handed Tru a pair of cotton gloves. "No food, drink, or photography is allowed in the rare book room. The door must be kept shut, as it's a climate-controlled space. The gloves must be worn at all times."

"Heard and understood." Although Callum obviously hadn't obeyed the no photography rule. Tru put the gloves on and followed the woman, who unlocked the door and stepped out of the way. "Thanks." Tru gave her another smile, but the woman was already on her way back to the front desk.

Tru went straight to the book Callum had been looking at and pulled it out. She carried it to the table, then had a closer look at the cover. She couldn't really make out the title. It was just too old and worn and not written all that legibly.

She opened it to the first page and found the book's title on the thin, yellowed paper. *The Lesser Arts of Theurgy*.

She had no idea what this book was doing in the Nocturne Falls public library, but then again, this was a town filled with supernaturals. Maybe one of them had donated it?

She did, however, know exactly what theurgy was.

How could she not? It was the ancient Greek magic that used rituals to harness the magic of nature and time, sometimes used to commune with the Olympian gods. The oracle ceremony was a form of theurgy.

A little shiver went down her spine.

Why on Earth would Callum be researching that?

Eamon felt twitchy. There was no other word for it. Waiting on news from Pandora had set him on edge. His nerves, at least. He'd played with Nemo and Yardy, who were getting on brilliantly. He'd done a load of laundry. Including putting it away straight out of the dryer, which felt like a major accomplishment. Written and revised the script for his next episode. Watched a cooking show with his uncle, who'd returned from doing the funeral service.

And thought about Tru. A lot.

He would have much preferred to go next door and talk to her, but he couldn't do that. Not until Pandora gave them some answers.

Which made him feel twitchy.

It was a vicious cycle.

Seamus had just gotten up to fix a cup of tea, leaving Eamon in the living room by himself. He didn't want anyone to die, but having work to do at the funeral home would at least give him something to do.

The front door opened. He twisted around to see Callum coming in. Eamon got up. "Did you get the name?"

Cal's cheery expression faltered. "No, mate. Sorry. It's

proving tricker than I expected. Any word from the witch yet?"

"No, nothing there, either."

Cal nodded. "Soon, I'm sure."

"I'm sure," Eamon repeated, hoping that was the case.

"Say, about your friend Tru. Is she going to go through with the oracle ceremony?"

"I'm not sure." Eamon frowned. "Why?"

Cal smiled and shrugged. "It would be a marvelous thing to watch. A ritual that's been around that long? All that ancient magic? Aren't you the least bit curious? Or maybe it's just the writer in me, imagining what an amazing thing that would be to see firsthand and then put down on paper."

"It hadn't occurred to me."

Cal, still smiling, nodded. "Just me, then. No worries. Do you think they'd mind if I watched?"

"I have no idea." Although the more Eamon thought about it, the more he imagined they would. Tru's aunts probably wanted their oracle secrets to remain just that: secrets.

Seamus came out from the kitchen. "Cal, you want tea? I've just put the kettle on."

"I'm all right, thank you, though. I'm off to my room for a bit. Going to dig into this reaper thing again, see if I can't find a stone I've yet to overturn." Cal headed up the steps.

Eamon turned to look at his uncle. "I'll have a cuppa."

"In that case," Seamus said, "I'll get some biscuits out.

Although I wish we had some of that cake from Delaney's."

"So do I." There was a bakery and sweet shop in town that sold the most delicious cakes, biscuits, and chocolates, Delaney's Delectables. Sometimes, Seamus stopped by and picked a few things up to bring home. "You should have stopped on your way back."

"Aye, I should have. I was too excited to see how Yardy was getting on."

"Next time." Eamon followed Seamus back into the kitchen. "I don't think Cal is trying very hard to find that name for me."

Seamus frowned. "What makes you think that?"

"I don't know. Nothing I can really put my finger on. But he's been weirdly preoccupied with Tru and her aunts. Or at least preoccupied with oracles."

"It is a curious business," Seamus said. "Have you ever run across one before?"

"No."

"And I'm sure Cal hasn't, either." Seamus got the biscuit tin down from the cabinet. "Considering he's a writer and researcher who specializes in history, I'd be more surprised if he wasn't interested in them."

"Maybe. But something feels off to me."

"Could it be that you're just anxious about what Pandora might have to tell you?"

"I won't deny that, but this is something else." He glanced toward the upstairs. "It's a feeling I can't shake."

Seamus pulled the lid off the tin and put a couple of

biscuits on one of the small plates he'd taken out of the cabinet for that purpose. The kettle started to steam. "Yardy seems to be doing all right, don't you think?"

Eamon nodded, fully aware his uncle had changed the subject. He took a few biscuits for himself and let the matter lie. Maybe it was just his mind trying to occupy itself with something besides the impending news from Pandora.

They fixed their tea and went back out to the living room. Yardy and Nemo were both dozing in the cat condo now.

"That's the life," Seamus said as he set his mug and plate on a side table and settled back into his recliner.

Eamon nodded. His mug and plate went on the coffee table. He snagged one of the chocolate-dipped shortbreads he'd taken and sat down. "And just think, they have nine lives to do it with."

"Lucky beggers."

Eamon was about to take a bite of the biscuit when his phone vibrated. He nearly tossed the biscuit back on the saucer in his effort to get to it in time. But it wasn't a call or a text from Pandora. It was a text from Tru.

Are you free to talk or are you with family?

He typed back, *Just Seamus but I can go outside.*

Ok. Calling in 30 seconds.

Eamon got up. "Be right back." As Seamus gave him a nod, Eamon went out through the back porch and into the yard. His phone rang. He answered. "What's up?"

"Probably nothing, but in case it's not, I thought I should tell you. I hope you don't think I'm crazy."

"I don't know what it is, so ..."

"Well, I was just at the library looking for some new books to read, and I saw Callum there."

Eamon nodded. "He's trying to figure out the name of our reaper ancestors. Although what he'd need the public library for, I don't know."

"He was in the rare books room. Wait, let me back up. He was talking to one of the librarians about getting access to the room where they keep all the old magic books. He even told her he was a supernatural."

"Was she one, too?" He walked toward the middle of the backyard. It was generally considered taboo to out yourself to someone who was strictly human.

"Not that I can tell. She was sort of acting like he wasn't making a lot of sense. Anyway, he ended up in the rare books room. When he left, I went in after him to see what he'd been looking at. It was an old book on theurgy."

Eamon shook his head. "I have no idea what that is."

"Boiled down, it's the ancient Greek practice of using rituals to access the magic in nature. The oracle ceremony is theurgy."

Eamon turned around and stared at the second floor of the house. "Why would he be looking at that?"

"That's what I want to know. Doesn't make a lot of sense to me. But it felt like something I should mention."

Eamon frowned in the direction of Cal's room. "He

was asking me questions when he got home. Things like whether or not you'd gone through the oracle ceremony yet and, if not, did I think he'd be able to watch."

"Yeah, that's a big no. The oracle ceremony is a very private thing. Strictly for oracles only."

"I figured it was something like that." Eamon didn't really want to admit he'd been snooping, but this seemed like a special circumstance. Plus, he didn't think Tru would judge him. "The other night, I got up to check on Nemo—"

"Aw, that's so sweet."

Eamon smiled and rolled his eyes. "He was fine, by the way."

"Good," Tru said. "Go on. You were up to check on Nemo ..."

"And Cal's laptop was on the kitchen table. I took a look at what he'd been working on. Nothing to do with our reaper ancestors, although he did have the Underwood family tree open. But he also had a search page open on his browser. He'd been looking for information about what powers oracles possessed."

Tru sucked air in through her teeth. "Why is he so interested in us? In oracles? Just because he met us? This feels weird."

It did to Eamon, too, but he was loath to admit it. "I said something to Seamus. He thinks it's just Cal's natural curiosity as a writer and researcher who loves history, and that meeting you and your aunts has sparked an interest in him."

"Do you think that's all it is?"

Nemo was at the screen door, crying to come out. Yardy was sitting behind him, watching to see if Eamon was actually going to open the door. "I don't know. I really don't. It feels like more to me, but then I'm a bit tetchy from waiting on Pandora."

"You're what?" Tru asked.

He translated it into American English. "Cranky, bothered, easily upset."

"Ah, right. Titchy."

"Tetchy." Eamon smiled. "Listen, until we know what Pandora has to say, keep your distance from Cal. Keep your aunts away from him, too. Not saying anything's going to happen, but a little caution never hurt anyone."

"Eamon, you're scaring me a little. Do you think he might do something?"

"No, nothing to hurt you. Cal's not like that." At least he'd never been like that so far. "He'll probably just continue to pester you with questions, but maybe if you ignore him, he'll work on finding that name for me instead. Oh, and another thing—as soon as Pandora gives you the all clear, I think you should get the oracle ceremony done. The sooner the better, really."

"I've been thinking that, too. I'll let you know, all right? And you keep an eye on Cal."

Eamon's gaze returned to the second floor of the house. "I will."

33

Tru hung up, took a breath, then organized her thoughts. She really needed to talk to her aunts before she did anything else. She went down one flight, but there was no one on the second floor. No one who wasn't feline.

She heard soft singing in the kitchen and found Aunt Cleo at the kitchen table, looking at her tablet.

She glanced up when Tru came in. "Did you find any books at the library?"

"Not really. Nothing looked good." She didn't want to tell her or Aunt Delly about Callum and what he'd been up to. Not yet, anyway. Tru was really hoping it was nothing, which it probably was.

Aunt Cleo nodded. "I have days like that, too. I just finished a book, a mystery. It kept me guessing. You want to give that a try?"

"Sure." Tru came closer. "How much prep time do you and Aunt Delly need to do the oracle ceremony?"

Aunt Cleo shook her head. "We've been ready. We were ready when you arrived."

"Right. That makes sense."

"Does that mean you're ready to go through with it?"

Tru nodded. "So long as Pandora says she hasn't

found any reason I shouldn't, then yes. I'd like to do it as soon as possible."

Aunt Cleo smiled. "That's great."

"What's great?" Aunt Delly joined them, a basket of laundry on her hip.

"Two things," Aunt Cleo said. "One is that we just got an email about doing some predictions for a company in Tokyo. They'd like to fly us out next month."

"Fantastic," Aunt Delly said. "I've always wanted to see that city. What's the other thing?"

Aunt Cleo looked at Tru. "Troula's ready to join us. Provided she doesn't get a reason not to from Pandora."

Aunt Delly gasped. "That's wonderful! We could do it tonight."

Tru hadn't been expecting it to happen quite that fast. "Tonight?"

Aunt Delly glanced at her sister. "Don't you think?"

"Sure," Aunt Cleo said.

"Okay. So then we just need to know what Pandora has found out and we're good to go." And then she'd be an oracle, really and truly. Tru felt great peace about that, which made her believe her decision was the right one.

Aunt Delly clapped her hands, clearly excited. "Maybe the business in Tokyo would like all three of us?"

"Maybe," Aunt Cleo said.

Tru thought that sounded like an amazing trip until she realized something. "Um, who takes care of the cats when you guys go away?"

"We have a pair of pet sitters that come," Aunt Cleo

said. "We've used them several times. They're very reliable."

"That's good. I suppose it'll be easier now that you're down to thirteen."

"About that," Aunt Delly started. "The shelter is looking for someone to foster a pregnant girl. I told them we could probably take her."

Aunt Cleo nodded. "Absolutely. We've got room now. When do we need to get her?"

"We can pick her up anytime. The sooner the better, because they think she's not more than a week out. Could be any day, really."

Aunt Cleo stayed at her computer. "Then let's get the nursery set up for her and bring her home. I'll head up and see what needs to be done just as soon as I answer this email."

"Perfect," Aunt Delly said. "That's why I was washing blankets and bedding. To make a nesting spot for her. I knew you wouldn't say no."

Aunt Cleo smiled as she typed. "I do love kittens."

Tru snorted. "You love cats of any age."

"I won't argue that. But the babies." She let out a happy sigh. "They're just their own kind of magic."

"Then let's go get everything ready and we'll go pick her up."

Aunt Cleo tapped a button on the keyboard and then got to her feet. "Sent. Let's go."

Aunt Cleo and Aunt Delly headed off to do whatever they had to do to prepare for the expectant mother. Tru went out to the screened porch. She was a little nervous about becoming an oracle but happy about it, too. Especially being able to do it without concern for her personal health and safety.

She thought about her mom and wondered if her mother had realized that her powers were too much for her when she'd gotten them or if it was something that gradually happened over time. Had she known? Had they affected her in any other ways? Had she gotten headaches? Or any signs? If so, she'd never told anyone. Certainly never said anything to Tru.

But then, maybe she wouldn't have either way. She wouldn't have wanted to frighten Tru. Not when she knew becoming an oracle was her daughter's destiny.

Tru sat in a chair and put her feet up on the ottoman. She closed her eyes and let the afternoon's warm breezes drift past her. Somewhere, a wind chime sent soft, dulcet notes into the air. Bird song joined it.

She was about to drift off when her phone buzzed with the sound of an incoming call. She was instantly awake. She answered it. "Hello?"

"Hi, it's Pandora."

Tru pulled in a deep gulp of air. "Hi."

"I'm sure you're anxious to hear what I found out, so I won't delay. The spells I cast all returned clear results. The only death I see in your future is just what you'll be dealing with as an oracle. Should you decide to become one."

Tru exhaled, happy to have that weight off of her.

"Oh, good. I am. Going to become one. Thank you so much."

"You're welcome."

"Can I ask about Eamon?"

After a brief pause, Pandora spoke again, but her tone had changed slightly. It was more serious than it had been with Tru's news. "I'm actually on my way to see him right now. I don't feel like I should share his results. I'm sorry. You must understand that, right?"

Tru closed her eyes. "Of course. It was silly of me to ask. Thanks again."

"Happy to help. And welcome to Nocturne Falls."

As they hung up, Tru stared at her phone, her own joy quickly fading. Pandora was going to see Eamon in person to talk about his results. That had to mean she was about to give him bad news. Because if it was good news, why wouldn't Pandora have just called him like she'd called Tru?

Her heart sank and she could have started crying, but mostly, she hurt for Eamon. It was so unfair that he wasn't getting the results he wanted.

Tru went very still. But did that also mean Pandora was about to tell Eamon he was right to stay away from Tru?

That would be even worse.

She stood up and stared at his house, wishing she could send a telepathic message into his brain and get him to ask her to come over so she could be there with him when Pandora gave him the results.

He wouldn't, though. She knew that. He would have called or texted already if that was going to happen.

Eamon was going to get his news alone. Maybe with Seamus at his side. But not with Tru. And why would he? He was already avoiding her to keep her safe.

She decided to call him anyway. Not to wheedle an invite from him. This was his business, and he was entitled to hear it however he wanted. But she could at least share her news. After all, they'd just talked about her becoming an oracle.

She'd just let him know that the ceremony was really going to happen. She dialed and put the phone to her ear.

He picked up right away. "I was just about to call you."

"You were?"

"Aye. Pandora's on her way over to give me the results. I don't think they're good."

"I'm so sorry."

"Did she talk to you already?"

"She did. I'm going through with the ritual. Probably tonight."

"That's grand. I mean it, Tru. I'm so happy for you."

She could hear in his voice how much he meant that. "Thanks. I'm worried about you, though."

"Och, I'll be all right. I've made it this far, haven't I?"

"Is your uncle going to be with you?"

She heard a door close and then Eamon came back on, his voice quieter than before. "About that. Would you mind if I came over to your house to talk to Pandora? I'd bring Seamus with me. But not Cal."

"Oh. Yes, of course. Actually, I think my aunts are about to go out, but I don't think they'll mind."

"You're sure?"

She knew her aunts. "I'm positive."

"Okay. I'm going to text Pandora and let her know. Thank you."

"You're welcome." Tru hung up, smiling, and went in to find her aunts.

They were upstairs in the small front bedroom. It had no bed, just an old easy chair, a small cat condo, a scratching post, and a fresh litter box. There was also an area set up like a low playpen filled with blankets and covered with puppy pads. No doubt where mama and the babies would spend most of their time. The room walls were a soft lilac with a border of bunnies. It actually looked like a nursery.

Aunt Cleo was putting litter in the new litter box, while on the other side of the room, Aunt Delly was laying down a rubber mat for a feeding station.

Tru stuck her head in. "This is a pretty nice setup. How often do you guys foster pregnant cats?"

Aunt Cleo sat back on her heels. "As often as we need to. And this room allows us to give the mama and the new babies some privacy. Plus, the kittens can grow up a bit in here before we add them to gen pop."

Tru laughed. "I love that. Will you teach me how to help?"

"Sure," Aunt Delly said. "That would be great. If you want to."

"I want to. If I'm going to live here and work with you, then I'd better know how to take care of the cats as well. Pandora called. I'm all clear."

Both aunts let out sighs of relief.

Tru held her finger up. "There's one other thing. Would you mind if Seamus and Eamon came over here to talk to Pandora? I don't think Eamon wants to have that conversation with Callum around."

"Why not?" Aunt Delly asked.

Tru just shrugged. "He just doesn't."

"Of course they can come over." Aunt Cleo got to her feet, a look of concern on her face. "Pandora called you but is coming in person to see Eamon? That can't be good news."

Tru shook her head. "I don't think it is."

Aunt Delly put her hand to her heart. "That poor boy."

Tru could only nod. Her own heart was already hurting.

34

Eamon sat on one end of the couch while Tru and Seamus took the chairs where Tru's aunts would have been, had they been home. A few cats joined them, but most seemed highly uninterested in whatever the humans were doing.

Pandora sat at the other end of the couch, smiling tightly as they all got settled.

Eamon didn't look directly at her, making eye contact with her knees instead. "Thank you for being flexible on the location."

"It was no problem. It's just next door. But it was nice of Tru's aunts to open their home like this."

"They would have been here," Tru said, "but they went to pick up a new cat to foster. A pregnant one."

"Is that right?" Pandora asked. "You know, I might be interested in a kitten. Pumpkin could use a playmate. A kitten would keep her busy. Let them know to keep me in mind when adoption time comes, would you?"

"Sure," Tru said.

Then Pandora took a breath and shifted her body toward Eamon. "I'm sure you're ready to hear what I found out."

He nodded. "Aye."

"Let's just get straight into it, then. The results weren't at all what I was expecting. There just wasn't anything straightforward about them. No real black-and-white answers. In fact, I ended up calling my mother and my sisters in to consult. They're witches, too, as you might have already known."

Eamon glanced at his uncle. Seamus was gripping the arms of the chair so tightly his knuckles had paled. Eamon brought his attention back to Pandora. "So what did you find?"

"Let's start with one of the first things you asked me to look into. Whether or not you might actually be affecting the lifespans of those around you."

He braced himself.

"I could only cast a spell using your blood and Tru's, since those were the only samples I had." Her mouth bent in a grimace. "Based on what I found, there is every chance your close proximity is shortening the lifespans of those around you."

He put his head in his hands. He'd already known as much, but hearing it confirmed was like a weight pressing down on him. One he was powerless to lift.

She went on. "I cast the spell again, using your blood and a sample of my own. The conclusion was the same, although not as strong as with Tru's."

"Because we've had contact," Eamon said. But he couldn't look at his uncle knowing he was probably harming him. The man who was like a father to him. The man he was slowly killing. All Eamon could do was pray the familial connection gave Seamus some kind of immunity. He found his voice. "Go on. Tell me the rest of it."

"I'm going to explain what I found as best I can. Ask whatever questions you want. Just know that I might not be able to give you great answers. Or any answers."

"I ken." Except he didn't. What else could she have found?

"The next spell I cast was to show me how strong your reaper bloodline was. I assumed it must be dominant due to you being able to see the hourglasses. Not only did I learn that it wasn't as strong as I thought it would be, but there are at least three separate reaper lineages present in you."

That picked his head up. "Three? Callum had said he'd narrowed it down to three possibilities. He never said it could be *all* three." He looked from her to his uncle. "Did you know?"

"Not a clue," Seamus said.

"That's not all," Pandora said. "Like I said, I thought the reaper would be stronger in you. I now believe your current ability exists because of the three types of reaper in your makeup. It wins by majority, if that makes sense."

Eamon just nodded.

Pandora went on. "But when I realized the reaper blood wasn't all that was there, I cast another spell to show me what other kinds of supernaturals exist in your gene pool." She let out a breath. "I was not prepared for the result. I cast the spell again, thinking I'd done something wrong. That's when I brought my mom and sisters in and had them recast it."

Eamon could barely stand it. "What did you find?"

"You are *many* different kinds of supernatural."

He snorted softly. "I already knew that. Our bloodlines are as muddled as a dirty winter stream."

"You did tell me. I just didn't understand how many. And that's exactly what I think is causing your issue. I don't know if I can explain this properly, but there are so many different remnants of power within you that the reaper power has come to the forefront because there are three strands of it. The other powers are too diverse to work together in the same way, which is why you can't really access them."

He didn't know what to do with that information.

She held up her hands. "But then I cast another spell to determine which of your other powers might have a chance of overtaking the reaper ability, mostly in the hopes that with the use of more magic, we could pull that power to the forefront and eliminate the hourglasses you see. Does that make sense?"

"Aye," he said. "You'd make a new ability the most dominant, instead of the one I have now." He already knew he was on board with that. Anything had to be better than watching death approaching.

"Exactly."

"What did you find?" Tru asked.

Pandora said nothing for a moment. "That's where it got more interesting. Or more confusing, depending on how you look at it. We cast the spell five times. And not once did we get the same answer."

Eamon shook his head. "What does that mean?"

"None of us are entirely sure, but I have a theory," Pandora said. "Just like I have a theory about why you don't see an hourglass over Tru. But let's talk about you first. My best guess is that your abilities are trying to protect you from something. I don't know what that thing is, but the way a new power kept popping up, it was as if the real you was being kept hidden for a reason."

"I don't understand." Eamon frowned. "I'm protecting myself from myself?"

Pandora laughed softly. "Maybe. I'm sorry this isn't more clear, but it's new ground for me. My mom and sisters, too. There is another very powerful witch in town, a woman named Alice Bishop, and we talked to her, as well. She did give us a possible solution."

Eamon went still. "What? Actually, I don't care. I'll do it if it means I can live something closer to a normal life."

"I don't know if that's what it means or not, but she said that you might have an easier time of things if some of those extra powers were bound. That would sort of eliminate them from your system."

"Can you do that with the reaper powers?"

"Yes, we can," Pandora said. "But the issue is we don't know what will take over when they're no longer front and center. It could be worse."

He scoffed. "What could be worse?"

"Eamon, I saw a lot of different powers in your blood.

Many of them were ... dark. You need to really think about this before you act. It's like that old saying about better the devil you know."

He looked away, frustration bubbling up in him. Of course that was what his options were. To suffer with his current burden or end up with something far more terrible. He stood up and walked to the windows. A calico cat lay sprawled on the windowsill. He stroked the wee creature's fur and tried to calm himself down.

Tru cleared her throat softly. "You said you had a theory about why Eamon can't see an hourglass over me?"

"I do," Pandora said. "I believe it's because you're in a kind of in-between place in your life right now. On the precipice of becoming an oracle, which will really be the beginning of the life you've always anticipated. I could be wrong, but I think once you go through the ceremony, he'll be able to see one over you like he can with everyone else."

Eamon didn't like the sound of that. One of the reasons being around Tru was so comfortable was because he couldn't see an hourglass over her. Keeping that status quo was enough motivation that he made his decision right then and there. He turned. "What are the odds that I'll end up with a benign power?"

"I don't know," Pandora answered. "We would certainly do our best to bind as many of the dark fragments and remove them as possible."

"What would you need from me?"

"Just for you to be present and another sample of your blood," Pandora said. "Oh, and according to Alice, we would have the best chance of success if you'd been awake for at least twenty-four hours."

"And you have everything else you'd need?"

She nodded. "With me, my mom, my two sisters, and Alice, we have the five necessary to perform the binding ritual. We still need to finalize our research on the ritual, but we can be ready by the time you are."

"By tomorrow morning? I'll have been up twenty-four hours by then."

"That should work," Pandora said. "I'll let them know we need to get cracking with our plans. But just to be clear, you understand there's no guarantee about what kind of power you'll end up with?"

Eamon glanced at Tru and his uncle. "I'm willing to take the chance."

Tru waited until Pandora had gone before approaching Eamon. "It's very brave of you to go through with this."

"Doesn't feel brave," Eamon said, pressing his thumb and forefinger together where Pandora had taken the blood. "Feels like something I have no choice about. I don't want to be a danger to you or anyone else around me. If there's a chance I can change that, I'm going to take it, no matter the cost. Anything would be better than how it is now."

She reached out to touch him, but he backed away. "Don't. I can't bear the thought that I'm hurting you just by being near you."

Seamus came up to them, his gaze filled with sympathy. "It's all right, lad. We're going to get through this. You'll see."

Eamon didn't look convinced. "Until the binding ceremony, I think I should stay in a hotel."

Seamus frowned. "Don't be daft. I'll not have you doing that now. You've been with me all these years and I'm fine. One more day isna gonna hurt."

"He's right," Tru said. "There's no reason to punish yourself like that. Besides, if you're by yourself and you start to fall asleep, there won't be anyone around to wake you up."

Eamon narrowed his eyes. "There won't be anyone around to wake me up anyway. Cal and my uncle will both be sleeping."

Seamus lifted his chin. "I will not be. I'm staying up with you."

A hint of a smile curved Eamon's mouth. "You canna stay awake for an entire football match. How are you going to stay awake tonight?"

"I have more reason to," Seamus said. "We'll drink lots of tea and play cards."

"Sounds like fun," Tru said. Watching soccer didn't really sound like fun, but maybe it would be. She'd never actually seen a game. "I think I'll come over and join you."

"No," Eamon said sharply. "Not with..." He trailed off, ending his words with a frown.

"Oh, let her," Seamus said. "Same as you being around me. One more day isna gonna hurt."

"That's not what he meant," Tru said. "He was talking about Callum."

Seamus looked confused. "What about Callum?"

Together, Tru and Eamon explained what had been going on.

Seamus shook his head. "I doubt he's up to anything other than indulging his natural curiosity. He's always been that way. Even as a wee bairn. He'd get into anything that wasn't latched tight. He means you no harm, lass, I swear it."

"All the same," Eamon said, "I think she should steer clear of him for a while."

"I know you do," Tru said. "But he'll be asleep tonight, so I won't have to worry about him. And with me there, it'll be easier for you to stay awake. Seamus and I can take turns if we need to."

Eamon glanced skyward. "There's no point in me arguing this, is there?"

"Nope," Tru said. She smiled. She was worried about him and what the result of the binding ceremony might be, but at the same time, she was proud of him for going through with it. Once it was over, they'd be able to be around each other. In all sorts of ways.

The side door opened, and Aunt Cleo and Aunt Delly came in. Aunt Cleo had the cat carrier in one hand. They came through but paused at the hall. Aunt Cleo lifted the carrier slightly. "As you can see, we got her. How did things go here?"

"Fine." Tru could only see a scared little face and big eyes peeking out from the carrier. "Go ahead and take her up. I'll fill you in once you get her settled."

"All right," Aunt Cleo said. She and Aunt Delly went down the hall and up the steps.

Tru glanced at Eamon. "You don't mind me telling my aunts, do you?"

He shook his head. "Not at all. Especially since you plan on spending the night at my house. They ought to know why before they come to some other conclusion on their own."

She grinned. "Right. So I'll see you two after dinner then? Maybe around eight?"

Seamus nodded. "Looking forward to it."

She said goodbye to them both, then went upstairs after her aunts. The nursery room door was closed. She knocked softly. "Is it all right if I come in?"

"Yes," Aunt Delly called out.

Tru went in, closing the door behind her. The mama cat was in the birthing area, looking very round and a little overwhelmed. "Hi, sweet girl."

Aunt Delly was sitting in the chair, and Aunt Cleo had the closet open where the shelves were filled with all sorts of supplies, including both wet and dry food. She was getting the cat a dish of canned food now.

Tru went closer and sat down. "How's she doing?"

"A bit stressed, but she'll be better once she realizes she's safe. And that her babies will be too," Aunt Delly answered. "How's Eamon?"

Tru sighed. "He's not great. Pandora told him he is definitely affecting the lifespans of those around him."

Aunt Delly let out a soft gasp. "Seamus?"

Tru nodded and thought about what Eamon had told her about his ex-girlfriend. "I'm sure. But if past history is correct, any time Seamus has lost should be regained once Eamon's powers are bound."

Aunt Cleo brought the food over to the feeding area

and set the dish down next to the bowl of dry food that was already there. "Bound?"

Tru explained all that Pandora had said and the ritual that Eamon would be undergoing in the morning.

"That poor man," Aunt Delly said. "He must be terrified."

"I don't think he is," Tru said. To her, Eamon had looked resolved. "He seems pretty okay with it all. I think he's just happy that there's a solution. Well, maybe not happy. Relieved is probably more accurate."

"I can imagine." Aunt Cleo sat on the floor beside her. "But he has no idea what the outcome will be."

"No," Tru said. "But it's got to be better than what's happening to him right now, don't you think?"

"Maybe." Aunt Cleo shook her head. "Then again, that first glimpse of his future I saw was very dark."

Tru blinked with an uncomfortable realization. "Wait a second. What if what you saw was his future after this ritual? What if it really does make things worse?"

"No way of knowing that," Aunt Cleo said. "But don't forget, that's when Nemo got on his lap and changed everything. And he's adopted Nemo. That final view of his future is the last one I saw. It's the one that matters."

Tru nodded, but it still worried her. She probably wouldn't shake that feeling until Eamon was through the spell and they knew what his outcome was.

Which meant it was going to be a long night.

The mama cat cautiously made her way to the bowl,

where she sniffed at the food, then finally she chowed down with gusto.

"It'll be okay," Aunt Delly said. "Alice Bishop is incredibly powerful. She helped create this town. She won't let anything bad happen to Eamon. And he's going to have four more powerful witches around him, all of them doing their very best."

"That's good to know," Tru said. It really was comforting information.

Aunt Cleo went back to the closet and got a larger dish. "I'm going to get her some water. You two be thinking of names."

"Yes," Aunt Delly said as she got out of the chair. "This poor baby needs a name. And then her babies will need names. We need to come up with something."

Tru looked at the cat. She was a soft dove gray with white feet and a little white on her chest. She was eating like she thought she might never see food again. "She's a real beauty, so she needs a pretty name."

"I agree," Aunt Delly said.

"How about Chloe? It's a Greek name."

Aunt Cleo came back in. "What's a Greek name?"

"Chloe," Aunt Delly answered.

Aunt Cleo put the water dish down. "In Greek, Chloe basically means fertility." She laughed as she looked at the very pregnant cat still eating. "That might be a little too on the nose, but I like it. Chloe it is."

"It was Tru's idea," Aunt Delly said.

Aunt Cleo nodded. "Good job. Now we just need to

name the kittens when they arrive. Which could be any day, according to the rescue."

"That reminds me," Tru said. "Pandora might be interested in one of the kittens. She said her cat needs a playmate."

"That's wonderful." Aunt Delly pressed her hands together. "I love knowing the babies have good homes waiting for them."

"So do I," Aunt Cleo said. Then she looked at Tru. "Are you ready to become an oracle? Because if you are, we are."

As Tru got to her feet, her stomach rumbled.

Aunt Delly shook her head before Tru could say anything. "We have to have dinner first. The oracle ritual should not be performed on an empty stomach. Chloe's probably tired of us hovering over her anyway. Let's go fix some dinner."

"Dinner sounds good." Tru followed her aunt downstairs, with Aunt Cleo coming along behind her. "Am I going to need any downtime after this ritual? I kind of promised Eamon I'd come over afterwards."

"You should be fine," Aunt Cleo said. "You might even feel energized by it."

"Great," Tru said. She *was* very ready to become an oracle.

But that didn't mean she wasn't nervous about it.

On the short walk back to the house, Eamon and Seamus had agreed not to say anything to Cal about the binding ceremony or anything else, really. Just in case.

Eamon knew Seamus thought Cal's sudden interest in oracles was merely the man's inquisitive mind at work, but Eamon didn't want to put Tru at any greater risk than she already was. He wasn't going to chance it.

Not saying anything seemed like the best plan.

They went into the house but found no sign of Cal. Eamon glanced upstairs, figuring he was still in his room.

Seamus went right to the back of the house and opened the sliding door onto the screened porch. Immediately, Nemo and Yardy went trotting out.

Eamon watched them go. Maybe he'd sit out there with them. He had nothing but time on his hands until tomorrow morning. And Tru wouldn't be here until eight or later, depending on what time they got done with dinner.

"Are you hungry?" Seamus asked.

"Not really, but I suppose I should eat all the same," Eamon answered. "What's for dinner then?"

Seamus narrowed his eyes like he was thinking.

"What food do you think lends itself best to being awake all night?"

"Probably nothing too heavy or I'll be out. I love carbs, but they put me to sleep. We haven't grilled steaks in a while. We could have them with a bit of veg or salad."

"Sounds good. I'll need to nip to the store. Won't take me long, though." Seamus patted his back pocket to be sure his wallet was there, then grabbed his keys from a bowl on the counter. "Give me twenty minutes, then start the grill."

"I'll take care of it."

Seamus started for the door, then stopped. "Could you feed the lads, too?"

Eamon nodded. "Sure."

As Seamus left, Eamon picked up the cats' bowls and brought them to the kitchen. He grabbed a can of food from the pantry and pulled the top off. At that sound, the two of them came running in from the screened porch. Obviously, the prospect of eating superseded watching the birds and bugs in the backyard.

He put half a can each in two clean dishes, then took them back to the blue feeding mat Seamus had bought. The cats danced around and meowed, but as soon as the bowls were down, they tucked in.

Eamon went back to the kitchen to clean up. He almost laughed at the enthusiasm on display by the feline duo. He picked up the can and had a look at what it was. "Apparently, Chicken Party is a very popular flavor."

He tossed the can in the bin, put the dirty dishes in

the sink to soak, then went out onto the porch. He settled onto the couch out there, kicking his feet up and tucking a pillow beneath his head. He wasn't really nervous about tomorrow. Whatever happened would happen.

Anything was better than his current situation.

But he couldn't help but wonder what other dark powers lurked within him. He wished he could talk to Cal about it, because if anyone would know, it was him.

But Eamon's trust in his cousin was too eroded. He didn't want to believe that Cal was up to anything untoward, but he wasn't willing to risk Tru's, or her aunts', safety.

Although maybe that was his own paranoia talking. Seamus didn't think it was an issue. Eamon sat up. Had he delved into the sordid details of too many unsolved murders on his podcast? Had that tainted his outlook on his fellow man?

He thought hard. It wasn't just the podcast that had tainted his views. He saw death everywhere. His job dealt with death. There was really no escaping it.

It was completely possible he was projecting a dark intent onto Cal that was wholly of Eamon's own making.

There was only one way to really know for sure. He got up. He had to talk to the man. He'd known Cal all his life. Eamon should be able to tell if his cousin was lying.

He went to the bottom of the steps and shouted up. "Cal? Seamus has gone to get steaks for dinner. We're going to do them on the grill."

A few seconds ticked by, then a door opened and Cal

appeared at the railing. "Sounds grand. What can I do to help?"

Eamon hadn't actually thought about that. "I'm going to get the grill going. Can you make a salad?"

"How hard can it be?" Cal laughed. "Let me close up shop, and I'll be right down."

"Good." Eamon went out to start the grill. Once that was done, he'd go back in and ask Cal flat-out about his interest in oracles. Well, maybe not flat-out. But he'd work his way to the topic and see if he could figure out just what Cal was thinking.

He was already in the kitchen when Cal walked in.

Cal immediately opened the fridge and started taking out ingredients. "I see lettuce and cucumber. Wait. Found a few radishes. What else is there for salad?"

Eamon grabbed the plastic basket of grape tomatoes and an onion from the tray of fruits and veg Seamus kept on the counter. He put them with the rest of the ingredients. "Here. That might be about it."

Cal closed the fridge and had a look at the veg Eamon had pulled. "I suppose it'll do."

He took the lettuce and cucumbers to the sink and washed them, then gave them a good shake and brought them back to the counter.

Eamon got him a big bowl while Cal took a knife from the block near the stove. Eamon watched Cal's face, looking for anything that might give his true intentions away. "Haven't seen you much today. Any progress on the reaper name?" He supposed the name didn't matter now that Pandora had cast all those spells, but Cal didn't know that.

"Not much. I'm sorry."

"What have you been working on then? You've been awfully busy."

Cal sliced the end off the cucumber, sighing. "I have. I'm sorry again. I hit a dead end with the reaper business, but then I got distracted."

"By?" Eamon figured he already knew the answer.

Cal shook his head. "Those women next door." He leaned in, eyes sparkling with curiosity. "Oracles. Real ones. The stuff of Greek mythology and you and Uncle Seamus live right beside them." He went back to slicing. "How could I not be intrigued?"

Eamon hadn't expected him to come right out with it. Eamon played dumb. "So you've been researching them?"

"I have. Can you blame me? A real oracle can see into the past and the future." He dumped the rounds of cucumber into the bowl, then moved on to the lettuce. "Do you realize they might be able to help us? You, specifically, but ultimately all of the Underwood men might benefit."

"How?"

"That's just it." Cal shook his head. "I don't quite know yet. But the answer's out there. I just need to keep digging. But with power that old and that deep, there has to be a way. To maintain that kind of power, they must keep their bloodlines very clean and pure. Or it's a different kind of magic. I don't know."

"Neither do I. All I know is they're Greek. But I still don't get how you think they can help us."

Cal roughly chopped the lettuce before adding it to the bowl. "I'll figure it out. But at the very least, I might write up a paper about them. There are supernatural journals that would publish it."

Eamon wasn't so sure Tru and her aunts would welcome that kind of publicity. Although maybe they would. He'd have to ask. They were in the business of predictions. Could be good for them in that regard. He popped a cherry tomato into his mouth.

Cal reached for the onion next. "Any word on when Tru might go through the ritual? I'm still keen to watch. It would be a great addition to the paper. If I write one."

Eamon shook his head. He imagined Tru would be doing the ritual very soon. Once again, he played dumb. He didn't want to tell Cal the ritual was off-limits. That might only interest him more. "Not a clue. I'd better go check on that grill."

He walked outside to the little stone patio where the grill was, keeping his back to the house, and sent Tru a text.

Cal admitted to researching oracles. He thinks you and your aunts could help solve the Underwood problems but didn't say how. I hope you go through the ritual soon. He still wants to watch.

He lifted the grill lid and held his hand over the grates, testing the heat. He didn't keep his hand there long. The grill was an inferno. He turned it down just as Tru's answer came in.

Doing it after dinner. I'll text you when I'm through.

Eamon wanted to type a wish for good luck. Or something. But nothing sounded right. So he just sent a thumbs-up emoji.

Which seemed dumb.

What he really wanted to say was, "Be safe and I hope it's an easy transition and that you become the best oracle ever and thank you for being so stubborn about liking me even though you should have cut me out of your life at the first sign of trouble."

But Tru was smart. Maybe she'd get all that from the thumbs-up.

Dinner was leftovers, which was just fine with Tru, because all she did was pick at the food. A bite here, a bite there, enough to stop her stomach from rumbling and interrupting the ceremony to come.

Her nerves were from the not knowing. She put her fork down and sipped her water as she looked at her aunts, both of whom were eating like nothing interesting was about to take place. "Can you tell me anything about what's going to happen? Just a little something?"

Both of her aunts shook their heads.

Tru sighed. That was the answer she'd expected, but it was still disappointing. "Is it going to hurt?"

Aunt Delly laughed. "What kind of ceremony do you think this is?"

"I don't have a clue," Tru said. "No one's told me anything about it."

"Because it's secret," Aunt Delly said.

Aunt Cleo speared an olive with her fork. "Well, there's no blood."

"Great, thanks, that helps bunches." Although that was good to know. At the sound of a meow, Tru looked down to see Butternut beside her chair. "I know. They're not being helpful, are they?"

Aunt Cleo waved her hand. "Don't give him any of that chicken. It's got garlic and onions in it. The cats can't have that."

"I know that," Tru said. "And nice attempt to change the subject. Why is this so secretive? It's freaking me out."

"You have nothing to worry about," Aunt Delly said, patting her hand on the table. "It's a simple, beautiful, peaceful ceremony, but it's oracle magic, and you can only know about it once you become an oracle."

"Are we doing it outside?" Tru asked. "In the backyard?"

Her aunts looked at each other. Then Aunt Cleo nodded but without a lot of conviction. "Something like that."

Tru realized there was no point in asking any more questions, but she no longer felt as nervous as she had been. Her aunts wouldn't let her get hurt or be in danger. Besides, she was becoming an oracle, not a ninja. How hard could it be? She finished the food on her plate, then helped clean up.

"Dessert?" Aunt Delly asked.

"Seriously?" Tru laughed. "How much longer do you want me to wait? I'm going nuts. Can we have it after?"

"Of course," Aunt Delly said. "Your aunt and I will finish in the kitchen. You go change."

Tru wasn't sure what was wrong with what she had on, which was jeans and a cute T-shirt. "Into what?"

Her aunts smiled. Aunt Cleo just said, "Into the outfit on your bed. Then meet us outside."

"All right." Tru had no idea what outfit that might be. Curious, she went upstairs to check it out.

There on her bed was a beautiful white gown. Next to it was a length of gold satin rope, tasseled on both ends. A belt, maybe? Beside that was a pair of gold hair combs.

On the floor were a pair of flat leather sandals, also gold. And in her size.

She picked up the dress and realized it was styled like a chiton, which was a Greek toga. That seemed very appropriate.

She had no idea when her aunts had put this here, but flowy, draped gown was incredibly beautiful, and the more she looked at it, the more appropriate she felt it was for what she was about to do.

She changed into the gown, tying the rope around her waist twice because it was so long. She used the combs to pull her hair back on either side, not really sure if that was how they were meant to be.

She put the sandals on, lacing them up around her ankles.

All done, she glanced at herself in the mirror. She looked nice. And very Greek. But more like someone from Ancient Greece. Which was pretty cool, actually. This was a ceremony that dated to that time.

Satisfied she'd put herself together as best she knew how, she went downstairs. Except for a few small lights that had been left on, the house was dark.

That made it easy to see her aunts were standing in the yard just beyond the screened porch. They were facing away from the house, their hands upraised toward the moon. They were dressed in white gowns, gold rope belts, and gold sandals, too.

She opened the door and walked out. A sense of calm filled her, and in her heart she knew this was exactly what she was supposed to be doing. "I'm here," she said softly.

They turned and smiled at her.

Aunt Delly nodded. "You look beautiful."

"I feel beautiful," Tru said. "And ready."

"Good," Aunt Cleo said. She held out her hand. "Come. Walk with us into the Grove of the Oracles."

Tru wasn't sure what that meant, but she came down the steps and took Aunt Cleo's hand. Then Aunt Delly offered hers, and Tru took it as well.

Suddenly, the world in front of her changed. Trees sprang up before her, trees that definitely hadn't been there two seconds ago. They looked like a thicket of willows, but there was an opening in them, a natural arch. Beyond that was a clearing.

She looked at her aunts. They shone as if lit from within by moonlight.

"This way," Aunt Cleo said.

Still holding her hands, her aunts led her through the arch and into the grove. The space within was much larger than she'd realized. The grass under her feet was soft and springy, and although it was still evening, pale light bathed everything in a gentle luminescence. Fireflies danced around the white-barked trees, and the sweet fragrance of flowers and damp earth filled the air.

They stopped in the center.

"Welcome to the grove of the oracles," Aunt Delly said.

"Did you make this place?" Tru asked.

"No," Aunt Cleo answered. "It's always existed. Any oracle can come here. They just have to use their magic."

"You have magic? Do I?"

"You will," Aunt Delly said. "Very soon."

All around them, women dressed in white gowns and robes stepped out from amongst the willows and joined them in the grove. Some of the women shimmered with so much light, they seemed transparent. Each one was accompanied by a cat. Or maybe there were more cats than women. It was hard to tell.

Tru looked around, trying to take it all in. Then one face made the breath catch in her throat. "Mom?"

Maria stepped forward, smiling. She was definitely translucent. "Hello, sweetheart. I've waited so long for this day."

Tru reached out to hug her mom, but her arms went right through her. She stepped back. "You're not really here, are you?"

"I am, but I am not. But you *are* here, and that's what matters. Today, you begin your new life as an oracle. I'm so glad my sisters are here to guide you." Maria glanced at Cleo and Delphina. "I've missed you both."

Cleo nodded. "As we have you."

Tru felt a tear slip down her cheek. "I had no idea I'd see you."

Her mom took Tru's face in her hands, but all Tru felt was a gentle warmth, like the sun was shining down on her. "The ways of the oracles are vast and mysterious, but I will always be here when you need me."

Tru nodded. "I'm so glad to know that." Seeing her mother and learning that she'd have access to her once again changed everything. Any doubt Tru had was gone. Her heart felt like it might burst. "You left too soon."

"I know," her mother said. "And I know you think it was because my powers were more than my body could bear. That will not be your fate. What happened to me was really and truly just a stroke." Once again, she looked at her sisters. "Thank you for taking care of her."

Cleo and Delly nodded and sniffed, their own emotions plain on their faces.

Tru wanted to ask how her mother knew what Tru's fate would be, but her mom stepped back into the circle of women who'd come out of the trees.

Aunt Cleo spoke in a clear, strong voice. "Sisters, a new oracle seeks to join us. Who will share their powers with her to awaken what lies within already?"

Every woman in the circle took a step forward, hand outstretched, and as a group, they said, "I will."

Aunt Cleo and Aunt Delly clasped hands on either side of Tru so that she was encircled between their arms.

"Now," Aunt Delly said. "Put your hands on our hands."

Tru rested her hands overtop those of her aunts, her arms reaching out on either side of her.

The women around them came closer, stretching their hands out to touch Tru's aunts. Hands came to alight on her aunts' arms and shoulders. The glow increased, traveling from the women to her aunts and into Tru.

The oracles' power filled her with warmth and peace and a sense of well-being she'd never felt before. The air in her lungs seemed to change into something cleaner and lighter, buoying her up. She had no idea if her feet were still touching the ground.

The expanding brightness made it harder and harder to see, until there was nothing around her but faint shapes lost to the brilliance of the power that surrounded her. Then those shapes disappeared, and there was nothing but light and energy.

Tru closed her eyes, giving herself over to the experience. The light faded and she felt grass give way beneath her feet. She opened her eyes.

She was standing in the backyard of her aunts' house, the two of them beside her. The grove, the women, the cats, and the light were gone.

Not all the light. Tru glanced down at her hands. She was still glowing.

"How do you feel?" Aunt Delly asked.

Tru shook her head. "I feel … all kinds of things. Incredible. Grateful. Happy. But overwhelmed. I can't believe my mom was there."

Aunt Cleo smiled. "I wish we could have told you, but the secrets of our kind must remain secret."

The glow was fading. "I understand." She glanced over her shoulder like the grove might still be there. "How do I go back there?"

"Just think of the grove, and it will come to you," Aunt Cleo said.

Aunt Delly leaned in. "You'll always return to your starting place."

"Amazing," Tru said. She'd had no idea. Her aunts were very good secret-keepers. Seeing her mother had made everything feel right.

"Well," Aunt Delly said. "I don't know about you two, but I could use some baklava and a nice cup of decaf."

Tru's stomach growled at the mention of the word. She laughed. "Apparently, I could, too. Let's go."

After a quick piece of baklava and a regular cup of coffee, because she wanted the caffeine, Tru went upstairs to change back into her jeans and T-shirt. She added a soft cardigan, just in case she got chilly over at Eamon's.

She smiled. She wished she could tell him about tonight. About the grove and her mother and all the women. She wouldn't, of course.

But it was going to be hard to pretend like nothing amazing had happened to her.

38

Eamon opened the front door right after Tru texted she was on her way over. He stood there, waiting, but not for long.

She was soon headed up the steps toward him. "Hi."

"Hi." There was still no hourglass over her head. But that wasn't what he was focused on. "You look ... different." She had a glow about her. Not exactly the oracle glow, but then he supposed that was exactly what it was. "Are you ...? I mean, did you ...?"

She nodded. "I did. And it was incredible, and I wish I could tell you about it, but I can't."

He smiled, glad she'd had such a good experience. "I understand."

"How's it going over here?"

He shook his head. "Pandora just called to say they're having an issue locating one of the necessary elements for the binding spell. She did her best to make me think they'd have it by morning, but she wanted to prepare me in case there was a delay."

Tru walked in. "Did she say what the element was?"

He closed the door behind her. "Something called aether. She tried to explain it to me, but I still can't tell you what it is." He frowned, making his next words come out in a growl. "Starlight and fairy dust, for all I know."

Her brows rose.

He exhaled. "Sorry. It's put me in a mood."

She smirked. "I can tell." She pointed at her head. "Do you see anything?"

He shook his head. "Still nothing. And you definitely went through with it, right?"

"I definitely did. I thought you'd be able to see an hourglass after that."

He smiled. "Well, I can't and I think that's grand." He could come up with only one reason why that might be. The universe, or the fates, or whatever it was, wanted him to be with Tru. He'd been drawn to her because she'd had no hourglass. Now she helping him like no one had been able to before. "Congrats, by the way. It was really good, then?"

She inhaled, then let the breath out in a contented sigh. "Really good. Again, I wish I could tell you but ..."

He nodded. "It's all right."

"Speaking of telling people, where's Cal?"

"Getting ready for bed, for all I know. He admitted he's been researching oracles. Like I said before, he wants to write a paper about them." Eamon rolled his eyes. "I'm sorry I made you worry. It's just Cal being Cal."

"No problem."

He reached out, wishing he could touch her. He dropped his hand back to his side. "Thanks for coming over. I think Uncle Seamus is already drifting."

She laughed softly. "It's a good thing I'm here, then."

"It is. You want some tea?"

She narrowed her eyes. "Is that supposed to help me stay awake? Pretty sure I'm going to need coffee for that."

He snorted. "You Americans and your coffee. Come on, I'll make you a pot."

"First of all, I'm a Greek-American, and secondly, tea is for old women," Tru shot back.

"Just for that, you're not getting any biscuits." That was a lie. He'd give her all the biscuits she wanted.

"That's all right," she said. "I like cookies better."

Grinning, he shook his head as they walked into the kitchen. Uncle Seamus was in his chair, half-asleep, with Yardy perched on the back of it. Seamus roused a bit when Tru came in. Football was on, but Eamon had lost track of which game it was.

Seamus rubbed at his eyes. "Hello, there, lass. Nice of you to come over and help keep our lad awake."

She shot him an amused look. "I'm not sure he's the one who needs the help."

Seamus smiled. "You might be right."

"I see Yardstick has settled in nicely. Where's Nemo?"

"Yardy's a good lad. Grand company, too." Then Seamus pointed to the cat condo, where the tips of two ginger ears were just visible over the edge of one platform. "Nemo's in his tower. He loves that thing."

"So cute," Tru said.

Eamon got the instant coffee down from the cabinet. "Will this do?"

Tru glanced over. "Seriously?" She laughed. "I guess it will. But when you're able to go out and be around people, you're taking me to get some real coffee at that place in town. Aunt Delly told me about it."

"The Hallowed Bean," Seamus said. "We just went there the other day. Good spot. Lovely sweets."

Eamon nodded. "I will take you anywhere you want to go." The thought of being able to be out among people and not see anything but their faces filled him with a sense of excitement unlike anything he'd felt before.

Having Tru there with him would make it all that much better. What would it be like to be out with her, holding her hand, unconcerned about the people around him and what their lifelines looked like?

He could only imagine.

He filled the kettle and turned it on, then fixed a plate of biscuits and put them on the table along with the cream and sugar and spoons.

Tru just leaned on the kitchen counter, watching. "I didn't know you had this domestic side to you. It's pretty sexy."

He glanced over at her. "Is it?"

She nodded, giving him an appreciative once over.

He waggled his brows. "Do you want to watch me wash some dishes, then?"

She laughed.

He got a pack of cards from one of the kitchen drawers and added them to the table. "Fancy a game?"

"Sure, if it's gin rummy. That's all I know how to play. That and Go Fish."

He shook his head. "I've no clue what gin rummy is."

"That's okay," she said. "I'll teach you."

They had tea and coffee and biscuits, and Tru taught Eamon the game. At the commercial break, Seamus came over, made himself a cup of tea, took a few biscuits, watched them for a moment, then went back to his chair.

Eamon had just won his first round when Cal came down the steps and joined them in the kitchen.

"I just found out there's a very nice chocolate shop in town. Delaney's Delectables." Cal smiled. "Anyone fancy a couple of chocolates if I run over and get some?"

"Everything they sell is good, but will it be open?" Eamon asked. It was going on nine. But he had a real weakness for the triple chocolate cake Delaney's sold.

Cal nodded. "Website says open until ten. Have you been there?"

"No, but Uncle Seamus gets us slices of their chocolate cake sometimes. It's the best I've ever had."

Seamus raised his hand. "I'll take a slice of that if you're going."

"Then I'll definitely bring some of that back. Anything else? Tru, do you have a preference for milk or dark chocolate?"

She turned to see him. "I'm not picky when it comes to chocolate—dark, milk, white, purple, I'll eat it."

Cal laughed. "I can appreciate that. I won't be long." He had his phone in his hand. "Just need to call a car."

Eamon wondered if the chocolates were Cal's way of making up for not finding the name of their reaper ancestor. "Take my car. Keys are in the bowl on the counter."

"Your Charger? You're sure?"

Eamon nodded. "It's all right. Just be careful."

Cal dug the keys out. "I will be."

He left. Eamon shook his head. "I think he feels bad about not being able to get the name of the reaper for me."

Tru looked up from her cards. "Did you talk to Lucien about that?"

"I did. He's going to be present for the binding ritual, just in case there's something he can help with."

"That's nice of him."

"It is."

They played several more games, but Eamon didn't win again, making him wonder if Tru had let him win the first one.

Cal returned in forty-five minutes. He had a very large shopping bag in one hand, but he replaced Eamon's keys into the bowl on the counter before he unpacked the treats he'd bought.

He named the items as he took them out of the bag. "Two slices of Death by Chocolate cake for my cousin and my uncle. A special assortment of handmade chocolate truffles for Tru, and a piece of raspberry cheesecake for myself."

He passed out the desserts, bringing Eamon and Seamus a fork along with their containers. Then he gave

Tru the good-size box of truffles. "I just asked them for an assortment of their most popular flavors."

She took the lid off the box and inhaled. "Oh, that is the most glorious smell in the world."

Eamon smiled. "Thank you, Cal. That was very nice of you."

"Very nice." Tru picked up a dark chocolate truffle drizzled with lines of hot pink. "I really hope this is raspberry." She took a bite, and a look of pure rapture came over her face. "It is. Oh my, that is absolutely decadent."

Eamon used his fork to cut off a big bite of cake and joined her in tasting what Cal had brought them. "Mmm ... so good." He pointed his fork at the cake. "Maybe we'll add Delaney's Delectables to our list of places in town to visit. What do you think?"

She nodded, still savoring the truffle. "I think that's the best idea you've ever had."

Tru didn't remember falling asleep, but she obviously had, because she was just now waking up. What was the last thing she remembered? Eating truffles. She'd had another one after the raspberry. A coconut cream. But after that, everything went fuzzy.

She yawned and tried to stretch, but her arms and legs wouldn't move. She was struggling to wake up, too. Her head felt foggy, her body slow to respond. And why were there no lights on? The TV had been on. She was sure of it. Seamus had been watching soccer.

A little more awareness came to her. She was lying down but not on a very comfortable surface. In fact, it was hard and cold. She tried to move her arms again. She was tied to whatever she was lying on. Her legs, too. Maybe strapped down was a better word for how she was feeling. And there was fabric covering her face.

She flattened her palms against the hard surface, trying to figure out what it was. It felt like metal. That made no sense. Where was she?

She tried to call for help, but her mouth was dry, and the word came out as a cracked whisper.

"Oh, good. You're awake."

The darkness disappeared as the fabric was yanked away.

She blinked at the lights above her, then they were blocked out by a face. Callum was standing over her, and from what little she could see, they were in a very sterile, clinical-looking room. "What's going on?"

He smiled at her. "Did you enjoy those chocolates? Didn't even taste the sedative I injected into them, did you?"

She stared at him, trying to make sense of what was happening. "You drugged me? Why would you do that?"

He leaned in, smile gone. "Because unlike my idiot cousin and uncle, I'm not okay with the piddling bit of power I've been allotted. I know there's more, and I want it. I've been searching for it all my life. And now I've found the very thing that will help me get it. You. You're the key to that."

"I am? How?" None of this made sense to her.

"Yes, you are. Or rather, your blood is." He walked away from her, over to a stainless-steel tray of instruments that she could just see by turning her head.

Was she in a hospital? It didn't quite look like that, but she hadn't been in enough of them to really be sure. "My blood? Where are we?"

He ignored her as he selected something off the tray. With his back to her, it was impossible to tell what he'd picked up. She looked around as best she could, trying to find something that might be useful. There was a big stainless-steel sink off to one side, some cabinets, and shelves that held jugs of chemicals.

Something told her this was not a hospital. So where was she?

He turned and came back toward her. He was holding a fat syringe with a long needle. There was nothing in the syringe, but that wasn't much comfort. "We are in the most convenient of places. My uncle's funeral home."

A shudder went through her. That seemed worse than a hospital. There would be people in a hospital. In a funeral home, there *might* be some people. But none of them would be alive enough to help her. "Are you telling me there are dead people in here?"

"Yes. And you're about to join them. Sorry about that. I know Eamon's sweet on you and he'll be fashed, but it can't be helped. I need a large quantity of your blood, and I can't be certain you're going to survive the removal of it."

"What do you think my blood is going to do for you?" She tugged against the restraints, but there was no budging them.

"You won't get free. You might as well stop trying." He leaned against the table she was on. "As for your blood, it's going to cure all of my ills. According to my research —and I promise you, it's been extensive—the blood of an oracle, one not yet turned, can cleanse the blood of another who suffers from confused powers and an over-abundance of abilities. That's the Underwood men in a nutshell."

Her first instinct was to tell him he was out of luck, that she'd become a full-fledged oracle just a few hours ago, but she thought that might cause him to kill her immediately. What she needed was time. Time for Eamon and Seamus to wake up and figure out where she was, if that was even possible. She had to believe it was, otherwise, she was doomed. "There's no way that will work. You'd be better off doing a binding ritual like Eamon's about to do."

Callum frowned. "What are you talking about?"

"Didn't Eamon tell you?" She paused, dragging things out as much as she could.

"No, he didn't tell me. Explain what you mean."

She sighed. "It would be easier if I could breathe better. These restraints are restricting my airflow."

"You're stalling." He held the syringe near her neck. "Talk now, or I'll decide my method is better."

She squirmed away from the syringe, but that didn't do much. "Pandora, the witch that lives down the street, she and her coven are going to perform a binding ceremony on Eamon to get rid of the worst of his powers and strengthen the good ones."

Mostly true, but she wasn't super concerned with being precise right now.

Callum hesitated. "You're just making that up."

"No, I'm not. First of all, how would I make up something like that? I had no idea it was even possible. Secondly, why do you think Eamon was drinking tea so late and trying to stay awake? The witches told him the spell would be more effective after he'd been up for twenty-four hours. That's why I came over. To make sure he didn't fall asleep. Of course, you ruined that by drugging all of us."

She shrugged as best she could. "I guess if you could stay awake, the coven could perform the binding spell on you instead."

A glimmer of hope flashed in his eyes. "You swear this is true?"

She nodded, which was hard to do lying on metal. "I swear. They're all ready to go in the morning. Just waiting on Eamon. I don't see any reason they couldn't perform it on you. Please, let me go and I'll make sure it happens. Plus, I swear on my aunts' lives that I won't tell a soul what you did. We'll just forget about it. What do you say?"

He looked doubtful. "I don't know."

She tried a different tack. "I can only imagine how hard it's been for all of the men in your family with these difficult, unreliable powers. You deserve better. Let me help you get the power that should already rightfully be yours."

Slowly, he began to nod. "It should be. The Underwoods were one of the most powerful families in all of Scotland once upon a time. Revered and respected. All of that stolen away by the weakening of our bloodlines."

"We'll make it right again, I promise." She was running out of options. If he didn't agree to this, she had no idea what to do next.

Could she get to the grove of the oracles? This was

not the best situation to be in for her first solo try, but it was better than giving up. Maybe she could stay there until it was safe to return to the mortal realm. She wasn't sure how that worked, but what other alternative did she have?

He straightened, his eyes narrowing. "I don't believe you. I mean, I do believe you about Eamon and the witches and the binding spell, but you like Eamon too much. You'll grass me out to him the first chance you get."

"I won't, I swear. I like living a lot more than I like him."

Callum didn't look like he believed her. "I'm sticking with my plan."

Anger and desperation bubbled up inside her. "I hope my blood kills you, then, because that's what you deserve." She took a deep breath, preparing to scream her lungs out just in case there was someone around to hear her.

Before she could get a sound out, the doors flew open, sending the stainless steel tray and all the implements flying, and Eamon appeared, Seamus right behind him.

"Tru!"

"Eamon! He's going to kill me!"

Callum spun around. "What the—" He dodged as Eamon threw a punch, skittering around to the other side of the metal table. "Don't you understand what I'm trying to do could help us all? She could hold the answer we've been looking for."

"Killing Tru isn't the answer to anything," Eamon snarled.

Callum grabbed an implement off the stainless-steel tray and threw it.

"Look out!" Seamus yelled.

Eamon ducked, then went after Callum, quickly latching hold of Callum's shirt.

Callum desperately tried to get free. "You're ruining everything, you bloody fool."

"You're the fool." Eamon pulled Callum in and punched him across the jaw, knocking his cousin to the ground.

Seamus ran over to her and started unbuckling her restraints. "I'm so sorry, lass. I'm so sorry. We had no idea ..."

Eamon undid the other restraint. A vein in his forehead seemed to be throbbing, and there was an angry storm in his eyes, but he said nothing.

"How did you find me?"

Eamon answered her. "We woke up, and you and Cal were gone. So were my keys. Eejit took my car. Good thing he did, because it has a tracker on it."

She exhaled and was finally able to move as the restraints came off. "Thank you for getting here when you did. I'm so glad it wasn't a second later."

Eamon looked at his uncle. "Use those to tie him up."

Seamus nodded. "Aye."

"So am I, lass." Then Eamon pulled Tru into his arms and kissed her.

40

Eamon had never felt rage like this before in his life. Tru had nearly been killed, and it was his fault. He'd *known* Cal was up to something, but he'd let himself be persuaded otherwise because the man was family and for so long, family was all that Eamon had had.

But Tru had almost paid the price.

As it was, she was probably so traumatized by what Cal had done that she'd never want anything to do with any of them ever again.

He wouldn't blame her, either. Cal's actions had tainted the lot of them.

He glanced over to where Cal was unconscious on the floor, trussed like a pig thanks to Seamus, then he looked at his uncle. "What are we going to do with him?"

"Call the police." Seamus sighed. "I know you don't want to, lad. I know you think it means telling them about your own troubles, but they don't need to know that."

Eamon wasn't sure that was accurate.

Tru returned from the bathroom where she'd gone to splash water on her face.

Eamon couldn't believe he'd almost lost her. He'd

have had to kill Callum if that had happened. "Are you all right? How do you feel?"

She nodded. "I'm fine. Mad. Shaken up. Possibly bruised." One side of her mouth quirked up in amusement. "But also very grateful that you thought enough of your car to put a tracker on it."

He shook his head. "Are you making jokes?"

She smiled. "Yeah, I am. Because I'm happy to be alive. Happy you two made it here before anything really bad happened. Happy nothing happened to either of you. I actually have a lot of reasons to be happy right now."

"But he would have killed you."

She glanced down at Cal. "Maybe. But part of me was a little curious to see what my blood would have done to him. After all, he was going on the assumption that I hadn't yet become an oracle. That's what he needed. The blood of an unturned oracle. Said it would fix all his troubles. Said he'd been researching it all his life."

Seamus nodded. "Eamon told me you made the transition, which I'm glad of. I don't doubt Callum thought he'd found what he needed in you. All he did was research and study our genealogy. We always thought he was looking for a cure for Eamon. Never thought it had more to do with himself."

Tru took a deep breath and wrapped her arms around herself. "What are you going to do with him?"

Eamon thought she ought to have some say in that. "What do you want us to do with him?"

"I think he should be turned over to the police. For everyone's safety. I told him about Pandora and the binding ceremony, so letting him go wouldn't be a good idea. Besides, I'd personally feel better if he were locked up."

"We're not letting him go," Eamon said. "No chance of that."

Tru shot him a knowing look. "But you think talking to the police would mean revealing your own power?"

Seamus put his hands on his hips. "I told him that wouldn't need to happen."

"I agree," Tru said. "That's not a detail you'd have to share."

Eamon thought the police would definitely want to know about that, but he pulled his phone out anyway. It didn't really matter what he had to say to the police. Cal needed to be punished for what he'd done. And he needed to be kept away from Tru. The law was the best way to go about that. "Your aunts are going to hate me for what happened."

Tru snorted. "You saved me from being murdered. If not for you, I'd be dead right now. I'm pretty sure my aunts are going to think you're the best thing since ouzo."

Eamon doubted that. It was at least partially his fault that Tru had been put in that position at all. He called the non-emergency police number.

"Nocturne Falls Sheriff's Department," a woman's voice answered.

"I'd like to report ..." He wasn't sure what he was reporting, actually. "A thwarted kidnapping, I guess. Can you send someone to the Underwood Funeral Home?"

"What kind of kidnapping?"

"My cousin kidnapped and threatened to kill a friend of mine, but my uncle and I intervened in time to save her. He was holding her at the funeral home. We have him here now. This is Eamon Underwood. My uncle Seamus owns the place."

"I see. I have a patrol car in the area. I'll get someone right out there."

"Thank you." Eamon hung up. "They're sending someone."

"Good," Seamus said. "Now, how about we go upstairs and wait for them in the reception parlor like civilized folk? The prep room is no place to stay."

"Prep room?" Tru looked around. "So this is where the bodies are ... prepped?"

Eamon nodded.

She pointed to the table she'd been strapped to. "Have there been bodies on that?"

He nodded again. "Aye."

"And ... bodily fluids?"

"That, too. But I promise you, it's thoroughly cleaned and sanitized in between uses." She looked a wee bit green around the gills. "You still all right?"

She swallowed and nodded. "Yes. But now I really, really want a shower."

It took the three of them an hour to talk to the police and give their statements. During that time, Callum, who Eamon had hauled upstairs and deposited onto the floor of the reception room, had come around.

He'd had nothing to say for himself, refusing to talk other than to mutter incoherently under his breath. Eamon wasn't interested in his cousin's excuses anyway.

Callum was now in the back of a police car. He'd been patted down and handcuffed, after which Eamon's car keys had been returned to him by the responding deputy, a man who surprisingly had no hourglass over his head. His badge read Lafitte.

Eamon was stressed, tired, and ready to go home. But he had to ask. "Forgive me for being so straightforward, but what kind of supernatural are you?"

The man jotted something down on the tablet he was using to fill out the report. "Vampire. What are you?"

That made sense. The man was technically dead. "I'm all sorts," Eamon answered. "But not enough of one to put a name on it."

"Which is why your cousin thought Ms. Kouris's blood could help him. Got it." The deputy pulled a card from his pocket and handed it to Eamon. "You need anything, you call me, now, you hear?"

Eamon took the card. "Thank you. We can go, then?"

Lafitte secured his stylus and closed the tablet's cover. "You can. I'll be by the house later to pick up the cake and candy your cousin used to drug you. We'll need that for evidence."

"Of course. Thanks again." Eamon went back inside, where Seamus and Tru were waiting on him. "We're cleared to go."

Seamus pushed to his feet. "I'll lock up. You get Tru back to the house."

"All right." He walked her to the car and opened the door.

She didn't get in. Just stared at the vehicle. "Do you think he put me in the trunk or the back seat?"

"I don't know. I don't really want to think about it, either."

"Yeah, neither do I." She got in.

He closed her door, then went around to the other side and got behind the wheel. He started the car, the engine's low rumble vibrating through him but without the satisfaction it usually made him feel.

Tru looked small and tired. He wished there were more he could do for her. A way to erase what she'd just experienced. She offered him a quick smile. "This thing must have quite an engine in it."

He nodded at her comment but said nothing. The thought that Callum had probably tossed her into the trunk without a care made him sick. He felt the muscles in his jaw tightening as his anger returned.

She put her hand on his arm. Her touch was warm and comforting, and he hadn't realized how much he craved it until that moment. "I know you blame yourself for this. At least partially. I want you to stop that right now."

"It's not that easy."

"Sure it is. After all, it's much more my fault than it is yours."

He squinted at her. "How do you figure that?"

"Because if I had an hourglass over me like everyone else, you never would have paid attention to me. Right?"

"That's not your fault."

"Okay, maybe it's not my *fault*, but it's the reason I caught your eye. You'd have ignored me otherwise."

He opened his mouth to answer but then closed it again and thought through what she'd said. "I don't think I could have ignored you if I'd wanted to."

She smiled. "You mean the drunk girl looking for Nemo in your backyard was really that captivating?"

He laughed, despite his mood. "Aye. Captivating is a very good word. And you forgot the part about her being beautiful."

Tru blushed and looked away to stare through the windshield. "Lack of sleep is making you loopy. You'd better get us home."

"I really am very sorry about all of this."

"I know you are," she said. "But I don't hold you one bit responsible. And neither will my aunts when I explain it to them."

He pulled out of the parking lot. "I hope they understand." He really did not want to be on their bad side.

"They will. Aunt Delly isn't about to let anything come between her and your uncle. I promise, you'll both come out of this heroes."

"I don't need to be a hero. I'm just glad you're okay."

She reached over and touched his arm again. "So am I. And there's a silver lining."

He frowned. "There is?"

"I now know the prediction about me meeting death had nothing to do with you or becoming an oracle. It was all about Callum. And now it's behind me. I don't have to worry about it anymore."

"I suppose that's true." He felt oddly relieved about that. Still not happy it had been Cal's doing but glad she was truly safe.

"Which means it's now time to focus on you."

He sighed and shook his head. "I was asleep because of the drugs he used on us. Speaking of, the deputy is coming by to pick up the stuff from Delaney's, since it's now evidence. But as for me, they'll have to postpone the spell until it's been a full twenty-four hours that I've been awake."

"Maybe. We should ask Pandora, though. Being drugged and being asleep aren't exactly the same thing. And you weren't out for that long." She looked at the time. "It's only a little after one in the morning. So maybe a couple hours? Might not matter."

"We'll ask. But if they don't come up with that fifth element, my lack of sleep will be the least of our problems."

Tru nodded. "That's something else I want to talk to my aunts about."

"You think they know what aether is?"

Tru hesitated. "I think they know people who might know. And that's all I can say about that."

41

Tru wasn't that surprised to find her aunts still up when she walked into the house. "I have Eamon with me." She gestured to him, which was obviously unnecessary, as he was standing next to her.

They were both reclined in their chairs in the living room, watching an episode of *Columbo* and looking very comfy. There were a handful of cats hanging out with them. Most of them were sleeping.

Aunt Delly turned the sound down. "What's going on? You both look like something's happened."

Tru nodded. "It has."

She nudged Eamon, then walked around to sit on the couch. He joined her, looking very much like he thought he was about to stand trial. Tru chose her words carefully. "First of all, the good news. Eamon saved my life tonight. Seamus helped, too."

Her aunts gasped.

Tru held up her hands. "There's more good news. The death prediction isn't something I have to worry about anymore. It's been dealt with."

Her aunts still didn't look happy. Aunt Cleo's gaze held all kinds of suspicion. She pursed her lips. "Start at the beginning."

Tru did. With Eamon's help, she told her aunts everything that had happened, right up to her and Eamon walking into the house.

"We should call a doctor," Aunt Delly said. "All three of you should be looked over. You have no idea what kind of sedative he used or if there could be any lasting effects. And you might be injured, Tru."

"I feel fine," Tru promised. "I'll probably be sore in the morning, but considering what could have happened, I'm in great shape."

Aunt Cleo put her hand over her mouth for a moment. "I am so glad you went through the ceremony when you did."

"Me, too," Tru said.

Aunt Delly used the lever on the side of her chair to lower the footrest. "Are you sure you're all right?"

"I swear it," Tru said.

Aunt Delly got up. "Then I might just run next door and check on Seamus."

Eamon nodded. "I'm sure he'd appreciate that."

"Cleo, you don't mind, do you?" Aunt Delly asked.

"No, go on." Aunt Cleo put her footrest down, as well. "This is very disturbing news. But it could have been much, much worse." As Aunt Delly went out the front door, Aunt Cleo looked directly at Eamon. "Our family owes you a debt of gratitude."

He shook his head. "My family caused this issue. You owe me nothing."

"We'll agree to disagree about that."

"There is something Eamon needs help with," Tru said.

"Anything," came Aunt Cleo's quick reply.

"The witches are missing one element to complete the necessary ingredients for the binding spell. Something called aether. Do you have any idea what that is and how they could get some?"

"Aether? Really?" Aunt Cleo seemed surprised.

Tru nodded, hoping that was a good thing.

Aunt Cleo smiled. "I know about it. And I think I have a way to get some. But I need to be sure." She looked at Eamon again. "When do you need to know? And when will you need the aether?"

"I have to talk to Pandora and explain about being out for the few hours that I was drugged. If that's not an issue, then I suppose I'll need it by sometime this morning. Whenever they plan to cast the spell."

Aunt Cleo got up. "All right. Leave me to work on that. In the meantime, Tru, you make sure he doesn't fall asleep. I'll text you as soon as I have an answer."

Tru and Eamon stood. For the first time since he'd burst through the door at the funeral home, he looked at ease.

"Thanks, Aunt Cleo." Tru gave her a knowing smile. Aunt Cleo was going to talk to the oracles in the grove, Tru was sure of it.

Her aunt hugged her, pulling her close. "I'm so glad you're okay."

"Me, too."

Aunt Cleo let her go and hugged Eamon next, surprising him as much as Tru, judging by the look on his face. "Thank you for saving her."

Eamon hesitated, then hugged Cleo back. "I'm glad I was able to."

Aunt Cleo released him. "You'd better check on your uncle. No telling what Del's doing to him over there."

Tru and Eamon exchanged a look, then both burst out laughing. Eamon nodded. "We're off."

Tru shook her head as they left the house. "I'm not sure your uncle cares what my aunt is doing to him."

Eamon snorted. "You might be right about that." They went up the front porch steps together, but Eamon paused, his hand on the doorknob. "Do you really think your aunt can get the aether? I'm not doubting her, it's just that Pandora seemed so uncertain about it, and Cleo acted like it was no big deal."

Tru didn't want to make promises she couldn't keep, but neither did she want to break the confidence bestowed upon her by the other oracles. "If anyone can, it's Cleopatra Kouris. My aunt can be a force of nature when she wants to be. And we have ... connections that I can't really tell you about. You'll just have to trust me."

"I do trust you. Maybe more than I've ever trusted anyone."

She smiled at him. "I feel the same way about you."

He started to open the door, but she put her hand over his, stopping him. He looked confused. "You don't want to go in?"

She shook her head. "Not until you kiss me."

Just the words sent a ripple of anticipation through him. "But we're not supposed to be in contact."

"If you can kiss me when I'm lying on a prep table in a funeral home, you can kiss me standing on your front porch. Besides, we already know that Callum was the real danger to me. Not you. And that's all about to be behind you."

He hesitated, like he was trying to decide what to do. Then he let go of the doorknob, threaded his fingers into her hair and planted his mouth on hers.

She gladly leaned into him, happy to be alive, happy to be near him, and happy that, very soon, he would be free to live the kind of life he'd always wanted. A life that would now include her.

At least, she assumed it would. Or had she assumed too much?

When he finally released her and tipped his head toward the door, he said, "Ready to go in now?"

"In a second. First, I have to ask you a question."

"Anything."

"Once you're free of seeing death over people, does that mean you're going to want to, I don't know, sow all the wild oats you never got a chance to?"

His eyes narrowed like he was trying to figure out what she meant. "I'm not quite sure. I'll want to go out more, that I know."

"Out with me? Or out with ... other women?"

He smiled, then started to laugh. "Och, you want to

know if I'm going to date my way through Nocturne Falls, aye?"

She pursed her lips. "Aye."

He kissed her again. "Dinna fash, lass. That wild oat has been sown, and I'm very happy with what's sprouted."

While the kettle did its thing, Eamon stood in the kitchen and texted Pandora at 5:30 a.m. Probably still too early, but he was tired of waiting.

Tru had fallen asleep on the couch. Nemo was curled around her head. Uncle Seamus was still in his chair, also asleep, with Yardy nestled in between his legs. Delphina was in Eamon's chair. She was snoring softly.

He sent Pandora a simple message. *Possible complication. Call/text when you can.*

Fifteen minutes later, she texted back. Perhaps it hadn't been too early after all. *Will call in a few. Need coffee first.*

A few turned out to be another fifteen minutes, which was fine. In that time, he had another cup of tea. He'd had so many he'd lost track. He answered the call, already dreading what she might tell him, but if there had to be a delay, so be it. "Good morning."

"Good morning. How was your night?"

He hesitated as he walked toward the front of the house so he wouldn't wake anyone. "I'm not even sure where to start."

"That doesn't sound good."

"Aye, it wasn't." Then he thought about kissing Tru and

smiled. He stepped outside and sat on the bench. "Although it wasn't all bad, either. My cousin kidnapped and nearly murdered Tru, but my uncle and I got to her in time. But that's where the complication comes in. My cousin only managed to kidnap Tru because he drugged us all with sedative-laced sweets. Don't know what kind of sedative."

There was no response from Pandora.

"Are you still there?" The sky was just starting to lighten toward the horizon. Day would be upon them soon.

"I am. Just ... processing. Wow. I'm sure there are more details, but you can share those later. If you like. So you were technically asleep from being drugged?"

"Aye. I was out for a couple of hours."

"But other than those hours, you were awake?"

"That's right."

"You should be fine. I mean, it's not ideal, but we're probably going to have to push the time back anyway, because as of 3 a.m. last night, we still didn't have a viable source for aether. I haven't checked in with Alice Bishop yet. It's possible she's found some but just hadn't let us know yet. If anyone can find it, it's her."

"About that," Eamon started. "Tru's Aunt Cleo is working on it, too. Tru seems confident her aunt will come through."

"Really? That would be amazing. I guess I shouldn't be so surprised. Oracles have roots that go deep into history, and aether is a very old element. So old we don't really consider it an element anymore. I've never used it for anything, and I've done some complicated spellcasting. But with this kind of intense magic, it takes an incredible amount of power. I mean, we're talking about removing parts of you, essentially."

He frowned. He hadn't heard it put that way before. "Just for my own information, how much is this going to hurt?"

She sighed into the phone. "I don't know. I've never participated in a binding spell like this, although I have helped with a powerful spell to bring *out* supernatural powers. My guess is that you're definitely going to feel it. I don't see how you couldn't. If there's an upside, it's that as tired as you are, you may just pass out."

He nodded. "Good to know. Is there anything else I can do to prepare myself?"

"Nothing I can think of. Oh, maybe don't eat breakfast. In case you get sick during the binding spell."

That was a comforting thought.

"And also, if you can make sure Cleo lets us know about the aether as soon as possible, that would be great. It's really the missing link at this point."

"And if she can't find it? And if Alice can't, either?"

"Then we'll just go to Plan B."

He exhaled in relief. "Brilliant. I was worried there wasn't another option. What's Plan B?"

She hesitated. "It doesn't actually exist yet, but we'll come up with something."

He closed his eyes. He should have known. "I should let you get to it, then."

"Talk to you soon." Pandora hung up.

He put his phone on the bench beside him and stared out at the street, into the darkness. It was quiet and peaceful, and he could almost imagine he was normal at this hour.

He doubted Cleo was up or had any information for him yet. He'd wait until Tru was awake, then let her talk to her aunt.

Instead, he contented himself to just be. The air was still and cool, and the approaching dawn had begun to wake the birds, which were now singing the day into exis-tence. Up and down the street, porch lights flickered off, alerted by the increasing brightness that they were no longer needed.

A soft *thap thap thap* reached his ears. He glanced to the right and saw a jogger coming down the street. An hourglass hovered over the man's head.

Eamon dropped his gaze to the lawn. Was it really possible that in a matter of hours, he might never have to see one again?

It was almost too much to hope for.

Maybe he should go in. He was about to get up when the door opened quietly and Tru slipped outside.

"Morning," she whispered.

"Morning." He moved his phone out of the space beside him. "Sit."

"I fed the cats. They were both hanging around by their dishes as soon as they realized I was awake."

"Thanks."

She took a seat. "You haven't been sleeping out here, have you?"

He shook his head. "Talking to Pandora. If your aunt can't find a way to get some aether, Pandora says they'll have to switch to Plan B."

"What's Plan B?"

"I don't know. And neither did Pandora, but she promised they'd come up with something."

Tru reached over and squeezed his hand. "My aunt will come through."

"You seem very sure about that."

"I am. Because I know where she's going to find out about the aether, and I promise you, it's a good place. Filled with people who will know."

She seemed so sure, he just nodded.

She looked at him. "Are you ready for today?"

"I have been ready for this my entire life."

"I guess you have been. I hope it goes really well. And that it's not too hard on you."

He glanced over. "You make it sound like you're not going to be there."

"I wasn't sure what the protocol was on that."

He thought a moment. "I'm not either, actually. But I'd like you to be there, if it's allowed. My uncle and your aunts, too. Lucien will be."

"Then I see no reason the rest of us can't join. If you want us, we're there."

"That's settled then." He studied her for a moment. Even after what she'd been through with Callum and how little sleep she'd had, she was still the most beautiful woman he could imagine. It seemed fitting to him that she was Greek, because the word "goddess" suited her perfectly.

She caught him watching her. "What? Do I have bedhead?" She touched her hair, running her fingers through it. "I guess it would be couch head. I didn't mean to fall asleep. Sorry about that."

"You have nothing to apologize for. Not after what Cal put you through."

"Shame he ruined all those perfectly good truffles."

Eamon snorted. Tru's sense of right and wrong was really something remarkable. "I guess I should let you go home at some point. I'd like to take a shower before this spell business, and you mentioned wanting to do the same."

"I do."

But neither of them got up.

A moment later, he realized Cleo was coming across the lawn toward them. "Morning. Del still in there?"

"Passed out in Eamon's chair," Tru answered.

Cleo shook her head. "Of course she is."

"Any luck with the aether?" Eamon asked. He was too tired and too anxious to pretend anything else interested him.

Cleo nodded. "Yes. I was able to get the answers I needed."

"From where I think?" Tru asked.

"Yes," Cleo said.

"I knew it," Tru said softly.

Eamon could barely contain himself. "So you have the aether?"

"No, but I know where to get some." She didn't look happy, which made no sense to him. This was good news.

"Where?"

She glanced at the house. "You've already got some. Well, not you exactly. But according to what I learned, there is aether in your house. Which makes so much sense, in light of the reading I did for you."

Eamon shook his head. "I don't understand. Please, tell me what you mean in plain English."

Cleo took a deep breath. "Aether is the very spirit of living things. It's an almost undefinable element, but to say that it is life itself isn't far off."

"And that exists in my house?" Eamon still didn't get it.

"In our house, too, but yes," Cleo said. "You have some. In the form of a small, orange cat." She smiled. "Nemo."

43

"Hold on," Tru said, a cold chill settling over her. "You don't mean you're going to offer Nemo up as some kind of sacrifice, do you?"

Eamon threw his hands up. "I am not doing that. Sorry. But if this requires the loss of life, especially that one, I'm out."

Aunt Cleo put her hands on her head. "No, no, no. Do you really think I'd do that?" She rolled her eyes. "Cats have nine lives. Nemo will only have to donate one of them."

"Still sounds like you're asking him to give up a life," Eamon said.

"I am," Aunt Cleo said. "But not the way you think."

"Cats don't really have nine lives, though. Do they?" Tru thought she probably looked as confused as she felt.

"Not nine *real* lives," Aunt Cleo said. "But they have a good portion of aether within them. It's that extra something that makes cats cats." She took a moment. "Aether was revered as an element in ancient Greece, which explains a lot about why Greek people love cats. And why the temples were always filled with them. You're just going to have to trust me on this. It's very hard to explain."

Eamon was still frowning. "I guess the Egyptians knew, too."

Aunt Cleo nodded. "They did."

Tru needed more information. "How do we get this aether out of Nemo without hurting him? Will he understand? It's not like he can give his consent. How do we know he's going to be okay with it?"

Eamon nodded. "I want to know, too, if it could hurt him in the future. If having less aether means he'll be more prone to sickness or injury, then ..."

"Does it have to be Nemo?" Tru asked.

Aunt Cleo shook her head. "No, it doesn't have to be, but considering this is Eamon's future we're talking about fixing, it seems right that it should be." She leaned against the porch railing and looked at Eamon. "Do you remember how your future changed when Nemo crawled into your lap?"

"Aye."

Aunt Cleo nodded. "I believe that was a sign that Nemo will be just fine with making the donation. He's only giving one life's worth. He'll have eight portions left. It won't cause him any harm."

"Okay," Tru said. "But how do we get that one life's worth from him?"

"I can extract it," Aunt Cleo said. "Not only was I taught how, but I was assured the donor wouldn't feel a thing."

"I must be daft," Eamon said. "But I feel like I ought to have a chat with the lad about this first."

"You probably should," Aunt Cleo said. "Cats are incredibly perceptive. I'd wager he'll understand more than you think."

He nodded. "All right. But before I do that, I should call Pandora and let her know. She's waiting to hear." He picked up his phone, then frowned. "I guess I'll do that inside. I need to plug in. My battery's about to die."

He stood up and gestured to the bench while looking at Aunt Cleo. "Please, take my seat. But if you could give me about ten minutes, then come in and help me explain to my uncle what's going to happen to Nemo, that would be grand, because I don't think he's going to care for it too much."

Aunt Cleo settled onto the bench beside Tru. "I'd be happy to."

"Thank you." Eamon went inside to make his call.

When the door closed, Tru leaned in. "You went to the grove?"

"I did. They knew exactly what aether was and where to get it, and they taught me how to pull a small portion of it from a cat." Aunt Cleo shook her head. "They were surprised. They said it's been a very long time since anyone's used aether for anything."

"And you swear it won't hurt Nemo?"

"Sweetheart, I wouldn't want him hurt any more than you or Eamon would. He'll be fine. If the oracles had told me differently, I would have informed you and Eamon that there was no aether to be had. I promise you, Nemo is going to be fine. And this fulfills what I saw. Nemo saves Eamon's life. I just never imagined it would be so literal."

"Neither did I," Tru said. "Kind of amazing, though, isn't it? That things have come together the way they have?"

"The fates know what they're doing. Maybe someday you'll get to meet them, too. Once in a very rare while, they summon us to the grove to help them make a decision. It's only happened once in my lifetime so far, but you never know."

"That would be very cool."

The door swung open, and a flustered Aunt Delly stood there, glaring at her sister. "Have you lost your mind? Eamon said Nemo has to give up his life for the binding spell."

From deep within the house, Eamon called out, "That is *not* what I said."

Aunt Cleo chuckled softly. "I'm coming in to explain right now, but listen to me, Del. He won't be hurt. This is all straight from the grove."

Aunt Delly blinked. "Really?"

"Really." Aunt Cleo marched past her sister.

Tru followed. She could hear Eamon and his uncle arguing.

Seamus was clearly upset. He was standing in the middle of the living room, clutching Yardy to his chest. "You're not doing it. I'll not let you hurt that wee lad. And don't look at Yardy, either. He's already lost a leg. If that doesn't put him down a life or two already, then I don't know what does."

"Uncle Seamus," Eamon said from the other side of the couch. "Nemo isn't going to be hurt. I swear it."

Aunt Cleo came to stand beside Eamon. "Seamus, he won't be hurt. On my life, I promise it."

Tru and Aunt Delly caught up with them as Seamus frowned even harder. He looked confused and ready to fight. "How does an animal give up its life and not be hurt? Are you telling me witchcraft can do that?"

Aunt Cleo shook her head. "It's not witchcraft. It's oracle magic. I'm simply going to extract a small portion of aether from Nemo. He won't notice or miss it. But it will allow the binding spell to be cast. And it will save your nephew's life. Yours, too. And Tru's. Because once Eamon's reaper powers are gone, he won't drain the life forces of those around him."

"Plus," Aunt Delly said, "Cleo saw Nemo's part in this foretold when she looked at Eamon's future. Nemo was destined for this." She went around the couch to stand beside Seamus. "None of us would hurt an animal, Seamus. You must know that."

A little of the steam went out of Seamus. "You all promise me he won't be hurt."

Aunt Cleo put her hand on her heart. It glowed softly for a moment. "I promise on my life as an oracle, Nemo will come to no harm."

Tru had to learn how to do that.

Aunt Delly repeated the action, her hand radiant over

her heart. "I promise, too. My sister knows how to get the aether without Nemo even realizing it."

Seamus sighed. "I dinna like it. But if the lad won't feel it, and it'll save Eamon's life, then do what you must."

Eamon seemed to untense. "Thank you." He glanced at Tru. "I haven't called Pandora yet."

"Go on. We'll talk to him a little more. Make sure he understands completely."

"Thank you." Eamon took off for the upstairs.

Tru offered Seamus a big smile. "How about I put the kettle on while my aunts explain it a little more?"

"Aye," Seamus said. "This is definitely the kind of thing I need tea for."

While Seamus and her aunts took seats, Tru went into the kitchen. She filled the kettle, then flipped the switch to turn it on, hoping that was all that was required.

That's when she saw that the cake slices and box of truffles from Delaney's Delectables were still on the kitchen table. She wasn't sure how those hadn't been thrown away yet. Then she remembered that Eamon had told her the police needed them for evidence.

The shopping bag Callum had brought them home in was still on the counter. She slipped on a pair of kitchen gloves so she wouldn't add any fingerprints, and put the treats back into the bag, then tucked that away at the far end of the counter.

She wanted to be sure no one ate them by accident, but that didn't stop her from feeling a little sad that such tasty things were going to waste. They might have been laced with dangerous sedatives, but they still smelled heavenly.

Just to be extra safe, she found a marker in one of the drawers and wrote Do Not Eat on the shopping bag. Hopefully that would do it until someone came to pick them up.

When Eamon had recovered from the binding spell, they were definitely taking a trip to Delaney's. Tru deserved to sample some safe varieties. It was the only way, she reasoned, to be sure chocolate didn't become some kind of trauma trigger for her.

Going to Delaney's was just an exercise in good mental health.

As soon as Deputy Lafitte had come by to pick up the evidence from Delaney's, Eamon had taken Nemo upstairs.

Now they sat on his bed. Eamon searching for words. He'd never had a heart-to-heart conversation with any animal, let alone a cat. But here he was, facing Nemo, and trying to choose the best way to tell the wee lad what was about to be expected of him.

"So, Nemo. Let me start by saying that I'm grateful for your involvement in introducing me to Tru. I can't be sure that wasn't you doing your part in saving my life already, but there's a very wise woman downstairs who's told me otherwise."

Nemo was near the foot of the bed, swatting at a loose thread on the duvet. Eamon had a feeling the cat wasn't paying attention in the slightest.

He went on anyway. "This woman is going to take something called aether from you. Just a wee portion. Enough to make it possible for me to have a very necessary spell cast over me. It'll fix me up, you see. Give me the kind of normal life I've never had before."

He thought about having that kind of life. It still

seemed like a far-off dream. "I'm really looking forward to that, I have to tell you."

Nemo lay down and stared up at Eamon, his big green-gold cat eyes just gazing.

"You're a cracking lad, you really are. I never thought I'd have a cat, but I'm glad I do. You're grand company. Clever as the day is long. And about the most handsome cat I've ever seen. But mostly I want you to know that if you do this for me, give me this aether, I swear to you that I will protect you with everything I've got for the rest of your life."

Eamon sniffed, not sure why this was making him emotional. He was glad he was alone. "I promise that if you ever need anything, I will provide it. Nothing will be too good for you. There won't be a vet bill too high. I'll sell my car if I have to. That's how serious I am about taking care of you."

Nemo rolled over and stretched a paw toward Eamon.

Eamon took the paw, holding it in his hand. "I pray it doesn't hurt you. I've been told it won't, but if it does, I'm sorry and I'll understand if you're mad at me. I'll buy you a nice treat. Some fish or something, all right? I'll drive you to the pet store myself and let you pick out anything you like."

Nemo got up, walked over to Eamon, and plopped down in his lap. Eamon decided that was as close to approval as he was going to get. He scratched the cat behind the ears. "Thank you, lad."

He sat a minute longer. He knew there were a lot of people downstairs waiting on him and Nemo. Eamon had already met the women who'd be casting the spell. Lucien was with them, too. But the moment he carried the cat down, there would be no turning back. The wheels would be in motion.

So Eamon spent a few seconds more just giving Nemo some love and praying everything would be okay.

For both of them.

At last, he scooped the cat into his arms and took him downstairs, telling him the whole time what a good lad he was. Pandora; her mother, Corette; her two sisters, Marigold and Charisma; and the elder witch named Alice were all in the backyard, preparing for the spell. Lucien was out there, too, standing a ways off and letting them work. But Seamus, Cleo, Delphina, and Tru were still in the living room.

Cleo got to her feet and faced Eamon as he entered. "All ready?"

Eamon nodded, then leaned down and kissed Nemo on the head and whispered, "It'll be all right, lad."

"He's going to be just fine," Cleo said. She came around and took him from Eamon's arms. "Aren't you, sweet boy?"

She carried Nemo to the kitchen counter and set him on it. As she gave him a few treats, Seamus, Delphina, and Tru came to stand around her. Eamon joined them, his entire body tense with worry.

Cleo placed her hands on Nemo's sides, petting him gently and whispering sweet words to him. She closed her eyes, and the oracle radiance shone out of her. She opened her eyes and the radiance traveled down her arms, through her hands and onto Nemo.

He sounded like he was purring. Eamon hoped that was true.

Cleo drew her glowing fingers up his sides, past his neck, and over his head. As she did, the luminance traveled with her hands, leaving Nemo's body as it had been before she'd touched him. When she released him, the glow left her, too, except for a sphere that remained between her palms. It shimmered and sparkled with a fluid movement that looked more like water than flames.

She held her hands a few inches apart, holding the ball of light between them. "I have the aether."

"That's it? That's all there was to it?" Eamon exhaled, completely relieved. She'd been right. Nemo hadn't acted like he'd noticed a thing. He was still sniffing around the counter for more treats.

Cleo nodded. "Now to add it to the binding circle."

They all walked outside, letting Cleo lead. A circle had indeed been set up in the backyard on an open patch of grass between two tall oaks. The circle was made of five small hammered-copper bowls positioned at equal distances from each other.

Eamon kept his gaze low. The witches all had hourglasses over them, he knew that much, but he didn't need to see them more than once. He glanced at Lucien, but the reaper was watching the witches.

Cleo walked to the bowl in front of Alice, where she bent down and placed the aether into it. Inside the bowl, the orb of power glimmered and gleamed, rolling around but not losing its spherical shape or any of the matter contained within.

Alice stared at it in amazement. Then she raised her hands toward the other women in the circle. "I begin this circle with aether." She nodded at Cleo. "Well done, oracle."

"Thank you." Cleo came back to stand by her sister.

Eamon stepped forward.

Alice met his gaze and gestured toward the center of the circle. "Please, take your place so that we may complete the circle."

He walked into the center and sat down. They'd already told him he'd probably end up on the ground anyway, so best to start there.

Alice nodded at Marigold.

Marigold picked up a small cloth sack by her feet. "I extend this circle with earth." She tipped the sack into the bowl, filling it with rich, loamy soil.

Next to her was her mother, Corette. By her feet was a glass carafe. She poured water into her bowl. "I extend this circle with water."

Pandora was next. She held up a fan made of feathers that she'd had in her hands before putting it in the bowl by her feet. "I extend this circle with air."

Finally, there was Charisma. She knelt by her bowl and used a steel and flint to make sparks. The alcohol in the bowl ignited into dancing yellow flames. "I complete this circle with fire."

The women looked to Alice again.

From her pocket, Alice pulled a small ball of red silk cord, not much thicker than thread. She unwound a bit, wrapped the loose end around her hand, then carried the ball to Marigold and returned to her original spot.

Marigold repeated the action, passing the cord on to her mother. It made its way around the circle until the other end of the silk was in Alice's hand.

Somehow, there had been just enough to make it all the way around.

Alice held both ends in her right hand. "We come here to bind your powers, Eamon Underwood. Those dark and secret fragments that reside within your blood. With the elements to protect us, and silk to bind these broken and unwanted gifts, we begin."

Alice opened her hand so that the silk cord rested on her palm. It had become one continuous piece of thread, no break anywhere. She closed her eyes and reached her other hand out toward him and whispered words in Latin he didn't know.

Pain shot across his body, and for a moment, he couldn't breathe. He tried to open his mouth, but the pain was too great. Then a shadow left his body and floated toward Alice, taking most of the pain and his inability to breathe with it. Alice quickly looped the cord around the shadow and tied it off. It was so pale, it was hard to see.

An ache in his side remained. It felt like the cramp that came from running without warming up. He pressed his hand to it.

"Are you all right, Eamon?" Alice asked.

He nodded. "Fine." Whatever pain there was, he would gladly put up with it for the end result. The cramp was nothing he couldn't endure.

Marigold went next, pulling another shadow from him. This one was darker, with a hazy quality. This time the pain felt like fire on his skin. He exhaled, trying to cool the pain. Just as Alice had done, Marigold tied the shadow into the cord.

He couldn't see Corette, but he knew when she drew an ability out of him by the contraction that caused his leg to spasm in the worst charley horse he'd ever felt. He doubled over, clutching at his calf and gritting his teeth. He rolled to his side and stayed there, closing his eyes and willing himself to persevere.

Pain after pain went through his body as the darkest of his powers were called out of him. His body ached, his head throbbed, his muscles cramped. He breathed open-mouthed, his skin feverish and damp. Sweat trickled down his neck and back as images danced before his closed eyes. Nightmarish things. Dark devils and scowling faces, teeth bared.

He squeezed his eyes tighter until all the points of pain merged into one excruciating mass of anguish. He willed himself not to give in or give up. This was what he'd wanted. The freedom he'd craved.

Then everything went black.

45

"They're hurting him," Tru whispered. She couldn't bear it. She wanted to run to him and do ... something.

Aunt Cleo grabbed her hand like she'd read Tru's mind and thought she should hold her niece back. "They're not doing it intentionally."

Tru nodded, trying to convey that she understood, but she couldn't speak. It hurt to watch Eamon in so much pain. Every muscle in his body was taut with it, his face frozen in a grimace that was hard to see.

She wanted to comfort him. To help him bear the pain. She knew she couldn't, but the desire was strong.

The five women around him were doing their own sort of battle. Beads of sweat gleamed on their foreheads, and they strained to pull the dark powers from Eamon, making it plain that the more they took, the harder it became.

It was as if his body understood what was happening and was fighting back, trying to stop it. Maybe that was really what was going on. Maybe a battle was raging inside of him. Or maybe it was something else Tru didn't understand, but the amount of effort being exerted for Eamon's sake was staggering.

Even Lucien's brow was furrowed in concern.

Eamon let out a low groan, then went still, sprawled on the grass.

"He passed out," Tru said.

Alice, who'd taken the last shadow from him, went down on her knees. "We can do no more. We have bound as much as possible. The cord is full."

Tru looked closer at the red silk. What had once been a shiny length of cord was now dull and dirty and snarled with knots.

Pandora dropped to her knees as well. Her mother and sisters followed.

Tru started forward, but Alice put her hand up. "Don't touch us or the cord. The ceremony is not yet complete."

Tru stepped back between her aunts.

The women rested a bit more, then Alice stood up and gathered the cord, winding it into a tangled ball. It was twice the size it had been when she'd first taken it from her pocket.

"Now we rid these powers from this world permanently." She put the gathered mass of cord on the ground inside the circle but a little ways from Eamon, then picked up the bowl of earth and emptied the dirt onto the cord. She put the bowl back in the same spot before taking the bowl of fire next. She poured the flaming alcohol onto the dirt and silk cord. Both immediately began to burn.

She returned that bowl, then picked up the feather fan. She waved it over the fire, wafting air over those flames. They jumped higher, consuming the silk and earth as they crackled and sparked.

She backed away and went for the bowl of water. She stood nearby, waiting a few more moments, then used it to douse the fire. Nothing remained of the dirt and silk but a damp splotch of ash on the ground.

Once that bowl had been replaced, she took the bowl of aether in both hands and walked to Eamon's motionless form. He'd yet to move since he'd collapsed.

Alice stood over him. "Take this aether to fill the gaps. Let the truest power rise so that you might be whole once again, however that may be." She tipped the bowl and slowly poured the aether over him.

The liquid light spread over him like a blanket, stretching out across his form until he was completely covered.

Alice quickly went back to her place in the circle. She put the bowl down exactly where she'd gotten it. She stared at Eamon expectantly. The four other women stood once more, joining her in watching him.

In the midst of them, Eamon had begun to move. Writhe was perhaps a better word. His movements looked painful.

Tru clenched her hands, trying to stop herself from reacting. She wanted to do something, but she didn't know what would be allowed. Probably nothing. She made herself stay put. Eamon hadn't come this far just to have her mess things up.

The glow from the aether was starting to fade into

him, like he was absorbing it. He cried out, a low, guttural, snorting sound that, to Tru's ears, wasn't entirely human.

What on Earth was happening to him?

His back arched; his head went back as another low moan spilled out of him.

Tru forced herself to breathe.

Lucien took a step forward.

Seamus twisted his hands together. "Hang in there, lad."

Alice raised her hand in Seamus's direction and nodded as if to say not to worry, it would all be fine.

Tru clung to that hope, because no other outcome would be acceptable.

As the glow disappeared, darkness seemed to take its place. Eamon fell into shadow, which should have been impossible with the sun climbing higher in the sky, but he became harder to see.

His moaning increased.

"He's hurt," Tru said. "Do something."

Alice shook her head but didn't take her eyes off Eamon. "There is nothing to be done. His body must make sense of the abilities left within him. What is deemed dominant will emerge when it is ready."

Tru had a bad feeling about this. What kind of ability covered a person in shadow and made them hard to see? What kind of ability caused pain and suffering? She didn't understand it at all. "I should go to him," she whispered.

Aunt Delly squeezed her hand. "Not yet, Troula. Not yet."

Eamon cried out, louder this time. He moved, maybe onto his knees. Or all fours. It was hard to tell. Crackling sounds, like joints popping or bones snapping, filled the air.

Eamon's shape grew and changed, and his moans became soft snorts of air being forced out of his body.

Tru grabbed Aunt Cleo's hand again and held onto both of her aunts. Whatever was happening, she prayed it wasn't as bad as it sounded.

The shape within the circle no longer looked like Eamon. It didn't even look human. As a group, they stared. The shape increased in size.

The shadows began to fall away from Eamon, and Tru realized what she was looking at. She inhaled and her mouth stayed open. Around her, the others gasped, too. Like her, they probably couldn't believe what they were seeing.

An incredible beast stood in the circle now. A creature of myth and magic that shouldn't exist. Not the sleek, glossy hide. Not the dark, glistening horn. Not the hard, stamping hooves or the regal bearing.

Eamon had become a unicorn, black as night even to the horn protruding from his forehead. He was beautiful and a little frightening.

"Saints preserve us," Seamus said. "I thought it was just a myth."

Tru let go of her aunts' hands and stepped forward. "Eamon? Is that really you?"

The unicorn turned toward her, whuffing softly and nodding his head. His eyes shone with a light that Tru swore she recognized as Eamon.

It was hard not to stare. "Are you okay?"

Again, the unicorn nodded.

Tru looked at Seamus. "You knew he could do this?"

Seamus shook his head. "All I knew was that family legend says the Underwood men once had the ability to shift into this form. It's why we've been pursued by so many different kinds of creatures over the years. Why we fell in love with so many of them and why our bloodlines got so muddled."

He stared at Eamon. "I've never known any of us who could actually take the form, though. Never even heard of one. This is nothing short of miraculous, if you ask me."

Tru glanced at Alice. "Is this permanent?"

She nodded. "I see no reason why it wouldn't be."

"Did the aether cause this?"

"Perhaps," Alice said. "We took so many random fragments from him that we had to refill all those empty spaces with something that would take the place of them. The aether did its job. My belief is that this form always existed inside him but was too repressed by all the other bits. The aether may have given it the strength it needed. An ancient element might have very well allowed an ancient form to be reborn."

Tru looked up at Eamon. He was the most majestic

creature she'd ever seen. Ebony from head to hoof. "I didn't even know unicorns came in black."

"Neither did I," Seamus said. "But unicorns aren't just part of our family history. They're also the national animal of Scotland." He shrugged. "Maybe it's not so surprising after all that this is what he turned into."

Tru smiled and reached her hand toward Eamon. He nuzzled his nose into her palm, his skin like velvet. He bent his head, and her hand traveled higher, to the black horn. It was hard as bone and cool to the touch.

She just shook her head, stuck in a place somewhere between astonishment and bewilderment as she stared into his dark eyes. "Well, it's surprising to me."

46

Tru's hand stroking his face felt like heaven.

Eamon leaned into it, content to do nothing else but stand there and let her caress him.

He knew what he had become. He couldn't see himself, of course, but he understood the form he'd taken as easily as if he'd been transforming into it all his life. It felt that natural that he should be standing in the midst of these people as a unicorn.

Not only was he comfortable, but he'd never felt so complete, either. Or so full of contentment.

Some of that was most likely because he couldn't see an hourglass over anyone's head. He wasn't sure if that was a permanent change or not. He hoped so, but maybe it was just a unicorn thing.

He laughed, but it came out as a breathy, horsey snort. He was a *unicorn*.

The bloodlines had always been there, obviously, but they'd become a family myth. A tale to be told and passed down about what had once been.

He never thought he'd be the one to bring that form back.

Tru stared up at him, the look in her eyes something

he'd never seen before in anyone. She looked mesmerized. By him.

He held her gaze, wishing he could speak to her. She really was the most beautiful woman he'd ever known. He was glad she seemed all right with his transformation.

Uncle Seamus came up to her. "Careful now, lass. The beast has the power to hypnotize you."

Tru kept her unblinking gaze on Eamon, a dreamy little smile playing on her lips. "He does?"

Uncle Seamus nodded. "Aye." He peered closely at her. "Blast it, I think it's too late." He frowned at Eamon. "Stop mystifying the poor lass. She'll be helpless in a moment."

Eamon hadn't been aware being a unicorn meant he had any sort of special powers. It wasn't like that part had been talked about. At least not to him. Apparently, Seamus knew. Good thing, too.

Eamon backed away from Tru and bent his head, breaking eye contact. He might have felt comfortable being a unicorn, but he realized in that moment he wasn't sure how to *stop* being one. How did he transform back into himself?

He stamped a hoof against the ground in frustration. Not having a voice made this more difficult. How had he become a unicorn? He wasn't sure, because really, he just *had.* Maybe he could become human again the same way. By just imagining himself as human.

Worth a shot.

He squeezed his eyes shut and pictured himself in his human form. He felt a soft breeze, but not much else. When he opened his eyes, he looked down to see he was once again the Eamon Underwood he was used to seeing in the mirror.

He glanced around at the witches. The hourglasses were well and truly gone. He could have wept. But transforming into a unicorn still fascinated him. "That was unbelievable. Is that really how easy it is to change forms?"

He imagined himself as unicorn again, and just like that, he was.

Pandora lifted a finger. "Um, you might want to be careful—"

He pictured his human self again and immediately returned to that form. He staggered sideways, lightheaded and feeling as if the world had tipped ninety degrees. That might have been too much shifting too soon.

Uncle Seamus grabbed his arm and held him upright. "Easy now, lad."

Tru grabbed the other one. "Are you okay?"

"Just lightheaded," Eamon answered, hoping things would get back on an even keel before he tossed his biscuits.

Pandora nodded. "That's a lot of back and forth for someone who isn't used to it."

"I ken that now." Eamon exhaled as things slowly went right again. "I canna believe I'm a unicorn."

"Neither can I," Tru said.

"It's in our blood," Uncle Seamus said proudly. "Never thought you had enough of it in you, though. And now you've brought it back." He looked at Alice. "That aether's not going to wear out, is it, now?"

Alice stepped forward. "No. The aether did its job of refilling the power gaps. It has permanently bonded itself to the truest and most potentially potent abilities left behind. The aether made his new form possible. It will always be with him."

Eamon looked at her. "So, really ... Nemo made this possible?"

She nodded. "He did."

He shook his head. "That wee beastie really did save my life." He looked around. "Where is he? Is he okay?"

"He's in the house," Uncle Seamus said. "I'm sure he's fine."

Eamon nodded, his head no longer betraying him. "I want to check on him, but I need to do something first." With a quick nod to Lucien, Eamon turned to face the five women who'd helped him. "The hourglasses are gone. Completely. I never thought it would be possible. Thank you seems insufficient."

Alice smiled. "You're welcome. I'm sure there will be something you can do for us someday. Unicorn hair is a very rare ingredient when it comes to spellcasting. My own supply is dangerously low."

He laughed. "You'll never have to worry about that again."

She nodded. "I'm pleased we were able to help you.

We'll let you be with your family now." She glanced at the women around her. "I think I speak for all of us when I say we could use a little rest."

He nodded. "I'm sure. Thank you again. Whatever you need, just ask."

The witches and Lucien said their goodbyes and left. Pandora lingered briefly to say something to Tru's aunts, then she slipped away home, too.

Eamon looked at his uncle. "You said something about me hypnotizing Tru?"

Seamus nodded. "It's one of the unicorn's powers. If you hold the gaze of a woman for long enough, you will enthrall her. She'll be enraptured by you for life."

Tru scoffed. "He didn't do that to me."

Seamus's brows bent. "Lass, another few seconds and you'd have been lost to his whims."

"Really?" Tru cut her eyes at Eamon. "Were you doing that on purpose?"

"No. I didn't even know I could do it." He scratched his head. "There has to be a way to get immunity to that."

"Aye," his uncle said. "A ring or bracelet woven from strands of unicorn hair protects the wearer from enchantment."

Tru's aunts joined them. Aunt Cleo nodded. "We'd best get that taken care of right away."

"Agreed," Eamon said. "I don't want Tru susceptible."

Aunt Delly shot him a look. "I think Cleo and I need the same protection, too. Just in case."

Eamon hadn't thought about that, but he didn't want

her aunts to fear him. He didn't want anyone to fear him, but especially not them. "Sounds like a good plan. I'll make sure that happens soon." He shook his head. "Blimey. I can't believe I'm a unicorn."

"Neither can I," Tru said. "I thought they were always white with white horns. But you're really something in that form. All that shiny black ... fur? Hair? Whatever it is, you're very pretty."

Eamon laughed out loud. "First, I turned into a unicorn. Now I've been called pretty. Today might be the best and oddest day of my life."

He put his arm around Tru, no longer afraid to touch her. "Come on. Let's go inside and see how Nemo's doing."

She nodded at him. "I'm so glad they were able to help you."

"Me, too." He'd never meant anything more in his life.

47

Tru, her aunts, Eamon, and his uncle all went back to Tru's house, where her aunts cooked them a quick break-fast of bacon, eggs, and toast. Tru and Eamon yawned their way through the meal, so when it was done, they all said their goodbyes.

Eamon and Seamus went back to their house, with Eamon promising to talk to her soon.

Then Tru said good night to her aunts and made her way to the third floor. She went to bed and slept like a cat the rest of the day. Having a full stomach contributed to her sleepi-ness, but it would have been impossible to ignore the urge to sleep anyway. Not after the night and morning they'd had.

She imagined Eamon had gone to bed, too. After all, he'd also been awake, but he'd undergone some pretty intense magic. That had to wear a person out.

All she knew was that being kidnapped and nearly murdered was incredibly exhausting. But she fell asleep with a smile on her face and peace in her heart.

Eamon's troubles were over. They could be together now. And she was a full-fledged oracle. Life was, as Eamon would say, grand.

Muted words woke her. Urgent tones. Happy ones,

though. Something was going on. She blinked her eyes a few times and yawned, struggling for a moment to remember where she was and what had happened.

The sounds were coming up the stairs. She tossed the covers back and looked at the time. It was four in the afternoon. The voices belonged to her aunts. It sounded like they were one floor down.

That was as much as she could figure out. She pulled her robe on and went to the second floor to see what was happening.

She found her aunts in the nursery, the door slightly ajar. Both of them were on their knees in front of the birthing area. She pushed the door open, yawning again. "What's going on?"

Aunt Delly looked over her shoulder. "Chloe's in labor. Baby number one is about to be—"

"He's here," Aunt Cleo said. She smiled at Tru. "A gray tabby."

"Babies?" Tru sucked in a breath as she took a step closer. "Can I help? Can I watch? I've never seen kittens born."

"Of course," Aunt Delly said. "Come on in and shut the door. The last thing we need is the whole clowder in here."

Tru came in and closed the door, then went to kneel beside her aunts. The newborn baby kitten was the tiniest thing she'd ever seen. Thankfully, Chloe didn't look like she was distressed. "Is she doing all right?"

"She's doing great," Aunt Cleo said. "But I'm still glad this is going to be her last litter."

"You know, Pandora wants one of the kittens," Tru said.

Aunt Delly nodded. "She told us that before she left this morning. We promised she could have the second pick."

"Second?" Tru said. "Why not first?"

Aunt Delly smiled. "We thought you ought to have first. Every oracle needs a cat to call her own."

"Really?" Tru grinned.

"Really," Aunt Cleo said. "Since Eamon and Seamus took Nemo and Yardy, we have the room. And every oracle really should have their own cat. So one of these little ones will be yours."

"What about Chloe? Who will she belong to?"

"We might try to adopt her out," Aunt Cleo said. "We just have to see how she does when she gets through her spay. Mama cats are full of hormones that can make even the most feral friendly. If she stays friendly, finding her a home, too, would be the best option."

"Then we have room to take another pregnant one in," Aunt Delly said. "Or another special-needs cat."

"Baby number two is coming," Aunt Cleo announced.

Over the next forty-five minutes, three more babies arrived.

The last one was smaller than the rest. "The runt of the litter," Aunt Cleo said.

"Will he or she be okay?" Tru asked.

"I hope so," Aunt Delly said, doing a quick check to see if the runt was a boy or girl. "If Chloe ignores him, we'll feed him."

But Chloe didn't ignore him, immediately getting to work licking him clean and caring for him like she had the others.

Tru sat back and watched the new family. All five kittens were nursing away. Chloe looked tired but happy.

After a few minutes, the kittens started to drift off, and Tru was able to get a good look at the last baby. "The runt is black and white."

"Mostly black but enough white that we can call him a tuxedo," Aunt Delly said. "And look at that white blaze on his forehead."

Tru could look at nothing else. "Kind of reminds me of a unicorn horn." She smiled. "That's my cat right there."

Aunt Cleo's eyes held concern. "Tru, he's the runt. There's always a chance he won't make it."

Tru shook her head. "He's going to be fine." She reached out and stroked a finger down the tiny baby's back. "Leo the Lion is going to be just fine."

While her aunts cleaned up the birthing area and put fresh food down for Chloe, who turned out to be ravenous, Tru went upstairs to take a shower. She wasn't sure how long she'd be awake for, but showering would help.

She checked her phone and saw that she'd missed a call from Eamon. She called him right back. As soon as he answered, she said, "I just saw I missed your call. Everything all right?"

"Everything's grand. I just wanted to see if you were hungry. I thought maybe we could go out. Now that I can."

The smile in his voice made her smile. "I would love to go out with you. Where do you want to go?"

"I'm not really sure. I figured we could go into town and see what looks good."

"Okay. Forty minutes or so? I was just about to shower." She wanted to tell him about the kittens and Leo, but that could wait until they were face-to-face.

"Just come over when you're ready."

"Will do." She took a quick shower, put on a little makeup, fixed her hair, then put on a cute blue and white sundress with a little jean jacket and white sneakers. She added jewelry, including her evil eye necklace, then put her phone in her purse and headed downstairs.

She stopped to see Leo and his mama on the way. Chloe looked like she was sleeping, but the kittens were nursing again, including Leo, so Tru let them be, but not before she kissed her finger and touched it to Leo's head.

Her aunts were on the first floor, doing laundry. She stuck her head in the laundry room. "I'm going out to eat with Eamon."

"Have fun," Aunt Cleo said. "And remind him about those unicorn-hair bracelets, would you? I'm pretty sure his unicorn power was what we picked up on when we performed the *vaskania* over you. Even if he didn't know what he was, his power was still there."

"I will definitely remind him," Tru said. Amazing that his power had been active even if his unicorn form hadn't been. "I won't be out late. I still haven't caught up on my sleep."

"You have your key?" Aunt Delly asked.

"I do."

"Tell Seamus I said hi."

Tru grinned. "I will."

She walked over to Eamon's. Seamus answered the door with Yardy in his arms. "Himself told me you were coming. In you go, then."

She came inside, giving Yardy a little scratch on the head. "Did you nap?"

"Och, did I nap? I was out like old Van Winkle. Yardy loves a good nap, too, doncha, lad?"

The cat responded by rubbing his head against Seamus's chin.

Seamus laughed. "Eamon's in the kitchen."

"Thanks." She went through and found him at the table securing something into a zip-top sandwich bag. Nemo was sitting next to him, fascinated by whatever Eamon was doing. "What's that?"

"Unicorn hair. From my tail. Which might be the two strangest sentences I've ever put together." He sealed the bag, stood, and handed it to her. He was in dark jeans and a white dress shirt, crisply pressed. He looked very handsome. He shook his head. "I tried braiding it, but that is not one of my skills."

She smiled and tucked the bag into her purse. "We'll figure it out. Thank you."

"Ready to eat? Seamus told me about a few good places in town, places we've gotten takeaway from but nowhere I've been, obviously."

"Wherever you want to eat is fine with me. Ready to go out in public without a care?"

He laughed. "So much."

"Then let's go."

He gave Nemo a scratch on the cheek, then kissed the top of his little ginger head. "Be a good lad, now." Then he and Tru walked out to his car. He got the door for her but hesitated before closing it. "You look lovely, by the way. Sorry I didn't say that earlier."

"Thanks. You look very nice, too." It was the first time she'd seen him in anything but black. "I like the white shirt."

He laughed. "I'm glad. It was the only thing I had that wasn't black."

He found a parking spot on Main Street, then they got out and decided to walk a bit. He realized, as they strolled, that he was keeping his gaze down. He lifted his head, holding his breath for a second.

But there were no hourglasses to be seen. Anywhere. Truly amazing.

Tru reached out and took his hand, glancing at him as if to make sure that was okay. He held tight and smiled back.

As they passed one block, he was surprised at how busy it was. "I wonder if it's always like this. This many people, I mean."

"I don't know. I guess we'll have to come out again some night and see for ourselves."

He laughed. "We will." Then he pointed up ahead. "That's one of the places my uncle mentioned. Howler's. Everything we've ordered from them has been great. It's not fancy, though. Sort of standard pub food. Burgers and such."

"I don't need fancy. Sounds good."

They went in, and a hostess seated them in a booth near the front windows, which gave them a nice view outside. They were looking over the menus when Eamon's phone vibrated in his pocket. He pulled it out and glanced at the screen. Not a number he recognized.

He set the phone screen down on the table.

"You can answer that," Tru said. "I don't mind."

"I don't know the number. Probably spam." But then the phone vibrated again. He checked the screen. Same number. This time, he answered. "Hello?"

"Eamon Underwood?"

"Aye, this is he. Who's this?"

"Hugh Ellingham. I was wondering if I might have a few minutes of your time. There's something I'd like to discuss with you."

Eamon knew who Hugh Ellingham was. He just had no idea what the man would want with him. "I'm at dinner at the moment."

"No rush. After you eat is fine. I'll text you my address. Come by when you're through."

"I'm not alone." He looked at Tru, who looked back at him with obvious curiosity.

"That's fine, too. You're welcome to bring Troula along with you, if that's what you'd like to do."

Eamon's mouth opened. "How did you know who I was out with?"

Hugh laughed softly. "Just an educated guess. See you in a bit. Enjoy your meal." He hung up.

Eamon put the phone down. "I don't know what to make of that. Hugh Ellingham just invited me to his house." His phone chimed with an incoming notification. Hugh's address, no doubt.

"Who is he?"

"He's one of the ..." Eamon looked around, then lowered his voice. "Vampires who founded this town. He said he has something to discuss with me. And that it's fine to bring you along."

"Do you want me to go?"

"I'd love for you to go with me, but if the idea of meeting a vampire alone at his house doesn't appeal, I can understand."

She blinked twice before answering. "He's not dangerous, right?"

"He could be, I suppose, but only if he had a reason to be. I doubt we have anything to fear. I don't know much about him other than he's part of the family that founded the town. He's married and has a son."

She nodded. "I'll go with you."

They ordered when the server came back with their drinks. Tru got the chicken pot pie, and Eamon had the prime rib special. The food arrived quickly, and as they ate, Tru told him about how the new pregnant foster cat had given birth that afternoon.

"I'm keeping the runt as my own," she said with a smile. "He's mostly black but he's got a white chest and belly, white feet, and a white blaze down his forehead." Her smile grew. "Reminds me of a unicorn horn."

He laughed. "Please don't tell me you're naming him Uni."

"No, I've named him Leo. I thought since he was the runt, he needed a good strong name. My aunts say there's a chance he might not make it, but I'm not going to let that happen. Neither will they if they can help it, and they know just about everything there is to know about cats."

He nodded. "I'm sure he'll be fine." He prayed the kitten thrived. He didn't want Tru to lose the wee one.

"Yeah, I think so. How did Nemo do today? That was quite a contribution he made."

"It was." Eamon smiled. "I will be grateful to that cat for the rest of my life. He did fine today. He was on the bed asleep when I turned in and still there when I woke up, so he must have needed the rest, too." Then he laughed. "I'm not sure Uncle Seamus left his chair that entire time, either."

Tru smiled. "I really like your uncle. He's such a sweet man. I hope he and Aunt Delly work out."

"So do I. My Aunt Sharon passed not long after they were married, and I wasn't sure he'd ever fall for another woman, but he certainly has warm feelings for Delphina."

Tru grinned. "I can confirm those feelings are mutual."

The server returned to see if they wanted dessert, but neither of them did. Probably because Tru was as curious about the meeting with Hugh Ellingham as Eamon was. He paid the bill, and they went back to the car.

"You're sure you don't mind coming with me?"

She shook her head. "Not at all. I want to know what it's about. I'm just nosy like that."

He laughed as he opened the door for her. "We'll know very soon."

They arrived at the Ellingham house about fifteen minutes later, Eamon's GPS taking them right to it.

They walked up to the front door together. The place was impressive and the landscaping flawless. Eamon knocked, half expecting a butler to answer.

Instead, the door was opened by a pretty woman with a bright smile on her face. "You must be Eamon and Troula." She stuck her hand out. "I'm Delaney Ellingham. Hugh and I are so pleased you could come by."

"Delaney?" Tru said, shaking the woman's hand. "Are you related to the sweet shop with that name in town?"

"Delaney's Delectables is my place, yes."

"That is very cool. Please, call me Tru, by the way."

"Tru it is." Delaney shook Eamon's hand, too, then stepped back. "Please come in. Hugh is in the living room. I'll take you there."

They followed her. Tru shot Eamon a look he couldn't quite interpret, but she seemed excited to either meet the woman who owned the sweets shop or Tru was happy that there was going to be someone else present. He couldn't really tell which.

Then he realized becoming a unicorn wasn't the only ability he'd gained. He could tell that Delaney was a vampire, too. Not sure how, he just knew.

Delaney brought them to a richly decorated room

that had all the trappings of money. "Hugh, Eamon and Troula are here."

A well-dressed man stood. There wasn't anything about him that screamed "vampire" to Eamon, but again, he could just tell. Maybe that was another benefit of having his powers sorted out.

Hugh smiled. "So glad you could make it. Please, sit. Make yourself comfortable."

"Thank you," Eamon said.

"You have a beautiful home," Tru said.

"That is so kind of you to say." Delaney remained standing. "Hugh told me you were coming from dinner. Would you like a little dessert? I have a chocolate raspberry fudge cake that I brought home from the shop today. I was going to bring it in with some coffee. Or tea. If you like."

Tru nodded. "That sounds delicious, thank you. Decaf, if you have it."

Delaney nodded. "I do. And for you, Eamon?"

"Cake and tea would be grand." He figured the meeting couldn't be about something too bad if they were being offered cake.

"I'll be right back." Delaney left them.

Hugh crossed his legs. "I understand you recently went through quite a transformation, Eamon."

Eamon blinked. How did Hugh know about that? It had only just happened.

Hugh chuckled. "You're wondering how I know that. I must confess, Alice Bishop is my grandmother's right-hand woman. Very little goes on in this town that we Ellinghams don't find out about. You must understand, it behooves us to be well informed. This town is everything to us and, as such, we want to protect it."

Eamon nodded. "I do understand that." Did they think having a unicorn living here was a bad thing?

"Have you recovered from everything you went through? It's been quite a while for me, but I still remember the transition from human to vampire as exhausting. I can only imagine what you endured."

"It was definitely exhausting. But life-changing. In the best possible way."

"I'm glad to hear that. As you might have guessed, that transition is why I called you here."

Eamon hadn't actually guessed anything about why Hugh had wanted to talk to him, but he braced himself for the worst. "I see."

Hugh nodded. "Unicorns are rare and powerful creatures. About as special in the world of supernaturals as creatures come."

Delaney came back in pushing a silver tea cart laden with plates holding slices of the fudge cake, each one dolloped with whipped cream. Next to them were two carafes, along with cups and saucers and all the necessary items to go along with those things. "Did you make the offer yet? Did I miss it?"

Hugh shook his head as he got up to help her serve. "I was just getting there."

"What offer?" Eamon asked as he accepted a cup of tea and a plate of cake.

Hugh helped Delaney pass everything out before he sat back down with his own cake and answered. He used his fork to take the pointed end off of his slice. "The offer is that I would very much like to make you an employee of Nocturne Falls."

Eamon hesitated. "I'm sure it's a wonderful job, but I already work for my uncle, and he relies on me. I can't quit that job. I have a podcast, too. I've been working at that for a while. I don't really want to give that up, either."

Hugh nodded. "As I'm aware. We don't want you to give any of that up. This job would really only require two to three hours of your time each week. As you saw fit, really. Whatever was best for your schedule, although there are certain hours which we consider peak times. Getting one or two of those in would be ideal, naturally."

Eamon nodded, but he had no idea what Hugh was talking about. "And this job would be doing what?"

Obviously amused, Delaney shook her head. "Honey, you have to tell the man what you want him to do before he can agree to anything."

Hugh smiled. "My wife makes a valid point. My apologies for getting ahead of myself. We would love for you to become one of our character actors. As I said, unicorns are rare. A black unicorn?" He shook his head as he helped himself to more cake. "Quite a find. I believe the social media alone could spark a new wave of tourism. Not that we're suffering, mind you. But I'm sure you understand that a fresh influx of business is never a bad idea."

Eamon narrowed his eyes. "I'm still not really sure what you want me to do. How would this work, exactly?"

49

Tru could tell Eamon still had a lot of questions. She did, too, and it wasn't even about her. But she had concerns as well. Eamon had only just become a unicorn. He might not want to share that part of himself with the world just yet.

Delaney put her coffee cup down. "First of all, let me back up, because my husband, in his excitement, has skipped a few things."

Hugh took another bite of cake. "You can't blame me. We've never had a unicorn. It's a very rare opportunity."

"I know, dear." Delaney looked at Eamon again. "I understand you haven't spent a lot of time in town due to ... reasons, but the town employs a wide variety of supernaturals to basically be themselves. All the witches and werewolves and, naturally, vampires, you see posing for pictures with tourists are really just citizens in their most natural forms. Even the gargoyles at the fountain are regular folks."

Tru laughed softly. "Calling them regular folks might be a bit of a stretch."

Delaney chuckled. "You're right. And they might not be in their most natural forms, either, because obviously, they're usually wearing costumes that accentuate their characteristics, but you know what I mean. We want you to be your true self. A unicorn. You wouldn't necessarily have to pose for pictures. But a gallop through town now and then or maybe around the lake at the shopping complex out there so that people could see you? It would just be the best thing ever."

Hugh gestured at Eamon with his fork. "You *could* pose for pictures, obviously."

Tru wasn't sure how that would work. She had to say something. "I'm not sure if you know this, but he can't speak in that form. It might be hard for him to manage time with tourists."

Eamon glanced at Tru and nodded. "She's right. I don't have a voice in that form."

"Hugh," Delaney said softly. Then she gave her husband a look Tru couldn't interpret.

Hugh nodded at Delaney. "You're right, of course."

Could they read each other's thoughts? Tru made a mental note to ask her aunts about that later.

Hugh returned his attention to Eamon. "That could be remedied if perhaps the unicorn had a companion. Say, a rider." He looked at Tru. "If it works better that way for Eamon, it works better that way for all of us. I understand this is something you'd both need to think about, so I don't expect an answer right away. But I can tell you the compensation package is generous. And the benefits are excellent."

"Wait," Tru said. "Are you offering me a job, too?"

He nodded. "I see no reason not to. Unless working together isn't something that interests you."

She wasn't opposed to it at all. "Just to be clear, I've only recently become an oracle, and I'm already committed to working with my aunts."

"We expect nothing less," Hugh said. "Again, this would be as your schedules allow. Up to you."

Delaney grinned. "You could dress up like a princess, if you wanted. Oh! Or a warrior queen. I kind of see that sort of woman riding a black unicorn into battle. Fierce and strong and—"

Hugh cleared his throat.

Delaney winked at Tru. "We can talk about that later."

Eamon looked at Tru. "What do you think?"

She honestly didn't know. "I think we need to talk about it."

Hugh picked up his phone. "I don't want to take more of your time than I already have. Eamon, I have your number, obviously. I'll send you a link to the PDF that outlines the compensation package we've put together."

"Thank you," Eamon said.

Hugh tapped at his screen, then looked up. "You can share that with Troula, as we'll be extending the offer to her as well. Take some time to think it over and then get back to us when you've made a decision."

Eamon nodded. "We'll do that."

Delaney got to her feet. "I have something else for you before you go." She left, coming back a few moments later with two big Delaney's Delectables shopping bags. "I understand you had a bad experience with some things from my shop recently."

Eamon shook his head. "Not through any fault of yours."

"I know, but all the same, I wanted to make it up to you. I put together a goody bag for each of you. Just to make up for what happened." Delaney handed them each one.

It must have weighed ten pounds. Or more. The sweet smell of chocolate wafted up.

"Wow," Tru said. "Thank you."

She and Eamon got to their feet as Hugh stood. He and Delaney walked with them to the front door. "Again, we appreciate you coming. If you have any questions, please call me anytime."

"I will," Eamon said.

Then Hugh looked at Tru and hesitated. "I know a little about what oracles can do." He held out his arm, pulling his sleeve up. "If you want to read me concerning this offer, if that might help you make your decision, please do."

Tru blinked. "I'm pretty new at this. I'm not sure you should be the first person I attempt to read."

Hugh chuckled. "There's not much that can go wrong, is there?"

Tru thought a moment. "Not if I'm looking at your future, no. All right then." She reached out and grasped his wrist. Then she closed her eyes like she'd seen her aunts do, and concentrated on the offer he'd made them and how it would affect the future.

A vision appeared in her mind of Hugh and Delaney out to dinner with a woman she knew was herself, even though the face was unclear, and Eamon. Of Hugh smiling and watching a gorgeous black unicorn stride down Main Street. Just like she'd known the woman at dinner was her, she knew the woman atop the unicorn was her, as well. Apparently, seeing yourself in a vision only resulted in a kind of pixelated version. Then one more vision came through of Hugh nodding with satisfaction at the gathered crowd.

Tru let go of him and opened her eyes. "Thanks for letting me do that. I'm glad I did. Everything I saw was positive."

Delaney took her husband's arm. "That's wonderful."

Hugh nodded. "It is. I hope we hear from you soon."

"You will," Eamon said.

Neither he nor Tru spoke until they and the shopping bags were in his car. He shook his head. "I was not expecting that."

"Nope," Tru said. "Wait. Do you mean the job offer or the chocolates?"

Eamon laughed. "Either one."

"Right. Yeah, no, me either."

He pulled out of the drive and got them headed for home, but when he got into town, he pulled the car over and parked in the first available spot. He turned the engine off and looked at Tru. "Are you as curious about the compensation package as I am?"

She nodded. "Maybe more."

He pulled out his phone and tapped the screen. "There. I sent the link to you."

Her phone chimed before he finished speaking. She took it out of her purse and opened up the message with the link. "Let's look at it together. On the count of three."

"Okay. One ... two ... three."

Tru tapped the link. The screen changed as the link connected her to the PDF file, which then downloaded to her phone. She tapped the arrow at the top of her screen to open up the PDF. Then she read.

Or rather, she skimmed. First, down the list of benefits, which included full health and dental. Very impressive. Then her eyes went straight to the payment. The salary was six figures and started with a two. "Are you kidding me?"

She looked at Eamon, who was staring at his phone like it had a ghost in it. "Did you see that number?"

"I could buy a new microphone. And a new mixing board. And pay off this car. And ..." He caught her gaze. "That is a *lot* of money. Especially for just turning into a unicorn and running through the streets two or three times a week."

She nodded. "It is."

"For that kind of money, I would be happy to pose for pictures."

"About that." She paused, then asked the big question. "What do you think about me working with you? I didn't mean to insinuate myself, you know. I was just thinking about how hard it might be for you if the tourists got a little out of control, seeing as how you can't speak and won't have hands."

He laughed. "I would be thrilled for you to be my companion in this adventure. I do think I should get some say in your outfit, however."

"Oh, you do, do you?"

He nodded, looking very serious. "That whole warrior queen getup. Would that be black leather, do you think?"

She snorted. "I have no idea. Are you voting for black leather?"

"I am a man. Why wouldn't I vote for black leather?"

She rolled her eyes but laughed all the same. "I'm happy to take suggestions. But seriously, I think we both need to talk this over with our families. It affects them, too. They rely on us to do certain things, so they should have a say."

"Good point." He put his phone away and started the car. "It would be nice to have the extra money, though. Being an undertaker isn't exactly a get-rich-quick scheme."

"I have no idea what being an oracle pays. Pretty well, I'd imagine, but I'm not sure brand-new oracles make the same as those who've been doing it for a couple decades. So yeah, the money would be really nice."

He nodded as he navigated traffic. "It would make it

easier for us to get a place together. Someday. If that's what we wanted to do."

She smiled as she leaned across the console to kiss his cheek, then stayed close to him to whisper softly in his ear. "I like the way you think."

He grinned. "Brilliant. Because I am mad about you."

She kissed him again before sliding back into her seat. "Well, I don't need a look at the future to tell you yours definitely includes me."

He reached over and took her hand. "I'm falling in love with you, Tru. If you hadn't figured that out yet."

"I'm an oracle. I totally knew," she teased. Then she shook her head. "I didn't. But I'm glad. Because I feel the same way about you."

His face held nothing but happiness. "I never thought I'd feel this way about a crazy cat lady."

"Says the man who kissed his cat on the head before we left."

Eamon snorted, but then his expression went serious. "He saved my life." He glanced over at her, his eyes filled with emotion. "So did you, you know."

"Then we're even, because if it wasn't for you, Callum would have done me in."

He squeezed her hand. "What do you say we go home, tell the families about the offer, then surround ourselves with cats, watch some mindless television, and stuff ourselves full of sweets?"

In that moment, her heart overflowed with the kind of joy that had no beginning and no end, the kind of joy that could get a person through better or worse, sickness or health. She might not be completely ready to say it out loud, but she loved Eamon and knew in her heart that she would marry him someday.

She nodded. "You are *definitely* the right man for me."

Want to be up to date on all books & release dates by Kristen Painter? Sign-up for my newsletter on my website, www.kristenpainter.com. No spam, just news (sales, freebies, and releases.)

If you loved the book and want to help the series grow, tell a friend about the book and take time to leave a review!

PARANORMAL WOMEN'S FICTION

Midlife Fairy Tale Series:

The Accidental Queen

First Fangs Club Series:

Sucks To Be Me

Suck It Up Buttercup

Sucker Punch

The Suck Stops Here

Embrace The Suck

Code Name: Mockingbird (A Paranormal Women's Fiction Novella)

COZY MYSTERY:

Jayne Frost Series:

Miss Frost Solves A Cold Case: A Nocturne Falls Mystery

Miss Frost Ices The Imp: A Nocturne Falls Mystery

Miss Frost Saves The Sandman: A Nocturne Falls Mystery

Miss Frost Cracks A Caper: A Nocturne Falls Mystery

When Birdie Babysat Spider: A Jayne Frost Short

Miss Frost Braves The Blizzard: A Nocturne Falls Mystery

Miss Frost Chills The Cheater: A Nocturne Falls Mystery

Miss Frost Says I Do: A Nocturne Falls Mystery

Lost in Las Vegas: A Frost And Crowe Mystery

Wrapped up in Christmas: A Frost And Crowe Mystery

HappilyEverlasting Series:

Witchful Thinking

PARANORMAL ROMANCE

Nocturne Falls Series:

The Vampire's Mail Order Bride

The Werewolf Meets His Match

The Gargoyle Gets His Girl

The Professor Woos The Witch

The Witch's Halloween Hero – short story

The Werewolf's Christmas Wish – short story

The Vampire's Fake Fiancée

The Vampire's Valentine Surprise – short story

The Shifter Romances The Writer

The Vampire's True Love Trials – short story

The Dragon Finds Forever

The Vampire's Accidental Wife

The Reaper Rescues The Genie

The Detective Wins The Witch

The Vampire's Priceless Treasure

The Werewolf Dates The Deputy

The Siren Saves The Billionaire

The Vampire's Sunny Sweetheart

Death Dates The Oracle

Shadowvale Series:

The Trouble With Witches

The Vampire's Cursed Kiss

The Forgettable Miss French

Moody And The Beast

Her First Taste Of Fire

Monster In The Mirror

Sin City Collectors Series

Queen Of Hearts

Dead Man's Hand

Double or Nothing

Standalone Paranormal Romance:

Dark Kiss of the Reaper

Heart of Fire

Recipe for Magic

Miss Bramble and the Leviathan

All Fired Up

URBAN FANTASY

The House of Comarré series:

Forbidden Blood

Blood Rights

Flesh and Blood

Bad Blood

Out For Blood

Last Blood

The Crescent City series:

House of the Rising Sun

City of Eternal Night

Garden of Dreams and Desires

Nothing is completed without an amazing team.

Many thanks to:

Cover design: Janet Holmes using images under license from Shutterstock.com
Interior Formating: Gem Promotions
Editor: Chris Kridler

Made in United States
North Haven, CT
26 May 2023